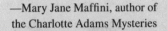
"This is a terr[...]
those cheese s[...]
wander aroun[...]
to have Lizzie[...]
body turns up."

—Mary Jane Maffini, author of
the Charlotte Adams Mysteries

"Who can't love a debut novel filled with mystery references and a pair of cats named Edam and Brie? And who
can't adore dedicated, saucy Lizzie Turner, a literacy
teacher with high hopes for her students? Readers should
have high hopes for this series. And thanks to the author's
fine research, readers just might find a delicious assortment
of new authors to browse."

—Avery Aames, Agatha Award winner and
national bestselling author of the Cheese Shop Mysteries

"Book a date with *A Killer Read*. Mystery-loving book
club members will keep readers guessing as they page
through clues to prevent themselves from being booked
for murder."

—Janet Bolin, author of the Threadville Mysteries

A Killer Read

ERIKA CHASE

BERKLEY PRIME CRIME, NEW YORK

THE BERKLEY PUBLISHING GROUP
Published by the Penguin Group
Penguin Group (USA) Inc.
375 Hudson Street, New York, New York 10014, USA

Penguin Group (Canada), 90 Eglinton Avenue East, Suite 700, Toronto, Ontario M4P 2Y3, Canada
(a division of Pearson Penguin Canada Inc.) • Penguin Books Ltd., 80 Strand, London WC2R 0RL,
England • Penguin Group Ireland, 25 St. Stephen's Green, Dublin 2, Ireland (a division of Penguin
Books Ltd.) • Penguin Group (Australia), 250 Camberwell Road, Camberwell, Victoria 3124, Australia
(a division of Pearson Australia Group Pty. Ltd.) • Penguin Books India Pvt. Ltd., 11 Community
Centre, Panchsheel Park, New Delhi—110 017, India • Penguin Group (NZ), 67 Apollo Drive,
Rosedale, Auckland 0632, New Zealand (a division of Pearson New Zealand Ltd.) • Penguin Books
(South Africa) (Pty.) Ltd., 24 Sturdee Avenue, Rosebank, Johannesburg 2196, South Africa

Penguin Books Ltd., Registered Offices: 80 Strand, London WC2R 0RL, England

A KILLER READ

A Berkley Prime Crime Book / published by arrangement with the author

PUBLISHING HISTORY
Berkley Prime Crime mass-market edition / April 2012

ISBN: 978-0-425-24703-7

BERKLEY® PRIME CRIME
Berkley Prime Crime Books are published by The Berkley Publishing Group,
a division of Penguin Group (USA) Inc.,
375 Hudson Street, New York, New York 10014.
BERKLEY® PRIME CRIME and the PRIME CRIME logo are trademarks of
Penguin Group (USA) Inc.

PRINTED IN THE UNITED STATES OF AMERICA

10 9 8 7 6 5 4 3 2 1

ALWAYS LEARNING   **PEARSON**

Acknowledgments

There are many people to whom I am grateful, and I'm certain to miss some, but please know, if we've met, you've played a role in my writing life.

My special thanks go to:

My agent, Kim Lionetti, who started me on this journey with invaluable advice and encouragement. To editor Kate Seaver for her thought-provoking questions, guidance and support. To Katherine Pelz, editorial assistant and person of great patience. To my anonymous copyeditor, the one with the eagle eye.

Mary Jane Maffini. Without her, this book would not have happened. She was the conduit; she was the constant source of encouragement, my go-to person for any and all questions; she is a dear and true friend. I probably owe her a spa weekend by now.

My longtime writing group, The Ladies' Killing Circle—Joan Boswell, Vicki Cameron, Barbara Fradkin, Mary Jane Maffini and Sue Pike—who, despite the name, have provided friendship and help as I've honed my writing skills.

Lee McNeilly, my sister and first reader. As in all aspects of my life, she's there for me, and she reads with a critical eye and a love of mysteries.

Tammy Rushing Lynn, for agreeing to be my "Southern" connection.

My two Siamese cats, despite the many attempts at "editing" by slinking across the keyboard at critical moments in a scene.

And, of course, to mystery readers everywhere. You're the ones we do it for.

Chapter One

◇◇◇

Some say life is the thing, but I prefer reading.

RUTH RENDELL

"I've got an idea, Lizzie . . . why don't you just do, like, brain surgery or something on me. Slice me open, pull out my brain, squish all this Shakespeare stuff into it, put it back and sew me up like new. Maybe that way I'll finally get it!" Andrea Mason punctuated her proclamation with a long groan.

Lizzie Turner internalized her own groan. She knew that Andie felt like she was being tortured, but Lizzie felt little remorse about the pain she'd inflicted. It was for her student's own good.

"Okay, Andie. I guess that's enough for today. I'll see you next Thursday, same time, same place, same English lit."

Andie groaned again, stroking her silver nose ring. She shifted from her terminal slouch to a more upright position and stuffed her book, notepad and pen into her black skull-and-crossbones backpack. "This sucks. It's so not what I want to be doing, Lizzie. Couldn't you just tell my folks I know it? Or I'm illiterate. Or something?"

"Listen, kiddo. You're not illiterate. Just undermotivated." Or totally nonmotivated was more like it. "I hate to restate the obvious, but you need your English in order to pass. And that means reading what's on the curriculum and hopefully, understanding some of it."

"Like that's going to happen." Andie pushed out of the chair and reached the door in record time. "This Shakespeare guy's just so boring, ya know? And I hate reading." Her lower lip slid out into a childish pout as she slammed the door.

Lizzie gritted her teeth and shoved her books into her tote. Words of dismay to a literacy teacher. *What's it going to take?* she wondered. Maybe she should give up tutoring, stick to the behind-the-scenes basics. *No, don't go there.* This was just one rebellious adolescent, not a critique of her skills. But it really bothered her. After two months of tutoring sessions, once a week, that girl was still a mystery.

"Yikes . . . that's it. I've got it! A mystery." Lizzie dashed out the door and caught up with Andie as she stood on the front porch, pushing her iPod earbuds into her ears.

"Andie, wait a minute." Lizzie touched Andie's arm to get her attention. She waited until the earbuds disappeared into the girl's pocket. "Have I got a book for you. Actually, tons of them. I want you to come to my mystery book club meeting tonight. I won't take no for an answer. Consider it part of your tutoring. In fact, for each meeting you attend, we'll skip the next tutoring session." She knew she was grasping at straws at this point. "Deal?"

Andie narrowed her brown eyes, already sinister-looking with layers of thick black eye shadow and liner surrounding them. "You mean, like read a mystery? Can I deep-six Will Shakespeare?"

Uh-oh. "Not instead of, not yet anyway."

Andie thought for a moment. "Okay."

"Great. Be back here at Molly's tonight at seven P.M."

Andie pulled her earbuds out, reattached herself to the iPod and left.

Wow, it actually worked. Lizzie gave herself a mental pat on the back. *Hope springs anew.*

Lizzie hadn't heard Molly Mathews come outside, but the slight wheeze of years of smoking signaled her presence.

"That child is tempting many fates. Do parents not teach their children manners anymore?" Molly asked.

"She's just doing her teenage thing, Molly. Besides, I know you like a gal with spunk. Which is a good thing because Andie's coming to the book club tonight. I'm hoping if I can get her hooked on a mystery, she'll keep reading."

"That ought to spice things up if it gets too boring." She hooked an arm through Lizzie's and steered her back inside. "I have some iced tea poured for us. I want to hear who all you've got lined up for our first meeting. Hopefully, it won't be the last."

"Why would you say that?" Lizzie slid along the padded cream banquette that followed the L-shape of the corner windows and took a long drink. "I think this book club has great potential. Another of your brilliant ideas."

"Nice of you to say so, honey. But it's no mystery that this here town needs a club that specializes in books with actual plots and resolutions."

Lizzie laughed. "Amen. But it is great of you to open your house to everything. First the literacy program and tutoring, and now the book club."

It really was the ideal location, Lizzie thought. The grand antebellum house with the prominent address had graced the acre of property for almost a century and was an Ashton Corners landmark.

Lizzie had often heard that people started to look like their spouses or their pets after many years of living together. She believed the same applied to people and their houses. Molly matched the house in grace and stature and, in one way, color: both she and the house were topped with gray. However, Molly's was a shoulder-length wave provided by

Mother Nature and styled weekly by Willetta at the Curl Haven.

Lizzie decided she'd better keep vigilant for the day her own long, straight dark brown hair started curling like the fanciful trim of her house or even paled to a matching taupe.

"Believe me when I say it's nothing, honey. This old house needs things happening in it to keep it alive. Claydon and I would throw great parties and have people over all the time. He loved to play the magnanimous host. And I was a real social butterfly. We did have a good life together." Molly sighed. "Now, enough of the past. Who all is coming tonight?"

"Well, there's Bob Miller." Lizzie chose a piece of blueberry bread from the plate Molly pushed toward her and vowed to add another half mile to her morning run. A part of her knew that at thirty-one years old, she didn't really need to worry about extra pounds just yet, especially since she'd been trim all of her life, but she wasn't about to take any chances.

"Now there's a surprise. Don't tell me y'all just asked Bob and he said yes?"

"No. His sister cornered me during the break at the Musica Nobilis choir practice—she stands behind me in the soprano section—and asked if he could come. She said she'd make sure he turned up."

"That makes more sense. Lucille always did have to be in charge of everything, and she couldn't be when he was police chief. Now that he's retired, I'm sure she's trying to take over his life again." Molly grimaced. "You know, I've known Bob since we were in diapers. His mama used to sew the most exquisite dresses, and she'd bring Bob along to play whenever my mama had a fitting. We tended to be in the same classes most of the way through school, but then we sort of lost touch when he got married. His Sue-Ann was the jealous type, even though she had nothing to worry about where I was concerned."

"Is she dead now?"

"No, honey. She up and left him way back, when their little girl was only eight years old. Said she couldn't take being married to a police officer. I think she meant to the *bank account* of a police officer. I heard she married a banker in Atlanta after the divorce came through. It's a shame about his daughter, Lily, though. I know he's aching to see her, but Sue-Ann did a number on that child and she wants nothing to do with Bob. People can be so cruel sometimes."

"I didn't know. That's such a shame."

"Yes, it is." Molly sighed again. "Now, who else is coming?"

"Sally-Jo Baker, of course. We try to get together at least once a week for dinner and a movie, but I don't think she's made too many other friends since moving here last winter. She's been wanting a way to meet more people. I hadn't given it much thought, having been born and raised in Ashton Corners, but it must be tough for someone my age to just plug into a whole new life."

"It is at any age, honey."

"I suppose. I think the best way to meet people is to get involved in things. That's one of the reasons I've invited Stephanie Lowe along, too. Hopefully, it will also reinforce the reading skills she's acquired in the literacy program." Lizzie glanced at the large red clock shaped like the state of Alabama, hanging above the kitchen door. "Yikes. Look at the time. I've still got to pick up some eats for tonight, get home and get changed."

"Wear something that'll knock them out, honey. My mama always used to say, along with the clean underwear bit, that you should always dress your best for the start of something new. Because you never know what might happen."

Lizzie's cell phone rang and she rummaged in her purse to find it. "Excuse me, Molly," she said before answering it.

"How interesting," she said a moment later, after ending the call and tucking her phone away. "That was Bob, and he asked if he could bring along a friend tonight."

Molly chuckled. "Probably someone for moral support. Did he say whom?"

"No. But it's a great way to start a mystery book club, don't you think? Having a mystery guest?"

Chapter Two

◇◇◇

I left looking on the bright side. At this rate, I might never have to learn how to bake.

THE CLUTTERED CORPSE—MARY JANE MAFFINI

Lizzie sampled a cheese straw from the plate in Sally-Jo Baker's hand. "You mean, you finished teaching today at three P.M., went home and baked three things to bring tonight?"

"Of course," Sally-Jo said with a nod. "I said I'd bring something."

Lizzie and Sally-Jo had met just after Christmas when Sally-Jo had moved to town to teach third grade at Ashton Corners Elementary School. They'd ended up in the school staff room one morning and over some bad coffee, found similar interests that had led to a good friendship.

"I know," Lizzie said, "but I didn't think you'd actually bake, not with LaBelle's Bakery practically next door to the school. I just find it so hard to believe that there are people who actually enjoy baking. And cooking, come to think of it. I'm always happy to be a sampler, though." She took another bite of the cheese straw to demonstrate. "Yum. So, who's arrived so far?"

Sally-Jo passed a china serving dish to Lizzie, who plated the cinnamon pecan drop biscuits she'd snagged at LaBelle's. "Stephanie Lowe was the first to show up. I guess she's also eager to meet new people."

"I'm glad she agreed to come. I don't think she gets out much other than to her waitress job at the Oasis Diner, and the literacy class, of course. I never see her hanging around with anyone during the break. It's going to get even worse when she has a newborn baby to care for all by herself. She'll never get out and meet people her own age then."

"Strange she never talks about her family or even where she comes from," Sally-Jo said. "She must be terribly lonely, and like you say, all she's got is work, class and being pregnant. I can't picture myself in her place."

"What—the job, the studying or waiting for the baby to arrive?"

"All of the above."

Lizzie couldn't picture herself in Stephanie's place either. At one point, just after high school, she'd been as anxious as many of her friends to find Mr. Right, settle down and have kids. But after a few years in college, where she'd tried darn hard to make up for not having had a steady boyfriend in high school, she finally arrived at the place of oneness, as she called it. The state of being happy on one's own, a decision made easier by the fact there wasn't a large pool of exciting, eligible men swimming around her. Except for the guys she met through the school system and her choir, dates were few and far between these days. Most of the Ashton Corners boys had been snapped up long ago, and if they hadn't, there was a reason. One she took to be a red flag.

"I wish we could get her to talk about herself and her family," Sally-Jo interrupted Lizzie's musing. "There's a story there, for sure. Here, if you take this tray, I'll handle the rest. Let the snacking begin."

"Lead the way!" Lizzie said as she held the door open.

As they were about to enter the library, the doorbell

sounded and the front door was flung open by Bob Miller. He smiled when he saw the two of them.

"Now that's what I call timing. Two of the prettiest gals in Ashton Corners, Alabama, and their hands filled with food. I told ya'll it would be worth your while to come, Jacob. Ladies, this here is Jacob Smith, my new neighbor and Ashton Corners's most recent legal mind."

Ahh, Bob's special mystery guest. Lizzie smiled her welcome.

"Pleased to meet you." Jacob smiled at both but moved toward Sally-Jo. "May I help y'all with something?"

"That's awfully sweet of you." Sally-Jo beamed up at him. "Maybe you could take this plate. I'm Sally-Jo Baker, by the way, and this is Lizzie Turner."

He nodded in Lizzie's direction but kept his eyes on Sally-Jo.

Lizzie had an instant vision of just what kind of help Jacob could offer. She pegged him at six-four since he had at least six inches on her, and Sally-Jo came up to his shoulder. The blond curly hair didn't hurt either. It made him look kind of cuddly, in a stocky, teddy bear kind of way—even with black-framed glasses. Put that next to Sally-Jo's short auburn pixie cut, snazzy pink glasses and size-two, five-foot-nothing build and that old adage about opposites attracting came to mind. One thing they did share was the glasses. Lizzie was sure she could come up with another dozen good reasons these two should be matched. On the other hand, she had recently sworn off matchmaking after her recent pairing of a soprano who stood near her in the choir and a new tenor had ended with one missing ferret and two suspiciously happy hounds. Surely, nobody could blame her that Kent's dogs managed to drive Marie's ferret out of the house, or worse.

"Jacob's quite the reader and new to town," explained Bob, "so I thought this would be a good spot for him."

"Not just for moral support then?" Lizzie asked, a twinkle in her eye.

"Sounds like something Molly would say," Bob muttered. "Might as well get started. We can't let the food go to waste."

Molly came up behind them, another plate in her hand. "I thought I heard your booming voice, Bob Miller. Even though I said I wouldn't believe you'd be here until I saw you. It's about time we broadened your horizons. And this is your friend?"

"Very astute, Molly," Bob said with a wink at Lizzie. "Jacob Smith, Molly Mathews, a mover and shaker in this community and truly one of the nosiest old broads I've ever known." He ducked as Molly reached over with a jab to the arm. "She's been trying to punch me out for nigh on sixty-five years now."

"It would be my pleasure, Bob," Molly said sweetly. "Now, come in here and get ready to contribute."

She ushered them into a large room, three walls of which were covered with dark oak bookcases. Two settees faced each other across an oriental carpet, and three club chairs upholstered in burgundy velvet had been pulled up to either end. The old-world elegance of the room was highlighted by brocade beige drapes framing a large picture window, which in turn framed the sprawling lawn at the side of the house.

Lizzie noted with disappointment that Andie wasn't there. Oh well, she'd have to come up with a different tactic to get her reading. Lizzie chose a chair next to Stephanie, welcoming her to the group.

Stephanie smiled. She'd pulled her shoulder-length mousy brown hair into a ponytail, which, along with her sweet expression and slightly nervous mannerisms, made her look even younger than her nineteen years. Lizzie watched as Stephanie stuffed her knitting into a bag on the floor by her chair only to whip it back out again. "Do y'all mind if I keep on knitting? It wouldn't be too rude or anything, would it?" she asked.

"No, that would be just fine, Stephanie," Lizzie answered.

Stephanie sat back and adjusted her stretched-out long cotton T-shirt over her bulging belly. *That needs to be ditched for a proper maternity top*, Lizzie thought, then wondered if Stephanie could even afford a new wardrobe. Maybe she should get some of the new mamas in the literacy program together for a maternity clothing exchange. *Food for thought.*

"I think we'll have a lot of fun with this," Lizzie began. "Thanks first to Molly for offering to host the meetings in her wonderful library here, and thanks to y'all for coming. I suggest we keep this short and sweet. I'm going to make an executive decision, even though there isn't any executive, that to get us started, we all take turns, alphabetically, choosing the books to read. Which means, Sally-Jo Baker goes first."

"Oh, wow . . . the power," Sally-Jo said. "Let's see. Well, I'm reading *A Veiled Deception* by Annette Blair right now, so I guess that would be my choice."

"I sure do hope that's a police procedural, little lady," Bob said, shuffling over to the desk where the food had been placed.

"Uh, not really. It's a cozy actually, about heirlooms and magic . . . lots of fun."

Bob stopped, his right hand holding a cheese straw halfway to his mouth. "I'm not so sure this is going to work. John Sandford's about as cozy as I get."

"Now y'all hold on, Bob Miller. That's the purpose of a book club, to expand your reading horizons." Molly leaned forward in her chair, pointing a finger at Bob. "I'll be more than happy to read one of your police procedurals when it comes your turn, although it won't compare with an Agatha Christie."

"Agatha Christie, oh boy, now you've done it, Molly. Ruined my evening." Bob winked at Lizzie as he sat back down, his plate filled with food.

Lizzie tried to get them both back on track. "Stephanie,

that means you're up next. Is that okay with you? Could you pick out a book to suggest at our next meeting, or do you want to wait a bit for your turn?"

"No, it's okay. Really. I already have an idea, but I'm sure Mr. Miller's not going to like it." She glanced at Lizzie. "It's *Finger Lickin' Fifteen* by Janet Evanovich. She writes about a woman bounty hunter, and the books are also funny and sexy."

Molly jumped in as Bob groaned. "I'd say we'll all be well on our way to broadening those horizons. And it won't hurt you one bit, Bob Miller." She smiled, leaned over and patted Stephanie's shoulder. "And we go by given names here, Stephanie. Or else y'all won't be allowed to stay. It's all informal here, honey."

Lizzie hid a smile at the thought of either Molly or her house being thought of as informal. This club was going to be anything but dull, she thought. And she was pleased that Stephanie was already into a series and reading beyond what she'd recommend in the literacy class.

"I'm real sorry, Ms. Mathews, I mean, Molly." Stephanie offered a tentative smile. "But I sure do have to use your restroom. It seems that's all I do these days."

"Why, don't you worry about it, honey. It's right through that door in between the bookcases. Real handy. Just up and use it whenever you have to, without asking."

Stephanie's smile turned into a grimace as she hastily stuffed her knitting back into the bag and pushed out of the chair. She'd just closed the door behind her when Andie burst into the room through the main door, without apology or explanation.

"There's a strange man standing in your hall, Ms. Mathews."

Chapter Three

◇◇◇

That was all she had been able to hear. She found
it interesting.

AT BERTRAM'S HOTEL—AGATHA CHRISTIE

B ob jumped out of his chair. "I'll handle this."
    Molly beat him to the door. "Don't be silly. It is my
house and it might be someone I know, even if the child
doesn't. Andrea, honey, help yourself to something to eat
and take a seat."

Lizzie gave Andie a reassuring smile and followed Molly
out the door. It might be a friend out there, but surely Molly
wouldn't get upset with her standing by. The man stood with
his back to them, closely inspecting an oil painting of the
Gulf coastline that hung at the bottom of the staircase.

Molly went up to him saying, "Excuse me, but what are
y'all doing in my house?"

He swung around, at the same time removing his Tilley
hat to reveal gray short-cropped hair, a nose much too big
for his face and a broad smile that lacked warmth. He wore
a tan golf jacket zipped to the chin and faded jeans. "I'm so
sorry if I startled you, ma'am, but I knocked and the door

just swung open. I'm in need of a phone, you see. I'm having a bit of car trouble." He nodded toward the street out front.

"And y'all thought that an unlocked door meant come right on in, don't try the doorbell, and don't, for heaven's sake, call out to see if someone is around?"

"Terrible manners . . . I do apologize, ma'am," he answered. "Now, if I could just use that phone. It's awful urgent."

Molly shook her head but gestured for him to follow her. "It's in the kitchen, in here. Do you need a phone book?"

"No, ma'am. Now, if you'll pardon me, it's private." He shut the door behind him.

Molly turned to Lizzie. "Well, I never. What a nerve."

"Maybe you should bring Bob out here," Lizzie suggested.

"Bob? It's still my house, young lady. I'll deal with this."

Lizzie joined her at the door, and they pressed their ears against it. All it netted them were a few sporadic words. ". . . you'll deal with me." "This ends it." ". . . warning you." They backed away quickly when they heard the phone receiver slammed down.

"That was the strangest call for a tow truck I've ever heard," Lizzie whispered.

The door pushed open, and the man headed for the front door, nodding at them as he passed.

"Excuse me," Molly said in a loud voice. "What did you say your name was?"

"Didn't." He turned, his hand on the doorknob. "Thank you, ma'am. Sorry to have disturbed you."

"Would you like to join us in the library for an iced tea while you wait?" Lizzie asked quickly. She wanted Bob to get a look at him, at least.

Molly glanced briefly at Lizzie but then caught on. "Yes, there's no need to wait outside." She walked briskly over to the man and looped her arm through his, pulling him toward the library.

He looked nonplussed for a moment. "Why, that's right neighborly of you."

Molly led him into the room and indicated an empty chair near the door. "I've asked Mr. . . . our visitor, to join us while he waits for a tow. And this is the first meeting of our local mystery book club. Now, just take a seat and I'll get you that tea. Lizzie, could you grab the plate of refreshments?"

"Of course. I'd suggest you try the cheese straws. They're amazing." She held the plate out to him.

"Having car trouble, are you?" Bob asked. "Maybe I could take a look at it. Might be able to save you a tow."

"Don't trouble yourself," the stranger answered. "Friend of mine has a truck. Said he'd be here shortly." He turned to Molly. "This is real hospitable of you, ma'am." He continued staring at her until Bob leaned forward with another question.

"Where did you say you're from?"

"Didn't. Mind if I have another of those?" He gestured to the plate Lizzie had set on the coffee table, but glanced up as the door to the restroom opened.

"I'm afraid I've used the last of your t.p., Ms. . . . er, Molly," Stephanie said as she entered. Then, seeing the newcomer in the room, she took a quick step backward.

A horn sounded in the distance. The stranger looked startled. Recovering, he quickly eyed the others. "You know," he said, bolting out of his seat, "I really should be waiting outside. He could already be here. Thanks."

He left with Bob in pursuit. A moment later, the group still in the library heard the front door close, and soon Bob returned. "Just wanted to make sure he left. And I locked the door. That was one hasty exit."

"That was all very strange," Molly said.

"Are you all right, Stephanie?" Lizzie asked. "You look a bit perturbed."

"Me, uh, sure. I'm fine. I was just taken aback to see

someone new here." She eased herself into her chair. "That's all."

Bob stared at Stephanie for a few moments before saying, "You'd better check around the main floor, Molly. Make sure he didn't stash anything in his coat. You've got real nice artwork and knickknacks."

"Knickknacks?" Molly huffed. "Knickknacks I wouldn't mind losing. But I'm sure he didn't have time to take anything. He was still in the hall when we saw him."

"Molly—"

"Not now, Bob. We have book club business to attend to. Y'all want more treats?" she asked and passed around a couple of plates of goodies.

Bob filled his plate again but sat with his eyes glued to the door.

"Well, I can tell ya'll one thing," Bob said as he pushed an arm through the sleeve of his khaki army surplus jacket. "I didn't expect to eat so much at a book club. This bodes well."

"I hope you didn't find that too hard to take," Lizzie teased. She resisted patting his slightly protruding belly. She'd learned the hard way that it was fine for men, her cousin Crawford in particular, to comment on Lizzie's creeping pounds as she bit into a second mocha truffle, but let her mention the words "beer belly" and he was quick to reveal to all at the family reunion the name of her secret schoolgirl crush.

"I figured the least I could do was uphold my share of the eating. Now, reading this here book could be a different matter."

Molly walked over to him. "Don't tell me y'all are going to try to weasel your way out of this." She had at least three inches on him when she chose to use it. Like now. "Especially since we all agreed on your suggestion for a name for the book club. Which proves you do actually read once in a while."

"That you did, and I think the Ashton Corners Mystery Readers and Cheese Straws Society is a damned fine name, too. No, I'll read it and weep . . . but I'll be back. Night, all."

"I've got an early day in court tomorrow," Jacob explained as he followed Bob out the door. "Uh, a very tricky case about a pet pig. Only in Ashton Corners." He shook his head and chuckled. "Thanks for tonight and see ya'll next month, if not before." He glanced at Sally-Jo, then closed the door.

The others were gathering their jackets when Bob came barging back in. "I'm afraid there's been a mishap outside. It's best if ya'll wait here until it's sorted."

"What's happened?" Molly asked.

"It isn't Jacob, is it?" Sally-Jo asked, a hint of panic in her voice.

"No. He's fine, just staying outside with the car. It's that stranger." He looked at Molly. "He's dead."

Molly gasped. "Oh, my Lord. Dead? He should have stayed inside. Was it a heart attack, do you think?"

"Not unless the bullet in his head precipitated it."

Chapter Four

◇◇◇

"You see, Mr. Pennington," said Race, "Mrs. Otterbourne was shot with your revolver."

DEATH ON THE NILE—AGATHA CHRISTIE

The police arrived within minutes. Bob went back out to join them while the others waited in the library.

"This is so cool," Andie said. "Way weirder than anything on the 'net."

Lizzie looked at her sharply and wondered what Andie's parents would think of Lizzie's grand plan to get Andie motivated. Although she certainly looked enthusiastic now.

"It's creepy, that's what it is. Do you think he committed suicide?" Stephanie shuddered. "If he had a gun, he could have killed us all." She seemed poised for flight.

"Cool," Andie repeated.

This time Molly glanced at her sharply. "We'll just have to wait and see what the police say. Hopefully, they won't keep us waiting too long. Now, let's focus on something else while we wait. Who wants more tea?"

No one answered, but they all found seats on the library's settees.

Lizzie mentally ran through their encounter with the

man. He'd seemed a bit grumpy and jumpy but not like someone depressed and bent on suicide. But what did that mean? It's not like she'd had any experience with something like this—except through fiction, of course. Still, she was itching to get out there and find out what was going on.

She should be more concerned about Andie, she realized. What would her parents think when they found out about the death, especially since Lizzie had yet to tell them about coercing Andie into joining the book club.

"It's all so strange," said Molly. "Why come in and call the AAA or whomever, then kill yourself while waiting? Not even Agatha Christie would put that in a plot. Although she did have Poirot investigate a suicide that proved to be a murder in *Poirot Investigates*. I think it was the second short story in that collection." She glanced around at them all. "What if that's what's happened here? What do you think, Lizzie?"

"I'd say that it's hard to find a new plot."

Bob and Jacob came back in and joined the others. Bob looked in a foul mood.

"Did they tell you anything, Bob?" Molly asked.

"That snotty-nosed punk of a chief told me to wait in here until he's ready to question us. Me. I was a cop for fifteen years and spent another fifteen as chief. He doesn't think I can help? Can't believe they made him chief. Never did trust that kid." Bob's face had turned a bright shade of red during his rant.

Molly took a glass of tea over to him and ushered him to a chair. "Maybe he's embarrassed to have your expertise involved. He'll ask you when the time's right, I'm sure. Do you think the fellow committed suicide?"

"Well, he had a gun in his hand . . . quite an old one, come to think of it." He paused as if visualizing the scene. "Could have been suicide, I guess."

Sally-Jo went over to pour herself a glass of tea. "I wonder what was so bad in his life that he killed himself. No matter how tough things get, I can't imagine suicide as an answer."

Stephanie bolted out of her seat. "I've really got to get going. They can't keep us here, can they? I need to go home. Now."

"Just hold on, there," Bob said. "They won't let you leave, girl. Best to just sit tight and stay calm."

"Look, you didn't talk to the guy or know him, so I'm sure they won't keep you long," Lizzie added. She just wished they'd get started with the questioning.

Stephanie sank back into the chair, a dubious expression on her face, and pulled her knitting out of her bag. Just handling it seemed to calm her.

They heard voices in the hall, and a moment later the door opened and two police officers entered. Lizzie could hardly believe her eyes. Mark Dreyfus, her high school crush, in person. He'd been a short-lived but heart-wrenching obsession in her junior year. A small gasp escaped her lips when he removed his hat. He was totally bald. Gone was the curly black hair that went so well with his dark, intense eyes. Even still, he looked as delicious now as he had back then.

"I'm Mark Dreyfus, police chief. I'm sure Mr. Miller has already informed you about what happened, and I'm sorry we're going to have to take your statements before you leave tonight," he told the group. He spotted Lizzie and smiled. "We'll talk to you all individually and then you're free to go, although I'd like you to stop by the police station tomorrow morning and sign a statement. Ms. Mathews, are there a couple of rooms we could use?"

"Why, sure. The kitchen's at the end of the hall and next to it is Claydon's study. Would those do?"

Mark nodded. "Hank"—he turned to the other cop—"you can take Mr. Miller to start with. Ms. Mathews, perhaps you would come with me. We'll take the kitchen."

"Don't you think you should be talking to me, Chief?"

Bob stood with his arms folded across his chest, glaring at the chief.

Mark barely glanced at him. "No. I think you'd be happier dealing with my deputy, Mr. Miller. And I need to speak to Ms. Mathews. It is her house, after all, and she may have been the last one to speak to the deceased."

Bob grunted but continued to glower as he followed the deputy out of the room.

The first two interviews took the longest, and then the others were quickly dealt with. Lizzie was the last of them, and Mark talked to her in the library.

"Hey, Lizzie. It's been a long time."

Another shock. She thought he'd never even noticed her in school. "It has and I can't believe you even remember my name," she said.

He chuckled. "You weren't hard to miss. You were always reading a book. In the cafeteria, on bus trips, at football games."

She felt mildly annoyed. Not the way she'd hoped to be remembered. She, on the other hand, could still picture all six gorgeous feet of him in his A.C. Gators green and yellow football uniform, surrounded by a squad of perky, blonde cheerleaders. She was dying to ask why he shaved his head but wisely didn't give in to the temptation. Instead, she said, "Football wasn't my thing. Do you know who the dead man is?"

"According to his car registration, he's from Carleton County. We'll have to confirm his identity before releasing a name. You didn't know him? I understand you and Ms. Mathews confronted him in the hall earlier in the evening."

"I'd never seen him before, and he didn't give his name. I was wondering if you found anything odd in his pockets? After all, he just invited himself in and was wandering around for who knows how long before we found him."

"What did you have in mind?"

"Well, stuff that didn't belong there . . . maybe something he might have taken from Molly's house?"

"Do you think his intention was to steal something? You didn't buy his story about calling for a tow?"

"I'm not sure. He did just walk into the house. I'm sure we would have heard the doorbell if he'd bothered to ring it. Nobody just walks into the house of a complete stranger. Who knows what he was up to before Andie Mason walked in on him. He may even have been casing the place."

Mark suppressed a smile. "Anything else make you question his story?"

"Well, we did overhear snatches of his conversation on the phone. Okay, we had our ears to the door but only managed to hear a few words. They sounded almost threatening."

Mark had been writing in his small black notebook but paused to look at Lizzie. His eyes are still the same, she thought.

"Do you remember any of it?" he asked.

"Well, something about doing it his way or not at all and this being the end of it."

"You're certain?"

"I'm a teacher, Mark. I remember things. What about his car? Was it disabled?"

"I can't answer that. I'm having it towed to the station, and we'll have it gone over there. Is there anything else you can think of . . . something he said or even just an impression you had?"

"Well, he didn't seem menacing to us, not real friendly though, sort of abrupt, and he wouldn't give his name. I found that a bit disturbing. And I know Bob Miller thought it suspicious."

"I'm sure."

"I have another question."

"Shoot." He grinned, then added, "So to speak."

"Why didn't we hear a shot? We were kind of loud at times, but shouldn't we have heard it?"

"Not necessarily. That's a long driveway, and if everyone was talking at once—"

"Okay. Did he leave a note?"

"A note? Why do you ask?"

"Well, don't suicides usually leave a note behind?"

"I don't expect to find one, Lizzie. It looks like he was murdered."

Chapter Five

✧✧✧

What do you mean, the police consider me a suspect?

CORPSE POSE—DIANA KILLIAN

Three miles was not going to do it. But Lizzie had run out of time. Her three-mile running circuit took her down Broward past the old Carnegie Library, now a Civil War museum, across the town square, and over to the bike path along Sawmill Creek; then, cutting through the park, she headed back along Madison and right on Sidcup, to the eighty-year-old two-story white clapboard house with the wraparound porch and two-bedroom addition that she called home.

Her landlord, Nathaniel Creely, had built the cramped but sunny quarters as an extra income unit when he retired. After his wife died a year later, he rented it out anyway, more to hear the occasional cough and slamming of doors than anything else, Lizzie suspected. She liked the coziness of the place, and being five blocks from the center of town was an added bonus. Creely had readily agreed to put in a paved driveway, paint the place in a cream color she loved and even plant a row of hibiscus by the front window. She'd immediately signed on the dotted line.

She delighted in the fact that every second morning, when she ran in the opposite direction, it took her along Cavendish Road and past the blue Cape Cod house she'd grown up in. Her earliest memories had her in the bottom left corner kitchen cabinets, the ones her daddy had removed the turntable shelves from and transformed into a playhouse. She'd spend hours sprawled on the cushions he'd added, playing school with her two favorite dolls, Becky with red hair and the blonde bombshell Barbie, surrounded by the sounds of her mama humming as she worked in the kitchen.

She'd outgrown her special place by the day the humming stopped. That shattering day when just before dinner, Chief Bob Miller had shown up at the door to tell them her daddy wasn't coming home again. He'd been killed in a traffic accident out on Broward Hill. It took another six months before her mama noticed ten-year-old Lizzie needed new shoes; another couple of years before she once again smiled. But the smile never reached her eyes. It still didn't, although Lizzie hadn't given up hoping.

A quick shower was followed by a breakfast of veggie protein drink with a banana chaser, and she was back on track. Her Siamese cats, Edam and Brie, had wolfed down the canned food she'd given them for breakfast and now awaited the usual dried food top-ups. She filled each of their bowls, giving the head-butting male Chocolate point, Edam, a few rubs under the chin. Brie, the more regal and older of the two, demanded a rub between the ears. Lizzie promised to brush them both when she got home from school.

The phone rang as Lizzie was pulling on a tangerine leather jacket. She answered, her free hand smoothing stray hairs back in place.

"Hello, Lizzie, honey. I'm sure glad I caught you."

"Molly, what's the matter? You sound upset."

"I surely am, honey. The police were just here, and it appears the gun used to kill that man last night was mine. Or rather, Claydon's." Molly let out a deep sigh.

"What? I don't understand, Molly."

"Neither do I, and I can tell you, I'm rightly frazzled. The police say it was murder and the gun used is an old antique. Everyone knows about Claydon's collection, so I checked in his study and there's a gun missing from the gun case. I'm not sure what to do."

"Did the police say anything else?"

"Yes. She told me not to leave town, and you know that's what they say in all our mysteries. They must think I'm the prime suspect." Molly choked on what sounded like an intended laugh.

Lizzie looked at her watch. She could stop briefly at Molly's on the way to school. A hug was definitely in order.

"Look, Molly, I'm sure they don't think that. They know you, after all. I can stop by for a couple of minutes before school, if you'd like. Maybe have a quick cup of coffee?"

"Would you mind, honey? I'd surely appreciate it."

Lizzie grabbed her large tote bag, called out good-bye to the cats and left. On the drive over to Molly's, her thoughts were a jumble of questions about the murder, so she tried to simply concentrate on the scenery. She loved this time of year, still early enough in fall for the autumn cherry trees to be in full bloom, their white flowers a bright contrast to the deeper-colored maple leaves.

She made a left on Sequoia and drove past the freshly painted Federal-style, two-story house belonging to the parents of her childhood friend Cindy Blake. How different the paths they'd chosen: Cindy, now a cardiac surgeon at a hospital in Atlanta, and married with two children; Lizzie, back in their hometown after five years away at college, a short stint working in Montgomery and more schooling—and she was still single.

Not that she regretted any of it. She loved her job, singing in the community choir was a passion, and she had many friends, old and new. Ashton Corners would always be home. She liked knowing she'd bump into someone she knew each time she went downtown, that memories of growing up could be sparked by a photo in the daily newspaper, and yet, the town had grown to offer enough variety so she could do something different every evening of the week if she so wanted.

Molly had two cups of coffee in china mugs and a plate of warm cinnamon buns on the kitchen table when Lizzie arrived. Lizzie sat on a stool at the counter that divided the kitchen work area from the banquette. After some tentative sips of the hot brew, a taste test of the buns and yet another pledge to herself to run longer the next day, Lizzie got to the point.

"Do you have any idea how the gun went missing?" She had her own idea, which started and ended with the deceased.

"I'm not sure how long it's been gone. I've not had a reason to check the display case." Molly smoothed an unruly strand of gray that had worked its way out of the red bow anchoring her hair at the base of her neck. She tucked it behind her right ear. The bow matched the red in her striped linen blouse, which looked snappy with her khaki pants. "It could have been taken months ago, for all I know. Or last night. Do you think maybe the stranger took it before Andie found him?"

"I'd bet on it. It's the simplest scenario, and that's usually the right one. The study is right next to the front door, after all. And we don't know how long he was in the house alone. Did you mention it to Chief Dreyfus?"

"No. It was Officer Amber Craig who came by. She said she's investigating the case."

That surprised Lizzie. Wasn't it important enough for the chief to stay involved? If Molly was being implicated, the case should be at the top of his priority list. Maybe she should talk to him. Or maybe she should butt out. For now.

"What's she like?" Lizzie asked.

"She's pretty new in town, so we hadn't met before. She seems efficient but not overly friendly. Like she must walk around with her teeth gritted all the time."

"How about talking it over with Bob Miller?"

"I don't want to unleash him on our poor chief," Molly said with a sigh. "Bob's already got a stick up his backside about the boy."

"Well, what about calling Jacob Smith then? He must take cases other than those involving pigs."

A giggle escaped Molly's lips. "Oh dear. I do suppose I should consult a lawyer."

"Just to be clear on your rights." Lizzie glanced at her watch. "I'm sorry, but I have to run, Molly, or I'll be late for the class. I'll see you tonight. It's literacy night, remember?"

"That it is. And, thanks, Lizzie. I appreciate you coming by."

Lizzie scrunched her into a big hug before driving off. Molly had slipped easily into the role of family member when Lizzie's Grandmama Beata, one of Molly's close friends, died and then again when Lizzie had to deal with her mama's illness and eventually choose a residence with the proper level of care for her. She knew it was thanks to Molly that the weekly visits took place in the brightly decorated sunrooms rather than a depressing bedroom. It helped to have pull with a board member and bypass the lengthy waiting list.

She owed Molly a lot, but she also cared and worried about her. Molly had been devastated when her husband, Claydon, had died suddenly of a heart attack many years before. Lizzie knew that the brave face she showed to the community was strictly that, even after all this time. This new trauma was not something Molly would have to face alone.

Lizzie made it to the school in record time. Ashton Corners Elementary School had celebrated its seventy-fifth anniversary last year. The halls were now painted a brighter, noninstitutional peach color, the windows in most of the rooms had been replaced by single-pane glass, the floors had been redone with a heavy-duty laminate, the old wooden desks had given way to new plastic ones, and even the blackboards had been replaced, but the character of the school remained in the twenty-foot ceilings, the crown moldings and the wide hallways.

Whenever she entered room 12, Lizzie had a fleeting memory of being back in sixth grade, listening intently to Mr. Bigelow, absolutely the most gorgeous teacher the young impressionable girls had ever seen. They'd giggled through many a lunch hour discussing his rumored romance with Miss Tays, the stunning fifth-grade teacher in room 8. Lizzie wondered now if that relationship had been pure adolescent fantasy or if the rumor had been true and the two were actually happily married after all these years.

And outside, the school had long ago shed its white and green government image in favor of an updated, smarter beige with taupe trim. The front boulevard sported mature oak and maple trees, and the schoolyard offered two play structures, one for the primary-grade students, one for the older kids; a paved area on which boards and boundaries for various games had been painted; and way back behind it all, a softball diamond.

Lizzie had never shined as a softball player, tending to close her eyes when the ball got into her comfort zone, but she'd spent many afternoons after class, lazing on the grass, reading while her pals played ball.

She made her way through the thinning groups of kids in the hall, entering the classroom at the same time as the teacher, and settled at the back to observe for the next hour. After class, she tucked herself into an armchair in the staff room and wrote down some observations of the class she'd just left. The teacher had her hands full with a couple of new students, and the disruption that caused for the other kids needed attention. Sometimes Lizzie wished she had a magic wand and, with one wave, could make everything run smoothly. But then she'd be out of a job.

Lizzie enjoyed working as a reading specialist. She'd been with the Ashton Corners School Board for four years now and loved the challenge of assessing young readers and suggesting methods to help them acquire the necessary reading skills, developing the programs when necessary. This allowed her to work with the children, their parents, the teachers and the school board administration. Never a dull moment.

The lunch bell jolted her out of her musing, and she slid her notes into her tote. After a quick stop at Tessa's Tex-Mex Cafe just around the corner for a spicy chicken burrito, she drove to a meeting at the school board office. Three tedious hours of listening to the ongoing debate of the merits of a proposed new statewide testing, and Lizzie wanted nothing more than to head home for a couple of hours of quiet.

She pulled into her driveway and by the time she'd gathered her tote and exited the car, a police cruiser sat near her bumper. Mark Dreyfus gave her a small wave as he emerged. He tossed his hat back in the car, locked the door and walked over to her.

"Hey, Lizzie. You got a few minutes to talk?"

"Talk or be interrogated? Or is there a difference? And should I have a lawyer present?"

Mark grinned. "A bit touchy today?"

Lizzie sighed and made an effort to relax her shoulders. "Sorry. It's been one of those days, as they say. Let me try that again. It's nice to see you, Mark. Please come in."

"That's much better," he said, grinning. "Got to get something out of the car. I'll join you in a minute."

Lizzie noted the slight limp as Mark walked to his car. She'd heard he'd been wounded shortly after he'd enlisted in the army, but had never learned the details. Maybe that's where he'd left his curly black hair, too.

The cats hadn't appeared when she opened the door, so she assumed they were in dreamland on her bed. She left the front door slightly ajar while she hung up her jacket and shoved the tote into the hall closet. This could be great timing. She might be able to get just as much information as she'd give. She checked her hair in the mirror at the bottom of the stairs but turned quickly as Mark came in.

"I thought you might like some refreshments . . . make it seem less like an interrogation." He held out a soda.

Lizzie burst into laughter. "Cream soda. I haven't had one of these in years. In fact, I didn't think they made it anymore. Thanks, Mark." *Is he being sweet, or is this to soften me up?* "I'll get a couple of glasses. Just make yourself comfortable." She pointed to the living room to the left.

He had his back to her, scanning the titles on the massive bookcase that covered one wall, when she returned. The white shelves held an eclectic mix of reference books, travel guides, classical literature, current mainstream novels and, of course, tons of mysteries. Lizzie wondered what he thought about all the books.

"This is a real nice place, Lizzie. I don't think I've seen so many books in one room outside of the library."

"A lot of them belonged to my daddy."

Mark turned around and smiled. "That's right, he was a writer, wasn't he?"

"Uh-huh. A newspaperman who then went on to write feature articles for *Life* and other magazines." Lizzie handed Mark a glass.

He flipped the tops off the sodas and poured both drinks, then sat on the green striped love seat. Lizzie chose the taupe wicker chair across from him and opened the window next to her. A soft wind blew the fragrance of sweet autumn clematis into the room. She breathed in deeply.

"You know, you do have a right to a lawyer and you don't have to answer my questions. But I'd really appreciate if you would," Mark said.

Lizzie sighed. "Thanks, but I don't need one and I will answer." She smiled.

He cleared his throat and took a long drink of his soda. "I'd like to know if you've thought of any other details, something you might not have mentioned last night."

"No, I haven't thought of anything else, and it's not from lack of trying. I couldn't get to sleep last night. It all kept replaying through my brain." She decided to let him be the one to mention Molly's gun. "Have you any more details? Or, better yet, a suspect?"

"No suspect and unfortunately, that doesn't happen very quickly unless someone's standing over the body with a gun," Mark admitted, "but that's my priority since it's been ruled a murder."

Lizzie flinched. That news wasn't unexpected but it was unsettling. "I'm not sure what else I can tell you."

"How about going through the events again from when you encountered Frank Telford in the hall." He answered the surprised look on her face. "He's been identified. He's from Stoney Mills. Seventy-six years old, lived alone. Does the name ring any bells?"

She tried to place the name with the face and match it to her internal Facebook. "No, I'm pretty certain I don't know him." She went through the events while Mark referred on and off to a black notebook he'd pulled from his pocket. Mark finished his soda before asking, "Did anyone else leave the room, other than you and Ms. Mathews going out to meet Telford?"

"Well, yes . . . Bob Miller went to check that the guy, Telford, had actually left the house, and to lock the door." Brie chose that moment to saunter into the room; she paused briefly, looking from Lizzie over to Mark, and then selected Mark's pant leg as the ideal spot against which to rub her sleek body. Lizzie grimaced. "I'm sorry about that," she said, pointing to his leg. "I'll get you a clothes brush before you leave."

Mark leaned down to absently pet the cat, ignoring the telltale beige fur on his gray pant leg. "How long would you say he was gone?"

"Oh, I don't know . . . maybe three minutes or so."

Mark nodded. "Anyone else leave during the meeting?" He'd pulled out a pen and begun to jot down notes as she talked.

"Let me think." She tried to visualize the library and place everyone in their chair. "Uh, Molly went to the kitchen again to refill the food tray, and Sally-Jo Baker went to the restroom at one point. So did Andie Mason and Stephanie Lowe. Jacob Smith, too, I think. And me. I got some more tea. Well, that would be everyone leaving at some point. Why are you asking?"

"Did anyone seem to take longer than normal?" Mark stared at her intently.

She bit her bottom lip and then shook her head. "I don't think so, but I wasn't timing anyone." She sat up a bit straighter. "Don't tell me you think one of the book club members is a murderer? That's ridiculous. We're readers, not killers. Besides, nobody knew him, so who would have motive?"

"Did anyone have a noticeable reaction to his being there?"

Despite the sodas, this Mark sounded very official, and she didn't like where it was heading. She thought briefly about Stephanie, then tried to erase the image. "I wouldn't say so."

He stared at her a moment. *Oh God . . . can he read my mind?*

"You know, I have to look at everyone in the book club, Lizzie, if only to eliminate them. Even you, I'm sorry to say. There might not be any connection between Telford's death and his appearing at Ms. Mathews's house or your book club. On the other hand, he could have deliberately gone there. And if so, that could implicate Molly Mathews, at the very least."

"Oh, come on now, you don't really believe Molly's involved in this?"

He didn't answer. She shifted uncomfortably.

She remembered Telford's excuse. "Did he really have car trouble?"

"Doesn't appear so. It started just fine for us. One more thing, Lizzie . . . don't leave town."

Her mouth dropped open, but she could not think of a thing to say.

Mark chuckled. "Sorry. I've always wanted to say that. Makes me sound like Lucas Davenport, don't you think?"

Chapter Six

When she needed a little space, music was the best
solution . . .

PINNED FOR MURDER—ELIZABETH LYNN CASEY

Friday night meant choir practice, and Lizzie realized
Mark's visit had put her a bit behind schedule. She gulped
down some leftover chili, only one day old, and, in record time,
changed into a charcoal cropped cardigan over a teal ruffle
blouse. She'd meant to get there early and talk to the music
librarian, hoping to replace some pages that had become
unreadable over the years due to an accumulation of coffee
stains and something that looked vaguely like strawberry
jelly.

The weekly practices were held in the basement hall of
St. John's Episcopal Church on Yancy Street. Over the past
few weeks—since the summer break ended—they'd been
working on music for the annual Christmas concert; Britten,
Rutter and some less-than-traditional carols made for a com-
pelling mix.

By the time Lizzie made it to the church, most of the
parking spaces in the adjacent lot were taken. That was the
problem with being located in the center of town: parking

lots were small, and leaving the car on the street meant
competing for desirable spots with store patrons taking
advantage of later shopping hours on Fridays. Her small
Mazda looked tiny next to Posey Daniels's monster Lexus
SUV. Lizzie often wondered why such a petite woman,
single at that, had to drive something so big. She was
tempted to peek in and see if extra cushions had been added
to the driver's seat.

Lizzie didn't meet anyone on her way in to the church. *I
must really be late*, she thought as she picked up some new
music left out on the table by the door to the rehearsal room.
She could hear the accompanist, Tommy McCann, warming
up on the piano. Chairs scraped the floor, and the sound of
a laugh, almost a screech, pierced the air. Judy-Lynn Jones
was there, at least. The door creaked as she pulled it open.

She nodded at her fellow choristers as she made her way
to her spot in the second row, third seat from the left. The
director, Stanton Giles, signaled for silence, asked them to
stand, and nodded at Tommy, who led them through the
scales.

"I was worried you might not make it," Lucille Miller
hissed from behind.

Lizzie gave her a small wave and shrugged her shoulders,
picking up the vocal run on the second go-round.

"I need to talk to you during break," Lucille said in a
loud whisper while Stanton demonstrated the next warm-up
exercise.

Lizzie nodded her head, anxious to get on with the practice. She knew Lucille wouldn't wait for the break, given
half a chance. She gratefully pulled out the Rutter as they
finished the warm-up and sat down.

An hour later, Stanton announced a ten-minute break,
and Lizzie headed for the kitchen. She'd forgotten to bring
a bottle of water, and the lingering humidity had made her
even more thirsty than usual.

"Lizzie, I thought we'd have a talk," she heard Lucille whine as she followed.

"You go ahead and talk, Lucille. I need a drink."

"Well, I've been dying to call and ask you if Bob actually showed up at the book club last night."

"He didn't tell you?"

"Well, no. He's been avoiding me. He likes doing that. Figures I interfere too much in his life. But somebody has to." Lucille tucked a lock of her curly gray hair behind her ear and pushed her black-framed glasses up to rest atop her head. "If not, he'd spend all his time fishing out the back of his house. Ever since he bought the old Stark place when he retired, he acts like that river and his fishing rod are the only important things in his life. He won't even come to Sunday dinner on a regular basis. And I don't know the last time I saw him in church. It's embarrassing for me, being in the choir and head of the Ladies' Guild and the Altar Guild. But he doesn't think about that. I think he's totally regressed into childhood." She took a quick breath. "Now, did he show up?"

Lizzie blinked, glad that Lucille had actually gotten back to the original question. "He did, and he even brought a friend with him."

"Friend? What friend? Bob usually doesn't have time for friends."

"His name is Jacob Smith."

"The new lawyer in town? Now I wonder how they met. I wonder if Bob's in need of lawyering services. I wonder what he's gotten himself into. You know, he never tells me. Anything. A lawyer. Hmm." Lucille helped herself to a cup of coffee from the urn on the counter. She also selected a piece of Bourbon pound cake, took a large bite, and chewed contentedly.

Lizzie wasn't about to get into that discussion. She knew she probably shouldn't say anything else, in fact. But she did. "So, you didn't hear that Bob found a body in a car outside Molly's house?"

"What?" Lucille almost choked on the cake. "You mean that story on the news? They didn't say much or I didn't listen carefully or something. You mean, Bob's gone and gotten himself involved in that? Wouldn't you know it. Can't take the cop out of the man. Just wait till I talk to him tomorrow. I might even go out to his place to do it. Yes, that's what I'll do. Who was the victim?"

"Nobody local. His name is Frank Telford, and he's from Stoney Mills. Or rather, he was."

"Telford. Hmm. I think there were Telfords living in Mobile. A banking family or some sort. Telford. Why does that sound familiar? Of course, everything sounds familiar at my age."

"So I've heard," Lizzie said just as the choir was called back into practice.

One hour later, Lucille hooked her arm through Lizzie's as she walked to the parking lot. "I think the Telford I remember hearing about had been up to no good."

Chapter Seven

Anything resembling free time is always a treat.

RED DELICIOUS DEATH—SHEILA CONNOLLY

By the time Saturday rolled along, Lizzie wanted nothing more than a few quiet hours spent in solitude. Physical exertion needed to be involved to make up for some missed runs earlier in the week. And since sunshine was forecast for the entire day, she decided to pack a small lunch and spend a few hours hiking along the Minto Country Nature Trail on White Mountain.

She felt a momentary pang of guilt for not calling Sally-Jo to join her, but she knew the talk would be all about the murder and after spending much of the previous day doing just that, she wanted at least a morning to herself. And no thinking. She added a lightweight beige fleece vest to the long-sleeved green T-shirt she wore and grabbed an Auburn Tigers ball cap from the closet before walking out the door.

She pulled into the dirt parking lot around eight A.M. and parked far away from the only other vehicle, a black Jeep Wrangler that was looking the bit worse for wear. No one was around, so she figured the owner must be well along the trail. She stuffed her cell phone and car keys in the front pocket of her small backpack, shrugged it on and set out.

The charm of these solitary walks lay in the overwhelming number of birdcalls. She knew only a few of them but appreciated the tunes that followed her along the well-worn path, through masses of pine, evergreen and oak. At this time of year the thick undergrowth was dying off, unveiling proof of the popularity of the trail. Most of the sports-drink bottles and candy wrappers were left by teens. One of these days, she mused, they'd realize the importance of nature and stop littering. But then, there was always a new gaggle of teens aging into their place.

She suddenly stumbled, grabbing at the protruding branch of a nearby pine tree to keep from falling. She looked down. At her feet, a booted foot stuck out at a strange angle to the ground. *Yikes! Not another body*, she thought as she dropped to her knees and spread apart the thick patch of lacy ferns.

"Shhh." A hand waved her away, and she sat back on her heels. After several seconds, the body pulled back out of hiding and sat up to face her.

"Good God, Mark. I thought it was a dead body I tripped over. Just what the hell do you mean, scaring me like that?"

He grinned. "Hey, Lizzie. I'm the one who got scared, or rather the flicker I was trying to photograph did." He held up his camera, long lens and all, for her to see.

"I don't believe it. You're the last person I would have expected to see here, taking pictures of birds." She clapped her hand over her mouth, wishing she could edit the words or pull them back in.

"I'll try not to take offense at that." He smiled again. "It's about the only place I can really get away. I don't tell anyone where I'm going, and I leave my phone in the car. What's your excuse for being here?"

She sighed. "Much the same, I guess. I love being out here. It's a good place to get away. Or hide away. And traipsing along the trail helps put things in perspective."

He stuck his camera in its bag and stood, reaching out a hand to help her stand. He brushed some dirt and twigs off the knees of his faded blue jeans and pushed his ball cap off his forehead. The ACHS Gators logo was so faded it was barely recognizable.

He removed the black plaid flannel shirt worn as a jacket and shoved it into his backpack. "Getting warm already. I think it'll be a perfect morning for a hike. Care to join me? You can tell me just what it is that you need to put into perspective today."

Lizzie nodded, thinking that she'd just been presented with the ideal opportunity to start quizzing him about the murder—until she realized that the murder was probably one of the things Mark needed to get away from. She'd go with his suggestion instead.

"Don't get me started on the three teachers who desperately need classroom evaluations on interactions, the group of six I meet with each week as part of the literacy program, or the one stubborn teen I tutor once a week."

He laughed. "I never realized the world of education could be so overwhelming. Shall we get started on a peaceful, relaxing, getting-away-from-it-all hike?"

"That would be nice," she said.

"Follow me then. I bet I know some trails you've never spied."

I'll just bet you do.

They walked alongside a small creek that slowly sloped upward. After about twenty minutes of climbing, with little talk except for Mark pointing to some wildlife caught unawares, Lizzie reached out to touch his elbow.

"I realize we have two different notions of 'relaxing,' but could we take a short break?"

He chuckled. "Absolutely. Sorry, I know I walk too fast. I do it without thinking."

"Your army training?"

He nodded and looked away. "Yeah, I guess."

His abruptness startled her. Was it a phase of his life he didn't want to talk about? She'd have to tread gently into that territory. She pulled her stainless steel water bottle out of her backpack and took a long drink, watching as he did the same. She could only imagine what horrors he'd gone through. She could remember her mama and daddy talking about their friends who hadn't made it back from Vietnam. She knew that a handful of guys from Ashton Corners had served in Desert Storm and now in Iraq, and they'd been lucky so far. Not one casualty from their town. Still, the psychological damage must run deep.

"Okay. I'm watered and I'm tough. Lead on," she said, resolve in her voice.

Mark glanced at her, then nodded, holding back a drooping branch until she stepped past. She followed him for another hour or so, waiting quietly while he stopped to take pictures of the occasional bird or deer. They reached a small clearing with a fire pit, obviously a favorite for meal breaks.

"Did you pack a lunch?" Mark asked.

She pulled a veggie wrap out of her backpack and waved it at him. He mimicked and countered with an unknown sandwich in a ziplock bag. They ate in companionable silence. She enjoyed the sounds of birds and a nearby waterfall, not feeling at all uncomfortable without verbal communication. She realized he had finished eating and was watching her.

"What?" she asked. Was he speculating on her ranking on the suspect list, after all?

"You surprise me, Lizzie, that's all."

Not what she'd expected to hear. "In what way?"

He leaned back against a stump. "Well, in high school you seemed so unapproachable. Like you had this inner circle of friends and your books and didn't want anyone else elbowing in."

She realized she was sitting there with her mouth hanging open. Not charming, as Molly would quickly admonish her.

"I guess that was pretty much like it was. I didn't think you'd noticed."

"Oh, I had."

She shifted to the right to get the sun out of her eyes. "You were the one in his own world, I'd say, what with all the jocks and cheerleaders and all."

"I didn't think you'd noticed," he said. A smile played at the corners of his mouth.

"Oh, I had."

Oh, boy. Now what?

He looked at her awhile longer, then smiled. "I'm sorry to say this, but I have to work this afternoon so we'd best be getting back. That is," he quickly added, "I have to get back. You don't have to head back right now, if you want to keep on going."

"I'd better get back, too. I have to get some groceries in the house and mark some papers, then go to a very special birthday party."

"Not your own?"

"Nope. This gal's much, much younger."

He stood up and put out a hand to pull her up. She was pleased when he continued holding it on the way back down the trail.

The phone rang as Lizzie opened the front door. She grabbed it as the caller hung up. No message but the caller ID pegged Sally-Jo. She dialed back.

"Wow, that was quick," Sally-Jo greeted her.

"I just came through the door, so that was great timing. What can I do for you?"

"I just wanted you to know that I had a call from Chief Dreyfus's office this morning and they've asked me to come in to talk to him at two. Do you think I need a lawyer or something?" Sally-Jo's voice sounded a bit more in the soprano range than usual.

"Why? You didn't do anything you need to worry about. He's probably going to be hauling us all in, making sure we're not changing stories or anything."

"Why would I do that? I told the truth, and I don't know anything beyond what happened Thursday night. Maybe I should have a lawyer with me, just in case."

A light dawned. "Actually, maybe it would be a good idea if you called Jacob Smith and asked his advice. Or maybe he could go with you. And then you could invite him out for a drink, as a thank-you. And he might ask you to supper. And you could ask him in later for another drink. And—"

"Okay. Thank you for your suggestion. I can tell where this is heading. And here I thought you'd given up matchmaking. I'll talk to you later. Maybe."

Lizzie smiled. "See that you do. I want to know all, you know."

"As always," Sally-Jo said with a small laugh. "Ciao."

Lizzie glanced at the clock sitting on the mantle. Time to get into high gear. Maybe shopping first, then the shower and later, the dinner invitation to a birthday party for a special four-year-old.

Chapter Eight

◇◇◇

"We're all good," she said. "All good."

FALSE IMPRESSIONS—TERRI THAYER

"**A**untie Lizzie! Auntie Lizzie! We been waiting. My mama says that's something like a watched pot. What does that mean? Where have you been? I got presents to open, Auntie Lizzie. Come on with me. Mama, Auntie Lizzie's here."

Birthday girl Jenna Raleigh grabbed Lizzie's hand and tried to pull her into the living room, a hard task for someone so tiny. Her curly blonde hair had been pulled back in a ponytail, held in place by a shiny red barrette that matched her red and white polka-dot T-shirt and red jeans.

"I'm sorry I'm late, Jenna. Hey, Paige . . . sorry to you, too. It couldn't be avoided. The flowers are for you, the wine is for Brad, and this"—she retrieved a large gift bag decorated with pink bunnies from her canvas tote—"is for the birthday girl."

"Yessss!" Jenna clapped her hands and grabbed the bag.

"Not yet, bunny. Put it with the other gifts. We'll open them when everyone's in the living room. Go get your daddy, please. How are you, Lizzie? It feels like just ages since I've seen you," Paige said with a deep sigh. Her own long blonde hair had been piled atop her head, held with a clip, but not securely enough to keep in check a bevy of tendrils that fell in a frame around her face. The long green cotton blouse she wore had the empire waist she'd favored since giving birth to her second daughter. Somehow, those last pounds and inches just wouldn't disappear.

Lizzie laughed. "I think it was last Sunday that I was over. It's been a hectic week for you, too, I'd guess."

"That doesn't begin to cover it." Paige hugged Lizzie. "And you've had quite the week, I hear. A dead body and all. Tell me about it."

Lizzie pulled one smaller gift bag from her tote before stashing it in the hallway. "This is for the non-birthday gremlin. I'll tell you all about the goings-on later. But it has been a weird few days. And you'll never guess who's investigating the case."

Paige grinned. "I'll just bet it's Mark Dreyfus. I knew you two would bump into each other at some point."

"Why didn't you tell me he was the chief? And isn't he awfully young to be chief? He can't be more than thirty-two or thirty-three."

"He probably got the job because of his army background, or maybe there weren't any other candidates. I forget the details, if I even knew them. And, I forgot to tell you because it happened when you were out of town taking that longer course, the name of which I always forget, and well, it just never dawned on me that you'd want to know. Does he still curl your toes?"

"You remember that!"

"Of course I do. In fact, I even saved some of the notes we used to pass in math class."

Lizzie groaned. "How much do you want for them?"

"No way. I plan to read them at your wedding, girl," Paige said with a laugh.

"That's okay then. They'll be too yellowed and crumbling to read by that point." *No point in adding fuel to the fire by telling her about our hike.* "Where's the rest of the gang?"

The shrieking of two small girls answered her question, as they flew through the kitchen door and flung themselves at her. Lizzie loved visiting the Raleigh household. She and Paige had grown up together, spending almost equal time in each other's houses. Their parents had been good friends, until the accident, when Lizzie's mama had cut herself off from everyone. Paige and her mama had been a big help to her, offering comfort and a second home. Paige was the sister she never had. They'd both known Brad Raleigh at high school, and Lizzie couldn't have been happier when the two of them finally got married. Now she was godmother to Jenna, and "auntie" to her and her sister, Cate.

After supper and the official opening of gifts, the girls went off to play while the adults took their coffees into the living room.

"What's up with that dead body, Lizzie?" Brad asked.

Lizzie stared at him a moment before answering. "You're growing a beard, aren't you? I've been trying to figure out what's different and that's it. Or else you're getting too lazy to shave these days."

"You're sharp tonight, Lizzie," Brad said with a grin. "My lady here is not overly pleased. I'd be rightly grateful if you'd tell her you like it."

"You know, Paige, it does give him a certain rugged man-of-the-bush appeal."

At six-five, Brad had kept his body as trim as the day they'd graduated. Not one for team sports, he'd been more an outdoorsman, hiking and hunting luring him away from town each weekend. Until marriage trimmed the number of outings and the frequency.

"Anyway," Lizzie continued, "Thursday was a strange evening." She told them about it in detail.

"They can't believe Molly had anything to do with it," Paige said in a shocked tone.

"They're checking us all very closely. They had Sally-Jo Baker in for an interview at the station this afternoon. I'm dying to hear how that went."

"So to speak," Brad said, straight-faced.

"Precisely. The police are trying real hard to find a connection between the dead man, Frank Telford, and one of us. Sally-Jo said they asked if she knew him before she moved here."

"Isn't she from out west somewhere?"

"No. Fort Myers. I think the police are really stretching. Although, when you think about it, we only know what Sally-Jo has chosen to tell us about herself. She's lived here for close to a year now, but I haven't met any of her relatives or friends from out of town." She paused. "But I'd swear she's not involved. And then there's Stephanie Lowe. She's not sharing any details about herself either."

"Oh, that nice young thing? She wouldn't hurt a fly," Paige observed.

"Why, because she's pregnant?" Brad asked.

"Now you just shush," Paige replied. "I think I'm a pretty good judge of character, and I'd say she's not a murderer."

"And how else do you know her except from eating at the Oasis?" Brad persisted.

Paige made a face at him. "If I weren't such a good judge of character, we wouldn't be married."

"Ouch. I'm not sure if that was a compliment or not. Just think I'll go do the dishes so you two can continue with your character assessments. Ladies." He gave a small bow before leaving.

Lizzie laughed. "Too bad you saw him first."

"Hah. I can't see you with two kids under the age of four running around your heels. And he wants more!"

"I seem to remember your thinking six was an ideal number of kids."

"That was when I was young, idealistic and a nonparent. So, what's it feel like to be grilled by Mark?" Paige grabbed a cushion and hugged it as she made herself more comfortable on the beige striped sofa.

"Grilled is right. He's probably a good cop, but I just wish he'd focus away from the book club. I'm certain no one in it is a murderer. He has help, though. Officer Amber Craig. Molly says she's new to town and that's who put her through the hoops. I haven't met her as yet." She paused and took a sip of her coffee.

"It's a real puzzle, though," she continued. "No one knew this Frank Telford. He was wandering around Molly's house, then made a phone call and then was found dead in his car. It's either a case of the wrong place, wrong time, or there's something tying it all together."

"Good thing you don't have to worry about it," Paige said. "Uh, Lizzie . . . you don't, do you? Or should I say, you won't, will you? Promise me you'll stay out of it. I worry about you enough already."

Chapter Nine

◇◇◇

The sweet tea was very refreshing. But Lulu had the feeling she was soon going to need something completely different: and alcohol based.

DELICIOUS AND SUSPICIOUS—RILEY ADAMS

Sundays always filled Lizzie with a feeling of exhilaration and dread. She took the liberty of going back to bed after grabbing the *Birmingham News*, delivered each weekend, and a cup of coffee, timed to brew about ten minutes before her inner alarm went off. She took a pass on her morning run and showered just before dressing to go to Magnolia Manor and visit with her mama.

If it was a good day, Evelyn Turner would be alert and would know Lizzie as her visitor, or better still, as her daughter, and they'd have lunch together in the dining room. If not, Lizzie would sit and talk until she ran out of news and idle chatter. She'd be sure to read a few more chapters of *Mansfield Park*, the Jane Austen novel they were currently working their way through—Lizzie planned to have all of Austen's books read by the end of next year, at which point they'd start on another novelist. She'd also help feed her mama in her room, and eventually, go back to her own world. Leaving was always hardest. *What if Mama remembers me just after I've left the room?* Lizzie wondered at the end of every visit, fearful of missing that moment of recognition yet all too aware that it was unlikely to happen.

This week's visit followed the latter pattern. Lizzie finished reading, then brushed her mama's hair, something they both felt to be soothing. Long gone was Evelyn's shoulder-length hair, often done up in a French twist or a bun. The current bob displayed more gray than auburn now. It always looked in need of an extra-conditioning treatment. The eyes that watched Lizzie in the mirror were a dull green, lacking curiosity and animation.

She remembered sitting on the edge of the bed, as a child, watching Mama getting ready to go out on a date with Daddy. He'd phoned her after meeting in town with someone, although Lizzie couldn't remember if she'd heard who or just forgotten those details. He told Evelyn to get all dressed up and to see if Lizzie could go to a friend's house for the evening because they were going out to dinner at the dining room in the old Sheridan Arms Hotel. Her mama had pulled a floral chiffon short dress over her head and then set about combing her hair, securing it behind her ears with a set of pearl barrettes. Her eyes had danced as she'd applied some red lipstick to her smiling lips.

She'd promised Lizzie they'd all go out on a picnic the next day. And they had. They'd chased each other around the park. It had been a day of laughter. Evelyn had been so full of energy and fun in those days. She'd love to take her mama out for a run now, something to get her muscles back in shape. To get her laughing again. *Not going to happen.*

The brushing done, Lizzie steered her mama back to her favorite beige lazy-lady chair, turned at right angles so that she'd have a view of one of the many colorful gardens surrounding the Manor. A stately moss-covered elm provided the backdrop.

A sharp knock at the door surprised Lizzie. She opened

it to find Molly cradling a large bouquet of freshly cut autumn flowers.

"I thought I'd find you here, honey. How's our gal doing today?" Molly asked, kissing Lizzie on the cheek and moving swiftly over to Evelyn Turner to do the same.

"About the same, Molly. We just finished reading, and I was about to go."

"Do wait for me, Lizzie. I just wanted to stop by with these. I think there's a large vase on the shelf in her closet." Molly looked as colorful as the bouquet, dressed in an orange and gold sheath, her hair held back with a large taupe bow.

Lizzie found it and filled it with water from the bathroom sink. "They're beautiful, Molly. They'll really brighten up the room. Thanks so much."

Molly nodded and passed the flowers to Lizzie, who arranged them in the vase. Molly sat down on an ottoman next to Evelyn and took her hands in her own. "Evie, I've been thinking about you a lot lately. I need to talk to Lizzie, so I won't stay. But I'll be back soon, dear friend, and we'll spend a lovely afternoon together."

She squeezed Evelyn's hands, gave her another kiss on the cheek and waited at the door while Lizzie said good-bye.

Once out in the hall, Molly grabbed Lizzie's elbow and steered her toward the front door. "I'm taking you out to lunch, honey. I'll bet you didn't eat here and besides, I do need to talk to you."

They agreed to meet at the Green Willows Restaurant, and Lizzie led the way out of the parking lot. At the restaurant, Molly asked for a table by the window, and they were seated overlooking the Tallapoosa River. Glasses of ice water appeared, as did the menus. Molly ordered them each a glass of Pinot Blanc.

"I think you deserve it and I need it," she said with a wink. They placed their orders, Molly choosing fried bass with a mixed greens salad and Lizzie opting for prawns and grilled vegetables, then toasted each other and took a long sip.

"Your mama is looking in good health, Lizzie. Did she do any talking today?"

"No, but she seemed to be trying to follow along with the story. She gets a look of concentration sometimes, like she's trying hard to come out of herself, but that just may be wishful thinking on my part."

"Nothing wrong with wishful thinking, honey." Molly slipped her boxy cream-colored jacket off and draped it on the back of the chair. "Now, switching the topic—and rather abruptly I admit, and I do apologize for doing so—but I'm wondering if you've had a conversation with the police chief lately?"

Lizzie wondered for a split second how Molly knew about their hike but then decided it was simply a question.

"Not about the case," she admitted. "Why? Has something else come up?"

"Well, I had a call from Stephanie, poor child, as if she doesn't have enough to worry about. Seems that new officer questioned her again. And Bob's all in a huff because she questioned him, too. I'll bet she didn't know he's the former chief, but I'm sure he set her straight in no time sharp." She chuckled, then sobered quickly. "It's like they suspect one of us and are hoping the others will give something away."

Lizzie put a hand over Molly's. "I think you've been reading too many mysteries. Don't take this personally, Molly. We were all there; they have to check and double-check our stories. I doubt they seriously think any one of us is the murderer, though." She tried to sound reassuring, although her true thoughts were far from calm. "I'm sure I'll be on that list, too."

"Well, you come and see me after they question you and we'll compare notes." Molly sounded a bit put out.

This would not do. Lizzie tried to mollify her. "I don't

mean to take your concerns lightly, Molly. And I am worried about this, too. But we know we're all innocent, so I can't imagine how they'll come up with any damaging evidence that says otherwise."

Molly sighed. "I guess you're right, Lizzie. It's just a worry, that's all. It's kind of like a Christie plot: the murder takes place offstage, the victim is someone we don't sympathize with, mainly because we don't know him and he did so rudely wander into my house, and although Christie didn't often use a gun as the weapon, it did happen. Problem is, Agatha Christie often had a second murder take place and that was often someone likeable. Someone who knew too much. But I guess that lets all of us off the hook 'cause to hear tell it, we know nothing."

"I wish the police would believe that."

"Ah, yes. That's the crux of the matter, isn't it? Also, well, I hate to mention it . . ."

"What is it, Molly?"

"Well, I seem to be missing a few small items, nothing that breaks the bank, but they were special to me."

"Like what?" Lizzie leaned forward.

"Well, a small cloisonné egg that Claydon gave me many years ago. And a ceramic thimble. Things like that. Nothing large. They were all in a small glass display cabinet I have in Claydon's study." Molly sighed and took a sip of her wine.

"Do you think that Frank Telford may have taken something after all?"

"I'm wondering. However, I'm also misplacing things these days. But I'm pretty certain I hadn't taken them out to dust or anything recently." Same as with the gun, Lizzie thought, and wondered fleetingly if Molly in fact might be getting more forgetful these days.

Their food arrived, and they didn't talk again until after the server left.

"That might give credence to the theory that Telford was casing your place and maybe pocketed some small items for himself, including the gun. Then he has a falling out with his partner when they met outside. And he ended up dead."

Molly nodded. "That would make sense. Maybe you could mention the items to the chief, see if he can locate them stuffed in the car or something. It might sound more convincing coming from you. They might think I'm coming up with this because it was Claydon's gun that was used."

Lizzie paused, fork in midair. "Or maybe the accomplice took them. Yes. He got mad that Telford tried that on his own, shot him and grabbed the evidence."

Molly smiled. "You've been reading a lot of mysteries yourself, honey."

She had. And maybe she should be proactive here. Not wait to be hauled in for more questioning but go to see Mark tomorrow, first thing. No, busy morning. She'd go right after school.

Molly seemed to relax a little and between bites of her bass shared her latest plans with Lizzie. "December 17 would have been Claydon's and my sixtieth wedding anniversary. I'm planning to celebrate with a wonderfully large Christmas party. Maybe an open house. Or a sit-down dinner. I haven't done one of those in so many years, and we used to love hosting them. I do believe the planning must begin now or I won't be able to stage it."

"That's a wonderful idea, Molly." *And a good way to get your mind off murder*, Lizzie thought. "Just let me know if there's anything I can do to help."

"Oh, there will be, honey. Thanks so much. I knew I could count on you. Now let's just hope this murder mess is all cleared up by then."

Chapter Ten

◇◇◇

Nothing is going to go wrong! I told myself firmly. I
hoped I was listening to myself.

FUNDRAISING THE DEAD—SHEILA CONNOLLY

Lizzie drove home by rote, deep in thought about Frank
Telford. She didn't like what was happening to her
friends. Despite what she'd told Molly, she realized that none
of them were really off the hook until the killer was in jail.
The police's persistence in questioning the book club members was evidence of that.

She wondered what had really brought Telford to Molly's
house. Was it merely a matter of coincidence? Maybe the
Internet held some answers as to why Frank Telford from
Stoney Mills would be at Molly Mathews's house one Thursday night. At the very least, she might learn more about
the man.

She felt a jolt of excitement when she turned onto Sidcup
Street and saw the police car parked in front of her house.
She had to admit, Mark hadn't been too far from her
thoughts since their hike the morning before. She pulled
into the driveway and took a quick, discreet look in the
rearview mirror. She'd meant to check her hair but instead

focused on the female police officer walking up behind her car. She quickly exited the car and turned to face her.

"Are you Elizabeth Turner?" the officer asked.

"Yes, I am. And you are?"

"Officer Amber Craig. I'd like to talk to you. It shouldn't take long. We can go inside or to the station." Her voice remained neutral, as if she were reciting this from memory and it was of no consequence to her.

Lizzie didn't like the "to the station" bit but tried to sound pleasant when she answered. "Inside is fine." She led the way and pointed the officer to the living room. She draped her jacket over the staircase newel post and followed. "Would you like some iced tea?"

"This isn't a social call, Miss Turner. I have some questions for you about the murder of Frank Telford."

No surprise there, thought Lizzie. "Fine. What would you like to know?"

The officer removed her hat, giving Lizzie a clearer view of her face. She looked to be in her midtwenties, long blonde hair pulled back in a bun, clear skin, angular features and icy blue eyes. In other words, someone who could make a certain police chief's mouth water. Lizzie sighed.

"Is this a big bother for you?" asked Officer Craig, her lips drawn into a stern line.

"No, not at all. I'm happy to help the police. I'm just not sure what I can help you with."

"I'll be the judge of that, Miss Turner. You were one of the last people to see the deceased?"

"Yes. As I said in my statement, in the hall at Molly Mathews's house."

"Now, that's not entirely correct, is it? Your statement says that when he left, you were in the library. Is that right?"

"Yes, it is. I first saw him in the hall."

"I'd like you to go over your entire statement again, right from the beginning, and don't leave anything out just because it's already in your statement. Or assumed."

Snippy little thing, Lizzie thought before beginning another recitation of the events of Thursday night.

"You didn't mention, this time, that you were the one to persuade him to wait in the library where the book club was meeting?" Officer Craig looked up from her notebook.

"Didn't I? I thought I did."

"You said, 'We asked him in.' In your statement you said"—she paused to read from her notebook— "'I asked him in.' Which is it?"

Lizzie thought a moment. "It was me. I asked him in."

Officer Craig nodded. "Why did you do that?"

"Why? Because I wanted Bob Miller to get a look at him."

"Why do that? Did you suspect Mr. Telford of something? Did you have prior knowledge of what he was doing there?"

"No. Of course not. I'd not met the man before. I just thought it odd he was so bold."

"So, it wasn't anything specific?"

"No. Just a feeling, a hunch maybe."

Officer Craig paused in her writing and sat quietly, looking at Lizzie.

She's trying to rattle me. I don't have anything to hide. I wish she'd stop that.

"And you still claim you didn't know the deceased and hadn't seen him before?"

Lizzie stiffened. She really didn't like Officer Craig's tone. "It's not a claim. It's a fact. Has the chief found out yet how Telford got hold off Molly Mathews's gun?"

"I'm not at liberty to discuss anything about the case, especially what the chief may or may not be doing."

She stood up abruptly and tucked her notebook into her pocket.

Lizzie felt desperate for some information. "Are you any closer to finding the killer?"

"Miss Turner, what do you not understand about what I

just said? That's all for now. I will be getting back to you at some future point, though." She nodded, placed her hat back on, taking care not to disturb her bun, and left.

Lizzie now knew exactly how Molly had felt. She wished she hadn't been so dismissive when talking to her at lunch. If all the book club members were going through the same thing, she needed to talk to them. Maybe one of them could deduce something from the various interviews and questions. Or, maybe someone had actually been told a piece of information that might help.

She soon found out that late Sunday afternoon was not a good time for catching people in. So, the calls could wait till later. Maybe she just needed to chill out for a while, put Officer Craig and Chief Dreyfus totally out of her mind. She found a jar of almond butter tucked in back of the condiments shelf in her kitchen, where she thought she might use it less and therefore cut down on the added calories and cost. But not today. She'd just dipped her spoon in for a second mouthful when the phone rang. Caller ID announced Sally-Jo.

"I see you called but didn't leave a message," Sally-Jo said without preamble. She often left out the salutations and good-byes. Her own form of shorthand.

"I did call but rather than leave a message, thought I'd call back later. You just get in?"

"Yes. Jacob just dropped me off. We drove out to the Wilkins Farmstead for tea. Just thought I'd throw that all in before you asked."

"Ah. A nice time, I'd imagine?"

"Very. And yes, I did call him yesterday and he went to the cop shop with me, then I treated him to a drink and we had dinner together. Dutch. Period. Stop. Nothing else happened last night." Lizzie could hear Sally-Jo pouring herself a drink of something.

"But it was a nice time, too—I'm just guessing now," Lizzie couldn't help but add.

"And you'd be right. So enough of my platonic dating life. What's on your mind?" Sally-Jo asked.

"First of all, tell me about your police interview. Who spoke to you?"

"You mean who interrogated me. It was Officer Amber Craig. And she really gave me the third degree. Everything except the rubber hoses."

"Why? What can she possibly imagine you'd know about the murder?"

"Search me. But she's suspicious since I'm a relative new-comer to town, as is Jacob. His appointment is tomorrow, and I'll bet he gets it even worse, being an attorney."

"Ah, but being an attorney, he knows how to stick up for himself. I'll bet she'll regret interviewing him." *What a pleasant thought.* Lizzie managed to pour a glass of water and chugged it to dislodge the remaining almond butter coating her teeth. "I had the privilege this afternoon. And I got to thinking, maybe we should reconvene the book club just to find out what's going on with everyone. Who knows, maybe the police let something slip that might give us an idea of where we're heading."

"Are you into the almond butter?"

"Yes." She tucked the phone between her shoulder and ear while hastily screwing the top back on the jar.

"Humph. Wasn't I supposed to ask you that from time to time and you were to say something like, 'Oh, dear, I forgot. I'll put it right away'? Whatever, a meeting might be a good idea. Actually, I thought she'd go easier on you, given your history with the chief."

"What history? We just went to the same high school." Lizzie felt her cheeks warming. Good thing she was alone.

"Hmm. That was then. I mean after yesterday's hike. Word does get around in Ashton Corners, you know."

"Oh, good grief. We need to talk about the murder, not my supposed love life. I'll check with Molly if maybe we can meet Thursday night and get back to you." She paused.

"If I time your call right, it may save me making another one—to Jacob. Two birds with one stone and all that," she teased.

Sally-Jo laughed. "I'm not rushing this one, Lizzie. So better keep your dialing finger in order.

Chapter Eleven

◇◇◇

"Maybe I'm fanciful," he muttered, "and yet I'd bet
there's something she has not told me."

THE MYSTERY OF THE BLUE TRAIN
—AGATHA CHRISTIE

Lizzie sorted through a stack of articles on reading exercises that she'd signed out from the school board office
earlier that morning. She'd borrowed the vice principal's
office for a couple of hours to put together a reading guide
for fourth-grade teachers, a list of short articles and chapters
from reference books that would reinforce anything Lizzie
might suggest. She wanted them prepared to hear her suggestions when they met, and hopefully, be better able to
visualize how to integrate the ideas.

She considered herself to be the shortcut between the
teachers and all that knowledge written for them to use.
Since they had so little time to even find what they needed
to read, Lizzie's method saved them many hours.

It took much longer than she'd planned, but by the time
she met with the first of her two student appointments in the
afternoon, the list had been forwarded to the school office for
distribution to the teachers.

She stayed on after school hours to answer some of their

questions and then rushed home to get ready for the literacy
class.

Two small literacy groups met at Molly's house, twice a
week, with Lizzie and Sally-Jo as the volunteer teachers.
These were the advanced new readers, most just a step away
from taking their GEDs. Lizzie's group met in the library
where the book club had met, while Sally-Jo's was in the
sunroom, an addition to the grand old house in the 1980s,
just before Claydon Mathews had died. The classes for those
just starting the long trek to literacy met in the Ashton Corners Community Center on Main Street. All were part of
the long-distance learning program attached to a community
college in Montgomery.

There had been talk of moving all the classes to one
central location last spring, but Lizzie had backed Molly's
request to keep some of the classes at her house. Lizzie
suspected, that in spite of all her community involvements,
Molly was lonely and still missed Claydon. She'd found
Molly one night, in the detached garage sitting in the front
seat of Claydon's 1960 Corvette, talking to herself. Lizzie
had been quick to leave and hadn't let on about it.

Sally-Jo had also been eager to remain at Molly's house,
partly, Lizzie suspected, because of their friendship. Even
though she'd lived in town for ten months now, Sally-Jo
didn't do a lot of socializing, spending most of her free time
fixing up her house, an old wood-framed two-story left to
her by a great-aunt. Excellent if sad timing. The house was
actually bequeathed to two of the six Baker girls, but Sally-Jo
eagerly grabbed the opportunity to move in and away from
the tightly knit family. Nothing like seven hundred or so
miles to ensure happy family relations, she often said. Lizzie
envied the thought of having sisters, but five did sound like
overkill.

"I have a short writing assignment for you tonight, based

on the book of photography that you read last week," Lizzie explained as soon as the four students in her group were seated and somewhat attentive. She noticed right away that Stephanie Lowe hadn't made it to class. She hoped everything was okay with her. She hadn't seen nor heard from her since book club. Troy Nebock, another of her students, was a no-show, also.

A hand shot up from the club chair in the corner by the window. Lizzie acknowledged Sonny Dolman with a nod of her head.

"I didn't git around to getting a library card, miss, so I couldn't take out a book." He looked very self-satisfied.

Not a big surprise. "I have a book right here, Sonny, that you can use." Sonny was doing well enough to be in the advanced group, but he liked to provide these little bumps along the way. The smirk left his face, and he tapped his left knee with his pencil. He sat slouched with his knees poking through the threadbare legs of his jeans, his thin black hoodie partially zipped up, showing off the top part of a purple T-shirt with skeletal designs on it. His long black hair was held back in a ponytail, allowing Lizzie to actually see his face for a change. He glanced over at the only other male in attendance, Dwayne Trowl.

Dwayne shrugged and held up his hand, although his arm remained lowered. He appeared to be wearing an identical T-shirt, although an unbuttoned multicolor flannel shirt covered his. His jeans were more intact. "What say we write about something real? Like that there murder right outside this here house last week?"

The two girls in the class shrieked and started talking at the same time. Sonny gave Dwayne a high-five sign.

Lizzie took a minute to consider the suggestion. That topic might work out better than their thoughts about a photograph. At least it would engage their attention and hopefully, their imaginations. Although a bit more advanced a task than she'd ordinarily choose to do at this point, it was worth a try. And she'd find it much more interesting to read the finished works.

"All right. Let's give it a go." Her gaze moved around the room. "Get your pens and paper ready and I'll give you the facts. Then I'd like you to write a page-long story about it. Tell me what you think led up to this murder, who this man was, and what happened. But be sure you incorporate all the points you've been checking for when reading."

She gave them a few minutes to get ready and then gave them the facts: that the Ashton Corners Mystery Readers and Cheese Straws Society was holding its first meeting; that a stranger was found wandering in the entry hall; that he asked to use the phone to call for help for his disabled car; that his body was found in his car, where he'd gone to wait for a tow; and that he'd been shot.

"Okay. That's what happened. Now, I'd like you to make that into a short story for me. It's due on Wednesday, so start working on it now. Ask me questions; I'm here to help with words, sentence structure, how you format this on a page, whatever you'd like help with. Are there any questions?"

There weren't any, so she again instructed them to get started. She sat thumbing through her notes on the original assignment, thinking she'd use it for a class later on. Then she decided to task herself with the same assignment, to see if she could make some sense of what had happened.

By break time, Lizzie felt she had a pretty good fictional outline, but nothing related to reality, she was sure. She needed more facts. At least she felt satisfied that, thanks to Dwayne, they were an interested group.

Lizzie pulled Sally-Jo aside as the students were leaving after classes. "We need to talk with Molly," Lizzie whispered. "Something's come up to do with the you-know-what." She didn't want to say any more with the others milling around.

Sally-Jo nodded. She slid her arms into the sleeves of the pale green shrug draped over her shoulders. "I'll see our charges out the door."

Lizzie found Molly in the kitchen, a pitcher of tea and three glasses on the table along with a platter of brownies and sugar cookies.

"You've got to stop with the sweets, Molly. I have absolutely no willpower and already too many extra inches around the waist."

"Nonsense, honey. Men like to be able to hold on to more than skin and bones. I don't care what the magazines tell you."

"Men! Have you looked around Ashton Corners lately? Bob Miller is about the most eligible guy around, and I think he has his eye on you."

"Pshaw. Now I know you're overworked. And I'd like to point out that Jacob Smith might turn many a young gal's head. And then there's Chief Dreyfus."

Lizzie spilled some of the tea she was pouring. "That's not likely to happen, Molly."

"Honey, I saw the way he looked at you the other night. And with a dead body outside and all. Seems he's able to focus on more than one thing at a time." Molly reached over and touched Lizzie's hand. "He was quite the catch when you were both in high school, as I recall. Things were a little tough for him when he returned from serving in Iraq, but I think he's landed on both feet with the job."

Lizzie looked up sharply. "I hadn't heard much about him after high school. You'll have to fill me in sometime. Anyway, he's just sizing me up for a pair of those orange coveralls, the kind so popular at the local jail. He's eyeing all of us as suspects."

Molly sighed. "I know, honey. Especially me. I've been wracking my brain about that gun and can't remember the last time I saw it or who might have been in Claydon's study."

Sally-Jo overheard the last bit. "You have so much going on in your house, Molly. You open it to the literacy classes, charity events, and now the book club. Isn't it possible someone slipped into the study without you knowing? But what's missing?"

Molly looked at Lizzie before answering. "Well, honey, the police say the gun that killed Frank Telford was one of Claydon's antique weapons, and I'm just trying to figure out when someone might have stolen it."

"That's shocking, and a worry," Sally-Jo said.

"It is. Especially since I usually lock the door to his study—it was Claydon's personal space, and I don't want just anyone wandering in there. But I must confess, occasionally I've found it unlocked. My memory is not always that sharp some days. I'll have to start writing down a 'To Do' list. And then place several copies of it strategically around the house."

Molly looked so dejected that Sally-Jo gave her a hug. "I've been locked into a 'To Do' list for years, Molly. It's simply overcrowding of brain mass."

"I wonder if someone on the fall house tour earlier this month may have gotten into the room . . . if I left it unlocked." Molly brightened slightly. "Maybe Frank Telford took the tour."

"I remember that tour," Lizzie said. "Didn't the Floral Society set it up?"

Molly nodded. "There were five houses in all. We provided tea and cookies after a tour of the grounds. Now, the interior of the house wasn't included in the tour, but someone could have just walked in. It seems unlikely though, doesn't it?"

"Well, if we assume Frank Telford deliberately came to your house last Thursday night and then took the gun," Lizzie said, "what was his motive? Had he spotted it during the tour and came back deliberately to steal it? It could be worth quite a lot to a collector. Or, did he just happen to spot it when he was snooping around, before Andie walked in on him? But why take it? To threaten the person he then phoned? And that person got the drop on him, took it and shot him?"

Sally-Jo grinned. "It pays to read all those mysteries."

She pushed her glasses up to sit on top of her head and rubbed her left eye. "But if that was the scenario, then the gun had to be loaded. Was it, Molly?"

Molly shook her head. "I have no idea. It never dawned on me to check. I guess it must have been because I know for certain, there was no ammunition in that study."

"And being an older weapon, it probably needed special bullets, something Telford probably didn't carry around with him on a regular basis." Sally-Jo looked pleased with her conclusion.

"Which doesn't really get us any further," Lizzie pointed out. "So much for reading mysteries."

"Well, I'd like to point out that in all those mysteries, the police usually arrest the wrong person to start with," Molly said with a shudder. "I don't want that to be me."

Lizzie snapped her fingers. "What about fingerprints? Molly, had you handled that gun?"

"Well, I've dusted it, but I didn't usually take it out of the case. No, I think my prints would be on the case, not the gun."

"That's great then. I'll call Mark tomorrow and ask about prints. I also want to find out if they checked to see whom Telford phoned from here. Oh, I almost forgot, Molly—we were thinking a special book club meeting is needed, Thursday night, if possible. We should all compare notes because I'll bet Officer Craig has grilled us all by now. I didn't get a chance to make any calls today, though."

"I'll take care of that," Molly said. "We'll meet here, of course." She sat up straighter, looking a bit happier. "Yes, I think a meeting of the Ashton Corners Mystery Readers and Cheese Straws Society is definitely called for."

Lizzie crawled into bed, willing her mind to follow the lead of her tired body. But it refused to cooperate. Molly was worried she'd be jailed; Mark had indicated he would investigate the members of the book club; and there was one dead body. She didn't believe for a minute that any of them were involved, but could the police be trusted to sort it out? Or would they stop at the first logical suspect, no matter how wrong a choice?

The last murder in Ashton Corners that wasn't spousal or family related had happened over two years ago. Lizzie remembered the media frenzy when the person arrested turned out to be innocent. Shortly after, Bob Miller had retired.

She heard the cats come bounding up the stairs and felt the thud as they landed on the bed, almost in unison. They chose to settle down side by side next to her, with one of them kneading the lightweight quilt with a contented purr.

Lizzie was drifting off to sleep when she heard a noise outside. She tried to place the sound. A screen door banging shut? Another sleepless night for Nathaniel Creely? Or a raccoon sifting through the garbage can? The cats heard it, too, and sat up abruptly. After a few uneventful minutes, they curled up again and went to sleep.

Chapter Twelve

◇◇◇

I didn't sleep much that night and I didn't sleep well.

FLASHPOINT—LINDA BARNES

Lizzie slept through her radio alarm the next morning and had to skip her run in favor of a bracing shower. She pulled a breakfast tortilla out of the freezer, nuked it and ate standing at the kitchen counter. She was booked to observe another class at nine and would just make it. She dressed in a gray pencil skirt, black blouse and lightweight tweed jacket, her no-thinking-required outfit, and pulled her thick chestnut-colored hair into a ponytail while slipping her feet into black pumps

As she locked the front door, she spotted a large manila envelope sticking out of the mailbox. The white label had her name typed on it. No address and no return information. She stuffed it into her tote and forgot about it until later in the morning when writing up her notes in the staff room. She opened the envelope and pulled out three chapters of a manuscript. Untitled. No name. Intrigued, she started reading. The lunch bell rang, but she continued reading until she finished. She looked up, surprised the staff room had filled so quickly.

Sally-Jo wandered over. "What's so fascinating?"

"Take a look at this." Lizzie handed her the papers. "It looks like the first three chapters of a manuscript."

Sally-Jo scanned the pages while Lizzie dug into her tote for her sandwich.

"That's what it looks like, but what's it about and where did you get it?"

"It reads like the setup to a mystery. I found it in my mailbox this morning with my name on the envelope but no return address."

"Maybe one of your literacy students dropped it off?" Sally-Jo suggested.

"Could be, but none that I know of are writing at this level. I'd better give it a more thorough read though, just in case."

"Heard anything further about the murder?"

"No, nothing new. But I was thinking, what if we drop over to Stephanie Lowe's later today? I had the strong impression she'd seen Telford before. We need to get her to talk about him, if that's the case."

"You may be right, but I'm betting she won't like it."

They took Lizzie's car and went directly after school, hoping Stephanie might be home. To their surprise, Andie answered the door.

"Oh, hey. Steph's in the can. Want to come in and wait?"

"Sure. Good to see you, Andie," Lizzie said. "I didn't know you and Stephanie were friends."

"We got to talking while waiting the other night, and she said I should borrow her Janet Evanovich books. Said I'd like them a lot more than Shakespeare. So, here I am." Andie stretched and casually pulled her tummy-hugger T-shirt back down. This one was a mass of miniature black skulls on a white background. Her low-rise jeans were a size too small; fuchsia flip-flops completed the look. Lizzie fleetingly wondered if they could work on her wardrobe once they got her reading.

"Are you okay after what happened?" Lizzie asked.

"Sure thing. It was way cool. I don't know anyone who's been involved in a murder before."

Sally-Jo shuddered. "'Involved' may be too strong a word, Andie. At least, I hope it is."

"Whatever." She dropped onto a faded green armchair, obviously Goodwill stock, and flung her legs over the worn padded arm.

"Did you tell your mama about what happened, Andie?" Lizzie asked, worried about the reaction on the home front.

"Uh-nuh. I didn't see her later that night. They went out to a meeting at the golf club and didn't get back till after I'd crashed. My mama never makes it up in time for breakfast, and my daddy's left for the office by the time I make it down-stairs. And she never said a word about it. So I never told."

She sounds so nonchalant about it all, Lizzie thought. She wondered what the family dynamics were like at other times of the day.

Lizzie glanced around the room. She'd met Stephanie when she'd registered for the winter term at the Words for Change Literacy Center, and knew she had moved to town last spring, gotten a job real quick at the Oasis Diner and lived alone. But Lizzie had never visited her home. The tattered chair and sofa were at odds with the bright yellow walls and fresh white trim. A chest of drawers, also white, and a small brown wooden table with two fold-up chairs, a rectangular coffee table with marred top, and a fifteen-inch TV on the kitchen counter rounded out the bachelor apart-ment. Tiny but tidy.

"Yo, Steph, you've got visitors," Andie yelled as a door closed in the hall.

Stephanie rounded the corner and looked pleased to see them. "Oh, hi there. It's nice of you to stop by. I'm afraid I don't really have anything to offer you, though, just some lemonade and Oreos."

"That's okay, Stephanie," Sally-Jo said. "We don't need anything and can't stay long anyway."

"I wanted to drop off the assignment from last night's class," Lizzie said, handing over an envelope, wondering what Stephanie would think of it and even more, what she would write. It might work out better than trying to get her to talk about it.

"Why, thank y'all. That's such a big help to me. I'm sorry I didn't make it to class, but I worked a full shift and got so tired and my back was aching."

"That's understandable and you're welcome. We also wanted to ask you a question about the night of the murder. Is that okay?" Lizzie asked.

Stephanie hesitated and then nodded as she eased herself onto the tattered mint-flecked sofa.

"We both noticed that you seemed startled at seeing the stranger in the room, almost uneasy. He's been identified as Frank Telford. Did you know him?"

Stephanie grabbed her knitting from a plastic Winn-Dixie bag on the floor next to the sofa and started a new row before answering. "No, the name means nothing to me." She didn't look up.

"Well, sometimes when you see someone out of context, in a totally different setting, it's hard to tell. Could he have been someone from your hometown?" Sally-Jo asked.

Stephanie flinched but answered, "Of course not. I'd know if I knew him, wouldn't I?" She glanced at Sally-Jo, almost glaring. "No, for sure. Now, how about that lemonade?" She set her knitting aside and made to push up off the sofa.

Lizzie glanced over at Andie, who sat watching the exchange intently. "No, don't trouble yourself. We should be going. I hope we'll see you both at the special book club meeting on Thursday?"

Both girls nodded.

"Do you think we hit a nerve or what?" Sally-Jo asked once back in the car.

Chapter Thirteen

◇◇◇

Nothing is as it appears.

A VEILED DECEPTION—ANNETTE BLAIR

Lizzie's first appointment on Wednesday at school had been cancelled. She'd planned to administer a series of tests to a sixth-grade student reading at well below his expected level. She knew the child's father had arrived home from an extended tour in Afghanistan the night before, so she wasn't too surprised the child had taken the day off. She thoroughly agreed with the family's priorities.

That left one student, Danny Beecham, before lunch and two after. She already had an idea of what might work with twelve-year-old Danny; she just needed to confirm her suspicions. She'd been allocated the vice principal's office for the day, so she set up her laptop, arranged the visuals, a series of cards, on the desk so they'd be facing Danny, then clicked open her Internet browser.

She planned to make good use of the few minutes before Danny appeared. Lizzie wanted to do a Web search on Molly and Claydon Mathews, a fact she thought better kept to herself. She wanted to see if Frank Telford's name

appeared. Why Telford had chosen Molly's house was gnaw-
ing away at her. Was there a connection from the past? One
that Molly might be unaware of or, heaven forbid, unwilling
to mention?

The hits on Molly Mathews went on for pages, not surprising with all her philanthropic works and her family's
long roots in Ashton Corners. Lizzie lingered over an article
mentioning Molly and her own grandmama, Beata Turner,
when they had founded a soup kitchen at the Methodist
church in the mid-1960s. It gave her a thrill to see her grandmama's name in print, and it added another valuable piece
of information to her own family history. But no mention
of Frank Telford anywhere on these pages.

Even though Claydon Mathews had died so many years
prior, he had too many mentions for her to check in one
sitting. She scanned the first few pages for "Telford" but had
to give it up when her student arrived. She shut down the
Internet connection and clicked to open her testing papers.

Despite growing up in an upper-middle-class home in
the well-heeled Guilleford area, Danny read at a fourth-
grade level. Lizzie took him through the visuals, the cards
on the desk, had him read a short paragraph in the textbook,
then asked him a series of questions related to the reading.
She set her face in an encouraging smile, trying not to show
young Danny how poorly he'd done.

Then she pulled a newly published graphic novel, very
similar to what he'd just read about the American Civil War,
from her tote bag. Danny devoured the graphic novel, scoring
high on comprehension when retested forty minutes later.
Mission accomplished. She found it easy to smile this time
as she sent Danny back to class. She'd send a reading list of
relevant graphic novels to his parents and secretly bet he'd
be reading along with his classmates before the spring break.

She made some notes about Danny as she ate her lunch
at the desk. She barely noticed the tuna salad sandwich she'd
thrown together that morning. After downing a bottle of

apple-pomegranate juice, she switched back to the Internet and read through several more pages about Claydon Mathews. She'd known he was a well-respected businessman in Ashton Corners, owning and running the local General Motors dealership for many years as well as having stakes in several other area businesses. He, too, had a reputation as a philanthropist and had held memberships in almost every fraternal organization in town.

A knock at the door interrupted her, and she absently called out, "Come in."

"You're a hard woman to track down, Miss Turner," Mark Dreyfus said, closing the door behind him.

Lizzie switched off and closed her laptop. "I do like to work, Chief Dreyfus. It gives me a paycheck, you know." She smiled and motioned to the chair Danny had recently vacated.

Mark sat, then shifted, trying to get comfortable. The charcoal gray uniform pants looked to be straight from the dry cleaner's. He wore a short-sleeved lighter gray shirt, even though the morning temperature had sent Lizzie back inside for a heavy sweater. She wondered if, on the cooler evenings, he missed having the warmth of hair covering his head. No way she'd ask that question, though. "I never did enjoy being sent to the principal's office," he said.

"Did that happen often?"

"Let's just say, we got to know each other real well. Now, it's going to be gratifying but embarrassing if I ever have to give him a speeding ticket." He chuckled.

Lizzie smiled. "Is that what you're here to do, give me a speeding ticket?"

"You might just have enough pull with the chief to have it knocked down to a warning." He was clearly trying for a straight-faced delivery, but his face crinkled around his eyes, giving him totally away.

"I'll remember that." *So what does he want?* She'd let him take the lead.

"I just need to ask if you know anything about Stephanie Lowe's background. She won't tell us a thing about where she's from or about her family."

"Your guess is as good as mine. I've chatted with her a lot since she moved here. But she doesn't do personal. She's in my literacy group, and now that she's in the book club, too, I'll be seeing more of her, so that may change. Why do you need to know? Do you think she has a connection with Telford? That maybe they're from the same place and knew each other?"

"That could be, or they might be from the same place with no direct connection, but she might be able to shed some light on him. And of course, there's her reaction when she first saw him in the room, something you neglected to tell me about."

Lizzie felt her cheeks glow red. "I guess, with everything going on, I forgot about it."

"Even though I specifically asked about people's reactions?"

"Even though." Lizzie checked her watch. "Was there anything else?"

"Not really, but it makes me wonder if there's something else you've not told me." He tipped his chair back, balancing on the back two legs.

"I'd think you should be talking more to Bob Miller. He's the trained eye in the book club. He would be the one to notice all these little nuances."

"In case you hadn't noticed, former Chief Bob Miller and I aren't exactly best buddies."

Lizzie leaned her elbows on the desk. "Tell me about that."

"Trying to sidetrack me?" Mark's eyebrows punctuated the question. "Let's just say, I saw a bit more of him, too, than I should have back in my youth. Those were not my proudest moments. I think he remembers the boy and won't accept a change in the man."

Lizzie shook her head. "That's too bad, for you both. Boy, I'm getting a whole new picture of you . . . not the Mark Dreyfus I thought I knew in school."

Mark grinned. "My misspent youth is behind me. Now—"

The bell rang, almost throwing him off balance in surprise.

Lizzie stood. "I'm sorry, Mark, I should have been getting ready for my next pupil, who will be here any minute. This will have to wait."

Mark nodded and walked to the door. "Are you busy tonight?"

"More questions?"

"No . . . I was hoping for a quiet dinner and maybe you could fill me in on the Lizzie Turner I didn't know in high school." He smiled.

Lizzie tried to ignore the tingle in her toes. "I'd like that, but I can't. I teach at the literacy program on Wednesdays." The letdown was enormous.

"How about a drink after class ends? What time do you finish?"

"At nine. I'll be home by nine fifteen."

"Good. I'll pick you up shortly after that?"

She nodded. His smile widened, and he opened the door to leave, surprising a red-headed ten-year-old with strawberry jam at the corners of his mouth, who had been about to knock.

Lizzie had been late leaving the school. She found Sally-Jo leaning against her car in the school parking lot, and they walked over to LaBelle's Bakery for a coffee and a chocolate croissant, which they shared.

"So, give," Sally-Jo said. "Tell me why the chief came to see you at school."

Lizzie pointed to her mouth, now filled with her first bite of croissant. She raised her eyebrows.

"How do I know?" Sally-Jo asked.

Lizzie nodded.

"Everyone knows. It was the talk of recess this afternoon. When you didn't leave in handcuffs, most of the teachers lost interest. But I want to know if he grilled you some more."

Lizzie nodded again, took a sip of her coffee and swallowed before answering. "Unfortunately, he did. He wanted to know about Stephanie Lowe and specifically why I hadn't mentioned her reaction to Frank Telford."

"What did you tell him?"

"Just that she hadn't told us much either. Before I got to that latter part, I was saved by the bell."

Sally-Jo cut her half of the croissant in half and ate one piece, chewing thoughtfully. She wore a hot pink shrug, the exact color of her eyeglass frames, and together they gave her face a glow. "Do you think he'd be mad if we did some investigating of our own? I bet he would," Sally-Jo answered herself.

"I'm sure you've got that right," Lizzie admitted and finished her remaining bite. "At this point I don't know how much we can actually do."

"But you're thinking about it, aren't you? Maybe the book club can come up with a game plan. We shouldn't let all those years of reading mysteries go to waste." She didn't look convinced, though. "I, on the other hand, have a bit of news." She took her time with her drink.

"Give," Lizzie demanded.

Sally-Jo grinned. "My loan approval came through at the bank, so I can get on with the reno plans for my house."

"That's exciting. But wow, what an upheaval. Have you decided what you'll start with?"

"The kitchen. I can't stand preparing another meal in that fifties-style kitchen. I know I shouldn't be carping all the time about the condition of the house—it was an inheritance, after all, and I should be grateful and just keep quiet.

But it so badly needs upgrading. And it'll do wonders for the resale value."

Lizzie nodded. "It will be really exciting to see those plans take shape. Just remember, if you can't stand it at any point, my guest room is available."

"Thanks, Lizzie. I'll keep that in mind." Sally-Jo sat back, a contented look on her face.

"Although, I'm sure others will be issuing invitations, too," Lizzie couldn't resist throwing in.

Chapter Fourteen

This was no time for nerves.

EXPOSÉ!—HANNAH DENNISON

Lizzie grabbed a bottle of peach juice from the fridge and sorted through the mail she'd picked up on the way in. A couple of bills, double the flyers, nothing of interest like a letter or an invitation. She wasn't sure whom the hypothetical letter would be from. Most of her friends from college were into email these days. It had been a long time since someone had actually written her a letter in longhand.

The invitation idea was just as elusive. Ashton Corners folks were more likely to pick up the phone and call. And if anyone were getting married or some such thing, she would have heard about it long before an invitation arrived. Not many weddings happening these days in her age group. She smiled to herself. Maybe Sally-Jo and Jacob would change that. *Just slightly rushing things there, girl.*

She saw the manuscript on the hall table where she'd left it last night. She grabbed it and settled into her favorite bucket chair by the windows. She noticed she sank a bit deeper into the fading paisley upholstery. Might be time to think about a new chair. Maybe next paycheck. Maybe not.

The first chapter, although containing some awkward sentence structure, was a grabber.

> *My pops, Harlan Fowks, rushed home from the bank, full of himself and like to bursting. At least, that's how my mama tells it. You see, there never was much money left over from his hiring out as a field hand. There wasn't much money to be had doing anything in small town Alabama in the early 1960s. But that Mr. Jenkins Parker had a good run of cotton and was raking in his own bankrolls, so the good luck spilled right over and Pops got himself a loan. And it was enough to put a down payment on the small one-bedroom wooden farmhouse at the far corner of the Parker place.*
>
> *My mama, Adele Risling Fowks, was both happy and scared by the news. She worried all the time, hoping that the crops would stay plentiful and her husband would stay healthy. But to hear tell it, my mama Adele was always a worrier and Pops just kind of laughed it off while he made plans to fix up the house before the baby, that would be me, Carla June Fowks, would be born.*
>
> *Mama always said Pops liked to take risks. That's what held him to the cotton fields instead of trying to get a job in town that might pay more money. But times were tough and not much there for someone like Pops who hadn't much schooling or such.*

Lizzie read on. There was little cash left over from his paycheck as a farmhand, so extras were infrequent, food being the main priority. A typical tale of poverty in Alabama in the 1950s and 1960s. But thirty-year-old Harlan Fowks had grit, a good Southern trait.

Where was this leading, she wondered after correcting some points of grammar. Glancing back over the last page, the red markings surprised her. She'd done it automatically because that's what she did. English grammar. Sentence structure. Nouns, verbs, adverbs. And wasn't that why the three chapters had been left for her?

She glanced at the clock. Yikes . . . time to grab something to eat and get ready for the literacy class, and of course, the date.

L izzie didn't know which emotion to go with as she rushed to get ready. "A date . . . with Mark Dreyfus . . . who knew?" she said aloud and laughed.

Nor did she know what to wear. She shoved a taupe sweater set back in the drawer and pulled out a fuchsia camisole and matching shrug. No, too much for the class. She scanned her closet, nixing a couple of skirts and a sundress. Too late in the season for those. She'd have to get around to rearranging her seasonal wardrobe one of these days. Even though fall temperatures in south central Alabama didn't turn alarmingly cold, the nip in the air called for heavier fabrics and longer sleeves in the evening. Or a jacket.

She pounced on a gold-toned jacket in cotton, matching it with a multipatterned blouse showing just a hint of cleavage, and taupe twill pants. Strappy brown sandals would still work. She checked herself out in the mirror. It would do nicely. Now, some blush and lipstick and she'd be all set.

Lizzie was pleased that most of the students were in attendance, with only Stephanie missing. Again. If this continued, Lizzie might have to work in some private tutoring classes for Stephanie, although she seemed to be progressing just fine. And of course, the book club would be a big help to her in her reading skills. Lizzie hoped she'd be back soon, though, as it was equally important for Stephanie to be out with others her own age. The socializing was all part and parcel of the program, offering a secure setting in which to put new language skills to use. Being pregnant really threw some unpredictability into the matter. Lizzie jotted down a quick note to herself to talk to Stephanie about it.

"First of all, I'd like y'all to hand in your assignment from last class, and then I thought we'd work with graphic novels tonight," Lizzie said, quickly getting their attention. "You know, reading is reading, whatever the format." She'd decided on using them after the success with her daytime student, Danny. Age didn't really matter when it came to enticing a nonreader to give it a try.

She grinned good-naturedly along with the others as Teesha Torres made a cheeky comment. The girl liked to think of herself as smart-mouthed and tough, but Lizzie strongly suspected it was all a ruse. She was hoping to see a change come about before the end of the year, but Lizzie acknowledged that she wasn't a social worker.

She handed around the novels and asked them to read the first chapter while she excused herself. She found Molly in the kitchen, reading an Agatha Christie and sipping a tea.

"How many times is it for that book, Molly?"

Molly looked at the cover of *The Murder at the Vicarage*. "About five or so. I never tire of Dame Christie; you know that, honey." She pointed to the stack of Agatha Christie novels perched on the bookcase at the end of the counter. Among them was a thick volume of short stories, plays and selected novels. "Everyone present and accounted for tonight?"

"All except for Stephanie."

"I should give that child a call," Molly said. "See if she's needing anything. She must be feeling so alone right now."

"That would be good of you, Molly, and could you try at the same time to find out more about her reaction to seeing Frank Telford? Both Sally-Jo and I thought it appeared that she knew him. Did you notice it, too?"

Molly thought a moment. "No, but I had my eye on

Mr. Telford and wasn't really looking at anyone else at the time. I'll try to see what I can find out, though."

"Thanks. I'm in need of a glass of water, and then I'd better get back to class."

She found all heads bowed in concentration. A good sign. By break time, they were still reading and seemed almost reluctant to stop. She waited until everyone had left the room to gather in the kitchen for some of Molly's cookies and coffee, and then went to find Sally-Jo, who was talking to a student.

When the conversation had ended, Lizzie said, "Sally-Jo, I'd like you to read the manuscript I showed you and tell me what you think of it. Okay?"

"Sure thing." Sally-Jo adjusted her glasses and peered over the top. "Am I looking for anything in particular?"

"I'd rather not say. I'd like your take on it, though."

"Fine. I'll do it when I get home tonight. I've finished my class prep for tomorrow, and there's nothing good on TV."

"Thanks. By the way, I love that blouse. Great shade of blue. Periwinkle, isn't it? That's a shade everyone can wear. Even me. Hint, hint."

Sally-Jo laughed. "Not that I don't love you, girlfriend, but I'm ever so glad to be away from a houseful of my sisters and their borrowing all of my stuff. From now on, what I own stays with me. Sorry."

Lizzie made a face. "In that case, we may turn up dressed as twins someday. Where did you say you bought it?"

"I didn't. Say, why don't I get the manuscript now in case one of us is tied up after class?" She followed Lizzie, got the papers and left as the class started returning.

Lizzie found the group ready for a lively discussion about what they'd read. Just what she'd been hoping for. She was taken aback though when Troy, usually so silent, took issue with Teesha's opinion of graphic novels in general. The discussion started getting heated, each pushing their opinions, when Troy abruptly stood up, grabbed his things and left the class. Lizzie let him go, hoping he'd cool off and rejoin them. By the end of the evening, everyone had moved on, even though Troy hadn't returned.

"Do you think graphic novels have a legitimate role to play in literature?" Lizzie asked as she collected the books.

Jolene, a nineteen-year-old high school dropout who held down two jobs, waitressing and housecleaning, moved forward in her chair and raised her hand. "Of course. I mean, I like them because it makes it easier to understand, and it's way more fun looking at pictures. So's if you want me to get into reading a whole lot more, like other things, like more real novels, that's how to do it." She looked around at the others. "Am I right?"

Sonny looked totally bored, while Dwayne appeared to be daydreaming, staring at the walls. Teesha, however, nodded in agreement. Jolene seemed pleased with herself.

Before dismissing them, Lizzie said, "You know, if ever any of you have any writing you'd like me to take a look at—aside from what I assign in class, I mean—I'm happy to do that."

"Like what?" Jolene asked.

"Well, maybe you want to write a short story. I think some of you are quite the storytellers."

Everyone laughed as they left. No one came up to admit that they'd already been dropping off bits of a story for her to read, which is what she'd hoped to hear. She checked with Molly, wondering if she'd seen Troy leave. She hadn't. Lizzie hoped he'd return at the next class. Sometimes they didn't. She hated to lose a participant, especially one who was so close to getting his GED. But she had a feeling Troy's thoughts were elsewhere. It happened.

She put all thoughts of the class out of her mind as she arrived home and did a quick touch-up to her makeup. The doorbell rang at precisely nine fifteen.

Chapter Fifteen

◇◇◇

Are you kidding? It'll be a lot of fun and to quote your words, it'll be no trouble at all.

A KILLER STITCH—MAGGIE SEFTON

"Hey, Lizzie," Mark said as she opened the door. He handed her a single large white chrysanthemum. She wasn't sure what surprised her more, the flower or Mark in a black long-sleeved sweater and black pants, giving him an edgy but oh-so-sexy look.

"You look great," he said.

"And you look very un-policeman-like."

"That's what I was hoping. I thought we'd go to the South Slide. You do like jazz, I hope?"

"Sounds perfect. And thanks for the flower. Let me just put it in water before we go."

He asked her about her class on the way, and she was happy to describe it, ever so briefly. By the time they were seated at a small table overlooking the river, the talk had turned to cooking.

"I can't believe you took a cooking class," Lizzie repeated.

"Well, it was that or starve. My mama was never much

of a cook. I think she had a menu of three items: fried grouper, hamburgers and of course, the ever-popular mac and cheese. And after my daddy left, my brother Mikey and I often just grabbed whatever we found in the fridge."

"How old were you . . . when your daddy left?"

"I was fourteen; Mikey was eleven. How old were you when your daddy died?"

"Ten. My mama gave up on cooking, too. In fact, she gave up on everything." Lizzie took a drink of the Merlot she'd ordered. "She had a wonderful network of friends who took over our feeding. They'd take turns, a week at a time, cooking extra for their families and dropping off part of it for Mama and me. I'm eternally grateful to them all, but it didn't help my cooking skills."

"I heard you went away to college in Auburn." He offered her some nachos from the basket that had been placed on the table, then some of the avocado chili dip before helping himself.

Funny, she thought. And she'd not heard very much about him. The usual small-town grapevine must work differently for men and women. "Yes, I got my bachelor of science in education and a master's at Auburn. Then I headed out with my degree to work for three years in the 'faraway' city of Montgomery, and then took my reading specialist certification at Alabama in Huntsville. It just seemed right at that point to come back to Ashton Corners."

"Never yearned to see a bit more of the world?"

"Oh, I had a part-time job and saved like crazy so I'd have enough to take the last couple of weeks each summer before school started and do some traveling. Still do. I went to Ireland this year. Loved it but totally stressed out over the driving."

"Left side, isn't it?" Mark leaned back in his chair, looking totally at ease. He was also totally focused on her, she realized. *Nice*.

"God, yes—and you can't believe how hard it is to keep

that in mind when turning a corner or entering a roundabout. And the country roads, so narrow and everyone driving so fast. I can't believe I made it out of the country without an accident. But I loved it. I'd even go back someday, but next time, I'll leave the driving to someone else."

Lizzie scrutinized him right back and realized she enjoyed being with this new Mark Dreyfus. She felt relaxed for the first time in days. "And what about you? You must have traveled in the army. But is there other traveling you'd like to do?"

His eyes clouded briefly, but there was no trace of it in his voice. "I've had more than my fill of travel for a while, but someday, a holiday somewhere with hot sun and sandy beaches would be great. And I'm just hoping I can afford to do it while I'm still young enough to enjoy it."

By the time he saw her to her door, she realized he'd avoided talking about his life in the army and what had brought him back home. *Next time*, she promised herself, knowing there would be a next time.

"I can't believe we've not talked about the murder at all," she said, sliding her key into the lock.

Mark laughed. "You're so suspicious. I told you it wasn't about police business tonight." He leaned forward and kissed her. "Tomorrow, though . . ."

L izzie didn't think to check her cell phone until lunch the next day. She'd had it on vibrate through her morning sessions, this time at Sheridan Middle School, but pulled it out of her purse as she finished her tomato and cheese sandwich in the staff room. This was her first session at Sheridan this fall, and teachers, old friends, kept sitting down beside her, anxious to catch up. She noticed she had six missed calls. She really should get caller ID, she thought for the hundredth time. Only one voice message. She just had enough time to listen to it before having to get to the next class. Molly's anxious voice asked her to call as soon as possible.

Lizzie excused herself from the group lingering at the table and stepped outdoors to make the call, wanting a few moments of fresh air, too. Molly answered on the first ring.

"Oh thank you, honey, for finally getting back to me," Molly said. "I've noticed something else missing, and I hate to say it, but I'm sure it was there before last night's classes."

"What is it, Molly?" Lizzie groaned inwardly. She'd been hoping the thefts weren't tied to the literacy program, although the thought had crossed her mind after none of Molly's missing items had been found in Telford's possession.

"It's a small jewel-encrusted table lighter. Again, not too costly but it did belong to Claydon."

"Where had you kept it?"

"Again, in Claydon's den, which was locked. I had it on a shelf along with his pipe and humidor and cigar case, above his liquor cabinet. I really am certain it was there earlier in the day."

Lizzie thought a moment. "You said the door was locked?"

"I'm certain of that, also."

"Wow. I guess we have to seriously consider the possibility that someone from the literacy program stole the items. So I wonder who among the students might be an accomplished lock picker? Molly, I'm sorry but I have to dash to class. We can talk about it some more when I come by after school for Andie's tutoring session, okay?"

"That would be good. I'm really sorry to keep bothering you with all this, especially when your plate is already so full. Maybe I should just bake us up a nice treat. My way of saying thanks."

Maybe I should run all the way over there, try to lose those extra calories ahead of time, Lizzie thought as she tucked her cell phone back in her purse. She hated to think that any of the literacy participants would take advantage of Molly's hospitality by stealing her things, but it seemed the obvious conclusion. And what about Troy leaving so abruptly? Could he be the thief? A part of her mind played with it while she went through the afternoon's appointments.

When she arrived at Molly's, she didn't have any other answers. She brought her laptop in with her and set it up on the kitchen table, next to the cup of hot tea and piece of fresh red velvet cake awaiting her.

"I thought we'd just run down these class lists," she explained, between bites. "Oh, Molly, so delicious, as usual."

"Well, y'all know I bake when I get nervous. Just like you and your almond butter. Oh, don't look so surprised. I've known about your addiction to the stuff for a long time now. At least it's healthy," she said with a small laugh.

"Yes, and fattening. Anyway, I'd hate to think of any of these kids as thieves." She turned the laptop so that Molly could also see the screen. "The first person who comes to mind, of course, is Troy Nebock. When he left in a tirade last night, maybe he broke into the den and helped himself to the lighter. But why only that one item?"

"It beats me. I've been wondering that myself. I mean, all the things stolen were beautiful with small jewels, fakes I should point out, so not of much value if he tries to resell them." Molly played with her watch on her right wrist, a Rolex. She loved jewelry, necklaces in particular, and bracelets, and had plenty to go with every outfit. However, she always wore the same watch. Lizzie would bet it had been a gift from Claydon. It had that elegant look that screamed "lots of money."

"Then maybe there's another reason for the thefts. Is there anyone else on these lists that you've heard anything about?"

Molly read through the lists carefully and shook her head. "There are several names here I don't know at all and couldn't even put a face to, even though I'm sure to have seen them, even talked to them. Isn't that just terrible? Let me go over this while you and Andrea have your session."

Andie barged in through the front door, meeting Lizzie in the hall as she came out of the kitchen. "Sorry I'm late," Andie said, bending over to catch her breath.

The skull on her backpack looked like it was crawling down her back to attack her head. She straightened up almost immediately. "Old Man Marley wanted 'a quick word' with me," she mimicked in an old man's voice.

Lizzie thought back to "Old Man Marley," as she and her classmates had also called him. She shuddered at the memory of him keeping her after class, several times that spring term, to drill trigonometry into her brain. Grade eleven, it was. She supposed she should be thankful; the extra study time was enough to get her through the year-end exams. She wondered if his specialty was still terrorizing students in math.

"What subject?" Lizzie asked.

Andie grimaced. "The dreaded math."

"No matter that you're a few minutes behind schedule. We still have lots of time," Lizzie added cheerfully.

Another grimace. "Yeah, whatever."

Lizzie's turn to grimace. She waited until Andie had settled onto a comfy club chair, rummaged through her backpack and pulled out her copy of Shakespeare's *The Taming of the Shrew.*

"Why don't you put your book away for now," Lizzie began. Andie looked surprised, then suspicious. "And just tell me, in your own words, what the story is about."

Andie leaned back and folded her arms across her chest. "I don't have a clue."

Lizzie had suspected as much. "You didn't find the Coles Notes any help?"

"Look, Lizzie"—she placed her hands on her thighs and

moved forward to the edge of her seat—"it doesn't matter what the notes tell me. When I read over the words, they're still like Greek to me. I just can't get it right."

Lizzie was ready for her. She pulled a DVD out of her bag and handed it to Andie. "I'd like you to watch this before next Thursday. It's the stage production of *The Taming of the Shrew*, and it's quite a delightful story. Really, it is. Maybe, after seeing the play, the words will come easier when you read it. I'd like you to give it a try, anyway."

Andie hesitantly took the DVD, a skeptical look on her face. "Yo, I'll try it, but it doesn't change Willie's words."

Lizzie hid a smile. "Trust me, we're working on that."

Andie flipped the DVD over and sat with her head bent for several minutes. Lizzie hoped she was actually reading the write-up on the back. However, the next question had Lizzie adjusting her hopes to Andie eventually viewing it at home.

"What's up with the murder?" Andie asked without raising her eyes.

Lizzie sighed. "Not much. The police are still working on it. Have they interviewed you?"

"Yeah. My mama had to be there, though, and she was none too pleased. But she'd make a good lawyer. Each time they asked me a question, she'd tell me I didn't have to answer it." Andie looked at Lizzie and made a face. "Like, I'd actually know something."

"She was protecting your rights."

"Sure. And she was in a hurry to get to her bridge club. Anyways, I didn't have a whole lot to tell them, did I?"

"She's right, though," Lizzie said. "If ever they want to question you and your mama's not available, I'll be happy to sit in. It just needs to be an adult, not necessarily a parent."

Andie nodded. "Yeah, okay." She looked back down at the DVD for a few minutes. "Is there anything I can do, you know, to help? I mean, like, we were there and all. And I know the cops are leaning on some of the book club members."

Lizzie felt pleased that Andie wanted to be involved, that she had bonded with the others. "I'll let you know, Andie. Although I really hadn't thought the book club would get involved in a real murder."

Chapter Sixteen

◇◇◇

I've got a tale and a half to tell, all right!

WISE CHILDREN—ANGELA CARTER

After Andie left, Lizzie joined Molly in the kitchen again. She grabbed a sugar cookie off the new plate that had been set on the table. Molly put a fresh cup of tea in front of her and said, "Nothing has come to me, looking at those class lists, except for the fact that I really don't know many of them personally. Now, I should do something about that. Maybe have a garden party on Sunday afternoon. I know it's really late in the season for this, but the weather's been so fine and warm up till now. And I heard the forecast says it will hold for another couple of weeks." Her face lit up. "Yes. Let everyone get to know each other better. I'm sure some of them could do with extra friendships. What do you think? Is this too short notice?"

"I think that you're the only person I know who could turn a manhunt into a garden party. Actually, it might not be a bad idea. We could keep a real close eye on the study and see if anyone makes another try." Lizzie nodded. "Yes, that's a great idea, Molly. I don't think it would matter much if you gave them two days' or two weeks' notice. But is that enough time for you to get it organized?"

"Of course. We're talking only, what, thirteen plus you and Sally-Jo and me—sixteen people. I'm sure I can twist a few arms and get a caterer. Worse comes to worse, I'll just stock up on food at the deli." She grabbed a piece of paper and pen and started making a list. "Let's see, I'll need some tables and chairs, too. And music. Oh, this will surely be fun."

"Okay. That's great. Just tell me what to do, and I'm sure Sally-Jo would love to help also. I can start calling the students before our meeting tonight."

"No, don't do that. I like the idea of printed invitations better. Makes it seem more special, and then they have the reminders right in front of them. I'll take care of that, print some up later tonight and then drop them off at everyone's houses in the morning. I'll just make note of their addresses here."

"That's a nice touch." Lizzie glanced at the clock hanging above the fridge. "I'd better get going if I plan to be back in time for the special book club meeting tonight. And I'm serious about the garden party. I'm ready to help, so just tell me what and when." She gave Molly a quick hug. "Thanks for the sweets."

"Y'all are welcome, honey. Now make sure you have a proper meal tonight, too. I worry about you and your cooking skills, or lack of them."

"I haven't withered away yet, have I?" Lizzie didn't want to get into another discussion about her often thrown-together meals, most of them missing one or two of the main food groups.

"Not yet," Molly acknowledged. "Say, why don't you stay here for dinner? That would save the drive back and forth. And I guarantee a complete, tasty meal."

"Thanks for the offer, but I've got some prep work for tomorrow that I want to get to now rather than later tonight. I'll see you in a little while." She gave a small wave and left before she could be persuaded to stay. She knew the routine with Molly, and she usually ended up giving in.

She'd never learned anything from her mama in the kitchen and usually didn't have the time or interest in doing something about it. Maybe she should sign up for some cooking classes. She could get a real good teacher's discount at night school. Now, Mark's taking cooking classes . . . that was a totally unexpected revelation. For some reason, she couldn't picture him in the kitchen, apron tied around his waist, whipping up a soufflé.

She wondered what Mark was cooking up for dinner.

A ndie Mason was the last to arrive at the impromptu book club gathering. Again. *I guess I'd better get used to it,* thought Lizzie with a sigh. *At least she's here.*

"Lizzie, what are you hoping we can accomplish by this meeting?" Jacob asked as Sally-Jo finished passing around the plates of cookies and cheese straws. He looked very much the lawyer tonight: dark suit and tie with a pale blue striped shirt, expensive Kenneth Cole loafers on his feet.

"I'm not sure, Jacob. I thought maybe if we pooled our thoughts about the past few days and what happened when we were each interrogated by the police, we might come up with some additional facts."

"And just what are you hoping to do with those facts, young lady?" Bob Miller chimed in, sounding still very much the chief. He was wearing his trademark faded denim jeans, a plaid flannel shirt that at one point must have been a vivid blue, and gray socks, clean looking but with a hole in the right heel. He'd left his shoes at the front door, as usual. Lizzie thought the look suited him far better than the gray police uniform he'd worn for so long.

"Maybe we can spot something the police haven't," she said.

"Help them." Bob snorted.

"Well, help them look in a direction other than our book club. I'm sure you agree with that, Bob."

He settled back in his chair and took a large bite of the cookie in his hand. "It would give me great pleasure to present the chief with the name of the killer, yes. But murder isn't something to play around with. I should know. I think you'd better leave this up to the professionals."

"It's not like we're going out there stirring up trouble," Lizzie said, looking at Sally-Jo for support.

"Lizzie's right," Sally-Jo agreed. "It seems like the police, one officer in particular, is focused on us, and that's the wrong direction. Maybe we can figure something out and give her a nudge in the right direction." She winked at Lizzie.

Bob harrumphed. "I certainly wouldn't have stood for any of that in my day. I figure, if nothing else, this new chief feels that way also. But"—he slowly looked around the room, his gaze lingering on the plate of cheese straws— "count me in."

He leaned over to Stephanie and whispered to her to pass him the plate, which she did after taking one for herself.

"So, does anyone have any information to share? Did the police say anything about their investigation or the murder that we don't already know?" Lizzie asked.

Stephanie shook her head and buried herself in her knitting. Lizzie noticed the short-sleeved purple cotton T-shirt she wore stretched a bit tighter around her swollen belly than the one she'd worn last week. Just a couple of months until she'd give birth. Lizzie made a mental note to find out if she had all the clothing and supplies she'd need.

Andie chirped up. "So did they haul any of you to the station in handcuffs?" She sounded excited at the thought.

"No, heaven forbid," Molly jumped in. "Officer Craig interviewed me here at the house, but she was very pushy about it. She didn't give anything away either. But she seemed disappointed when I told her I was born and raised in Ashton Corners. In fact, I haven't lived anywhere else.

Claydon and I traveled abroad a couple of times and out to the West Coast, but we were really homebodies and thought we had all we wanted or needed right close by."

Bob nodded and leaned forward, elbows on knees. "I did my stint in the army, stationed at Fort Bragg and then overseas in the Vietnam War, but that's about it.

"How about you, Jacob?" Bob asked. "Did they try to pin some connection on you?"

Jacob shook his head. "I had our intrepid Officer Craig, also. She really wanted me to have been in Stoney Mills at some point, but I haven't, so she eventually gave up. It helps being a lawyer. I'm really adept at turning the questions back on her." He grinned.

Bob snorted. "These days I can take some pleasure in that ability. Sure used to get my dander up though, dealing with lawyers."

Lizzie had been watching Stephanie for several minutes. She was concentrating solely on her knitting, trying to appear small or even invisible, it seemed. It would be tricky, trying to get her to talk, but it needed to be done.

Just jump right in, Lizzie told herself, and then asked, "Stephanie, did Officer Craig question you, too?"

Stephanie took a deep breath and looked up at them. "Yes."

"Not pleasant, I'll bet."

"No, not a bit."

"It's hard when people start prying into your personal life, I know," Lizzie said. And thought, *She's not going to say anything with all of us staring at her. I'll try seeing her alone. Maybe if I keep slowly chipping away, I can get some answers.*

Molly looked from Stephanie back to Lizzie. "So, what we're saying is the police are looking for a past connection, but what I want to know is, why did Frank Telford come here, to my house?"

"That's right," Lizzie said. "The question is, did Telford

know about our meeting and come here for that reason, which is highly unlikely because the book club wasn't widely advertised. But if it is the reason, the question still is, why?"

"One of us could have told him," Bob interjected.

"You're right, but that would mean that person knew Telford. And we've all claimed we didn't know the man." *Or won't admit it.* She looked around the room at everyone. She couldn't believe any of them were involved. "Why would he want to come to this house?"

Bob scratched his head and tried to smooth the long, gray strands of hair over the thinning spot right on top. "That's a good question. But here's another: was it all just a coincidence?"

Lizzie felt a buzz of excitement. Lots of questions and no answers, as yet.

"If Agatha Christie were writing this," Molly said, "then she would use the ordinary. Her solutions often came from everyday things, like people's names. Although I don't see many clues in the name Frank Telford, I must admit. But perhaps we should look at the most obvious, basic elements of this case."

"Agatha Christie," Bob said in mock disgust. "Molly, we've got to broaden your reading horizons. Let's say I just bring over some James Lee Burke for you."

Molly glowered at Bob but said nothing.

"Well, not that anyone asked me to, but I went online and searched for Frank Telford," Andie said. "And he doesn't have a Facebook site, go figure. I guess no one that old does."

Molly raised an eyebrow.

"That was a great idea, Andie." Lizzie meant it. "How about searching further on the Internet and see if he's mentioned anywhere else?"

"Sure, I can do that." Andie actually grinned.

"I wonder if we should go to Stoney Mills and ask around about Telford. See what we can dig up on him," Lizzie suggested.

Bob intervened. "That's not a good idea, young lady. There's a killer out there, and if he gets wind that someone's trying to track him down, who knows what he'll do. This calls for someone with some professional experience." He thought for a few seconds and then nodded. "Yeah, I could take a drive over there and do some checking. I'll do it in the next day or two, if the fish aren't biting." He stood up and went over to take another cheese straw off the plate, turned back to his seat but changed his mind and grabbed the plate to pass it around.

Molly couldn't hide her astonishment as she took one. Lizzie gave it a pass. He sat back down, looking pleased with himself.

Molly asked, "What can I do? It was my house, after all, and I'd like to get in on this."

"You could go undercover," Andie said with a wide grin. "You and Chief Bob could do it together."

Bob took up the thread. "Now, that's a great idea. Molly, you and I could pretend to be looking to buy us a house. It would be real natural to ask around about the town and the people before actually putting down our small nest egg." He was almost smirking.

Molly drew herself up to her full sitting height. "Miss Molly Marple. It has a ring to it. All right, I'll do it . . . but don't you go getting any funny ideas, Bob Miller."

Chapter Seventeen

◇◇◇

I was in no mood to deal with any more of this
nonsense.

THE DIVA RUNS OUT OF THYME—KRISTA DAVIS

The doorbell startled her. Lizzie turned on the light in her
kitchen and checked the clock. She'd been raiding the
fridge before heading upstairs to bed. She didn't usually get
guests calling at midnight. She peered through the peephole
before opening the door. Awfully late for her landlord to be
dropping by.

"Nathaniel. What are you doing here at this hour? Is
anything wrong?"

"I hope I didn't scare you, Lizzie. I've been waiting for
you to get home." He handed her a large manila envelope.
"I saw that cyclist again tonight, and he left this in your
mailbox. I wanted to bring it to you and make sure everything's all right. You know, I saw him the other night and it
looked like he had a big manila envelope that night, too.
That's real strange, him stopping by so late again."

Lizzie ripped open the envelope and pulled out more
chapters. "It's the next part of the manuscript," she said, to
herself rather than her landlord. She flipped through the

pages quickly, then asked, "Would you like to come in for some tea, Nathaniel?" She knew he often watched old black-and-white movies until the early hours of the morning, and although she longed for bed, he might want the company.

He'd thrown a navy nylon shell over his beige knit turtle-neck sweater, and had on brown khaki pants and a pair of worn moccasins. His wire-rimmed glasses were pushed up on his forehead, as was usual. Lizzie often wondered why he wore them. Sometimes he'd pull them down to read some-thing, other times, not. The same went for looking into the distance. He didn't own a car or drive, so no need there. His thinning white hair was straight and on the long side, although never unkempt. Perhaps the glasses acted as a head-band, keeping the hair back and out of his eyes.

"No, thanks. It's getting late, but I wanted to check on you. This is nothing distasteful or threatening, is it? Should I be calling the police the next time I see him?"

"I don't think so. Someone is dropping off a manuscript, section by section. It's an interesting story, but that seems to be all."

"Well, I should get going then. You'll be wanting your beauty sleep, not that you need it. The beauty part, that is." He gave an embarrassed chuckle. "Lock up tight, now."

"I will. Good night, Nathaniel." She closed the door behind him and took his advice about the locks. But instead of heading to bed, she poured a glass of Shiraz and settled down with the latest pages. Another three chapters, she noted, wondering how long the manuscript would be and if it were finished.

It seemed the more my pops had, the more he wanted. But it was all for the family. He weren't the sort to go out drinking and gambling. He tried to make sure the house had a washing machine, at the very least, for when the baby came along.

*It was sure hard with just his field hand salary,
though. But he managed to start a small savings
account, also, which made Adele happy. She didn't want
much out of life but a clean, dry house and food on the
table. And a healthy baby.*

*Harlan would often sit and watch his wife and his
baby girl, wishing he could give them a real fine house
and clothes. So, when one day the smooth-talking land
developer came to Stoney Mills, Harlan Fowls was all
ears.*

*He heard the man talking to a group of townsfolk
outside the barbershop, and stopped to listen when he
should have been down at the general store buying up
some food. This stranger was a real good talker, painting pictures of the land on the south side of town being
turned into lots of houses, with some parks, and at some
point even, a school. Maybe even another church for
Stoney Mills.*

Lizzie read on and turned over the final page, then looked
at the clock. One A.M. Really time to head to bed. She re-
checked the doors, turned off the last light and went upstairs.
While brushing her teeth, she thought about what she'd just
read.

Despite continued money problems, the family was a
happy one. The daddy, Harlan Fowks, struggling with ways
to bring in more cash, liked what he'd heard, and when the
man from the neighboring county talked persuasively about
the deal he was putting together to bring some housing and
industrial development to town, Fowks was hooked. It was
the promise of a healthy return on his money. After several
more meetings with the man and another couple of serious
investors, Fowks decided to take another mortgage on his
house and sink all his funds, meager as they were, into the
deal. His wife, Adele, when told after the fact, was enraged,

then scared about what would happen if the deal fell through and they lost everything. She had a young baby to worry about, after all.

Chapter six ended on that ominous note. Lizzie could almost predict where this was heading. It wasn't an original story line, but the characters held her attention. She changed into cotton pajamas and crawled into bed, still thinking about the story. It had potential. And could develop in so many directions. It might even turn out to be a mystery. The character could rob a bank, to get more money. Or even worse.

She toyed with the idea of asking the book club to read it, to get a variety of takes on it. The cats joined her, Brie settling in on her left side while Edam took time for some kneading of the quilt before curling up on her legs. She must remember to cut their nails, she thought and then fell asleep.

She arrived at the Ashton Corners Elementary School about twenty minutes early and stopped by Sally-Jo's classroom, catching her writing some math tables on the board.

"Oh, to be a student again," Lizzie said. "I did so enjoy arithmetic first thing in the morning."

Sally-Jo peered over her glasses at her. "I'm thinking there's a 'not' in there."

Lizzie laughed. "Totally. Even at this tender young grade. Anyway, I won't keep you. Just wanted to tell you that Molly has planned a garden party this Sunday for the literacy students. It starts at one P.M., but I told Molly I'd be over around eleven to help out. Does that work for you?"

Sally-Jo didn't skip a beat. "Sure. No problem. Jacob and I are going to the Stoney Mills Fair on Saturday, but Sunday is free. What can I bring?"

"You'll have to consult Molly on that. And what's this about you and Jacob? Another date?"

Sally-Jo squared her shoulders. "Date number three, if anyone's counting. But this time it's all in the name of duty, Lizzie. We thought it couldn't hurt for more of us to be asking the same questions in Stoney Mills."

"That's actually a great idea. By the way, I got another few chapters of the manuscript last night."

"Wow . . . that's so weird. And it reminds me, I've got the chapters you gave me right here. What was it you wanted to know?" She went over to the desk and searched through her tote.

"Mainly, what your take on it is. Do you think it could be a true story?"

"What makes you think that?"

"The writing style, for one thing."

"Umm, it's hard to say." Sally-Jo handed over the earlier pages while she gave the question some thought. "It could very well be. I'm happy to read more of it, by the way."

"That's super. I want to read all the chapters together, then I'll pass it along to you." Lizzie glanced at her watch. "I'd better run. Good luck on Saturday, and I'll see you at Molly's on Sunday." She gave a small wave and left.

Lizzie finished her meeting with a fourth-grade teacher just before two thirty. She'd been in meetings all day long and was keen to get outside for some exercise. She was due back for a staff meeting in an hour, which gave her just enough time for a brisk walk to LaBelle's Bakery to stock up on some treats for that evening's choir practice. Each of the four voice sections took on refreshments for a month, which meant her turn at helping out usually rolled around once a year. She and two others were providing the goodies tonight.

Her cell phone rang as she left the bakery, tantalizing smells emanating from the cloth shopping bag swinging from her hand.

She fumbled with the bag as she dug into her purse for the phone. After almost dumping the entire contents of the purse on the ground, she managed to say, "Hello, Lizzie speaking."

"Lizzie, it's Mark. Do you have a few minutes? We need to talk."

She maneuvered her arm so that she could glance at her watch, as she rounded the corner. "Ten minutes, that's all I can spare. I have a staff meeting at school shortly."

"Good. That should be all it takes. I'm parked in the school parking lot, and in fact, I have you in my line of sight."

She looked up and tried a wave when she spotted him leaning against the police cruiser. He gave her a small wave in return and stuck his cell back in his pocket.

"I'd offer you a cinnamon pecan drop biscuit or a sugar cookie, but they're for choir tonight," she said as she reached him.

"That's okay. I'm trying to keep off sweets."

"Surely, not a weight problem?" she asked, with a smirk and an exaggerated once-over of his body.

He laughed. "Only if I continue with the sweets intake. I didn't realize the unforeseen hazards of this job. Why, last week, I talked to three separate little old ladies in one afternoon and each of them pressed me into eating some of their home baking. It's awfully hard to say no to a woman with gray hair and a plate of molasses cookies."

"I'll keep that in mind for the future. I'm sorry but I can only spare a few minutes. As I said, we have a school staff meeting, and I have some materials to finish in preparation for it." They started walking toward her car.

"This won't take long. I just thought you might know something about an older couple, who looked suspiciously similar to Bob Miller and Molly Mathews, who were poking around asking questions in Stoney Mills this morning." Mark reached out to hold her bags while she unlocked the car.

Lizzie was pleased to hear that Bob and Molly had gotten

right to it but hesitant about sharing the group's plans with Mark. "News travels fast."

"Well, they asked a Realtor, who I happen to see on a regular basis out at the shooting range, about houses for sale and then about Frank Telford. Kevin had heard he'd been murdered here, so he called me. Now, I have a feeling you know all about this."

"I haven't spoken to either of them today, so I can't really tell you anything." Partly true. Maybe she should change the subject. "But I'm thankful you're the one asking. I'd hate to be grilled by Officer Craig again. She doesn't have much in the way of people skills, does she?"

"She doesn't really need them in this job. Besides, it's her first homicide. Mine, too, come to think of it. I thought it would be good training for her to get out there asking questions."

"I just wish she could do her practicum elsewhere," Lizzie said, placing the bag on the backseat and locking the car door again.

Mark laughed. "Now, I know you didn't mean it this way, but I take that as an endorsement of her policing skills. It will take all of our skills combined to solve this rather than having to bring the state police in."

Lizzie thought about that. "I do hope you're able to solve it, Mark, but I also hope I'm not paid a visit by Officer Craig again. Besides, no one in the book club is a murderer, so if you concentrate your efforts elsewhere, you might just find the killer. I'm sorry, I have to get going now."

"Fine. We'll talk again."

"Fine." She marched off, trying not to think of either police officer.

Chapter Eighteen

◇◇◇

A ball of frustration gathered in the pit of my stomach. I didn't like secrets.

THE LONG QUICHE GOODBYE—AVERY AAMES

Lizzie waved at Nathaniel Creely as she eased her 2004
Mazda 3 into the driveway. He had disappeared back
into his house by the time she exited the car. Her first
thoughts were of a much-needed shower followed by a quick
meal, and then she would be off to her weekly choir practice.
She hummed the soprano line of Rutter's "Nativity Carol"
as she kicked off her shoes and ran upstairs.

The front doorbell stopped her in the midst of shedding
her blouse. Rebuttoning it, she retraced her steps to the door
to find Nathaniel, with a plate of spiced figs in his hand.

"I thought you might have a few minutes to join me in an
appetizer. I know it's your choir night, but I suddenly thought
about this fig dish this afternoon—Charlaine used to make
them all the time—and I had a strong desire to taste them
again. They complement a glass of white wine so nicely,
you know."

Lizzie smiled and opened the door wider. *There goes the
shower.* "What a great idea, Nathaniel. I just happen to have

a bottle of Pinot Blanc in the fridge. You get settled in the living room, and I'll get the glasses and wine."

He must have had a lonely day, Lizzie thought as she pulled out a pewter tray and some wineglasses, and uncorked the Pinot Blanc. The thought of inviting him to join the book club flittered through her mind, but she knew he didn't really enjoy reading. Now, a gardening club would be a different matter entirely. She wondered why he hadn't thought of that but knew the answer. He might be lonely, but he was also shy. She racked her brain to think of someone, preferably female, she knew whom she might get to invite him on a gardening adventure. There was that matchmaking urge again. She'd best stow that one.

Nathaniel had set out some colorful cocktail napkins— white daisies on a blue and yellow background—he'd brought over and cleared a space in the center of the coffee table for the appetizer plate. Lizzie made a bit more space for the tray, then poured them each a glass of wine and bit into a fig covered in a spice mixture, still warm from the oven.

"These are delicious, Nathaniel. Your culinary skills never cease to amaze me. You put my own efforts to shame."

"That's very kind of you to say, Lizzie. My Charlaine was a very talented lady both in the kitchen and out. I sometimes can taste one of her tempting dishes in my mind and am spurred to re-create it. It never tastes quite the same, though."

"Well, I love these. And if I don't ask you for the recipe, perhaps you'll make them again for me."

He chuckled. "I'd be delighted, my dear. You know, your late-night delivery has been on my mind most of the day. Everything is all right, isn't it?"

Lizzie paused as she leaned over for a second fig. Good question. "That's sweet of you to be concerned, Nathaniel. Yes. I think so. It's the second set of chapters of a manuscript. I'm just not sure who it's from, maybe someone from the literacy program, but it's odd that it's being dropped off so late each time and there's no name or even a note with it."

Nathaniel finished his mouthful. "Well, you know, if there's ever any problem you can always just give me a call. I'll be over here in a shot, so to speak."

Lizzie smiled. "Thanks. I do know that. This seems quite harmless. We did have something unsettling happen at our book club last week, though. A body was found in a car outside Molly Mathews's house. The police think it was a murder."

"I did read something about it in the paper. How is Molly taking it? She was always a bit fragile, you know."

Molly, fragile? Lizzie would never have used that descriptive for her. She wondered how well Nathaniel knew Molly. She'd not given it much thought before. There was a lot she didn't know about her neighbors and their relationships, even though she was a hometown girl. Of course, Nathaniel could be thinking every Southern gal was still of the genteel ilk.

"Molly seems to be fine, although she's a bit disturbed that the dead man had been in her house just a couple of hours before. He wanted to use the phone and had just wandered into the house. She didn't even know him. Frank Telford was his name. Does that ring a bell, by any chance?"

"There is something familiar about it. But a lot of things sound familiar. Doesn't mean they are. You know how it is at this age . . . but, of course, you wouldn't. You're such a young lady."

Lizzie laughed. "Nice of you to say that. Sometimes I feel anything but. Depending on how my day went at work, of course. Can I freshen your drink?"

"No thank you, my dear. I know you have to get ready to go out, and I have a dinner to fix." Nathaniel finished his remaining bit of wine and pushed himself slowly out of the chair. "I'll just leave the rest of the figs here, if I may?"

"Why thank you, Nathaniel. You know they won't last long." She followed him to the door.

"By the way, I bought several flats of yellow and white chrysanthemums at Clifford's Home Hardware today. I know it's getting on in the season, but I thought they'd make a nice autumn trim right across the front of the house, that is, if you like mums?"

"Of course I do. It should look great. I'm lucky to have a resident gardener on the premises," she said.

"Was a time I could do a lot more than that." He gave her a wink and left.

Lizzie closed the car windows and sang through a series of vocal exercises on her way to choir. She liked to do her own, even though the first ten minutes of every rehearsal was always warm-up time.

She noticed right away that Lucille Miller wasn't there. She felt a bit relieved, not wanting to be quizzed about Bob and the book club again. She greeted some of the others, then pulled out her score for the Raminsh piece. She loved the first soprano line, which, as usual, was mainly the tune but crossed over the second sopranos at one point, ending with the soprano solo above them all.

It was easy to get lost in the music, to concentrate totally on the score, striving to stay in pitch. Lizzie loved the start-and-stop routine of rehearsals, the demands on the brain to set aside all other works and learn this new combination of notes and words, usually learned not in the order they were written, and the eventual coming together of the parts. She tried to find time in her day for half-hour practice sessions, but this past week in particular, she'd found it difficult to do. She knew that would have to change if she wanted to get up to speed before the concert. Their director, Stanton Giles, had high expectations of the group of amateurs under his guidance, but they were lucky to have him and Lizzie wanted to make the most of it.

At break, one of the tenors, Tim LaBelle, who owned the bakery near the school, shuffled over to Lizzie, coffee in hand.

"That's a nasty business, the murder happening right outside Molly Mathews's home. I hear the gun used belonged to Molly. I can't imagine someone so kind and concerned being involved in something like that."

"What? Where did you hear about the gun?"

"Why, it was in this week's issue of the *Corners Colonist.*"

"Well, you know Molly, Tim, and you know she's not involved except to be so unlucky as to have her gun stolen, well, her late husband's gun, and to have the murder take place on the street outside her house."

Tim nodded. "I was certain it was something like that. Nobody in his or her right mind would think poorly of Molly. I was sort of surprised to see the story."

Lizzie bet it was the doing of Officer Amber Craig, trying to stir up matters and maybe even get a confession. She grunted, too mad at Officer Craig to say anything more.

"You know," he continued, "the name Telford sort of sounds familiar, but I can't place it. I wonder if he did some work in Ashton Corners at some point."

"Do you think you might have met him?"

"I don't know, seems unlikely, though. At least, I'd hope I would have remembered his name, if that was the case." He shook his head. "No, I really can't say for certain, Lizzie."

They heard the accompanist play a short fanfare on the piano, their cue that break time had ended and everyone needed to be back in place. Stanton Giles took a few minutes to remind them that the choir would be singing at the church fundraiser in three weeks, a part of the Fall Fest Indoors. It was a thank-you to the church for allowing them to hold rehearsals in the hall.

"It's all music we've sung over the past couple of years,"

he said, "so it shouldn't take too much extra rehearsal time to refresh it. The pieces are being passed around as I speak."

Lizzie thumbed through the well-worn copies, pleased to note some titles she counted among her favorites. They spent half an hour on two of them, then finished with the Rutter.

As she drove home, Lizzie found her thoughts wandering back to Frank Telford. She wondered who else in Ashton Corners might know the name. Maybe they were searching for information in the wrong town. Maybe the answers weren't to be found in Stoney Mills after all. She made a mental note to spend some time at the offices of the *Ashton Corners Colonist*, the local weekly newspaper, as soon as possible, going through old files.

Chapter Nineteen

◇◇◇

She leaned back in her chair, lacing and unlacing
her fingers together in excitement.

A KILLER PLOT—ELLERY ADAMS

Lizzie eased her Mazda into one of the two remaining
empty parking spaces in front of Scissors 'n Snips Hair
Salon on Calvin Avenue Saturday morning. She was long
past her monthly trim, and even though a missed appointment didn't really show with her long hair, the bangs, which
she was trying to grow out, needed to be kept shapely during
the lengthy process. Each time she went in for a cut, she
debated whether to continue the growing out or to hack them
off at eyebrow length. And then she'd remember that she
looked ten years younger with the bangs, which would be
great when she hit the big four-O, but was not quite what
she was going for now.

Her usual hairstylist, Amanda, had phoned in sick, so
she sat through an hour of Patti-Lynn patter, as she thought
of it. As she left her tip and paid the bill, Lizzie realized she'd
had to say only about three sentences the entire time. She
smiled and waved at Patti-Lynn as she left, thankful to be
outside with only the noise of traffic around.

She went into the Winn-Dixie next door and bought some raspberry frozen yogurt that she'd been craving all week. A quick stop into Toby's Pharmacy just down the street, and then she went into the Book Bin, Ashton Corners's only independent bookstore. Jensey Pollard nodded at her, finishing up with a customer at the cash register before walking over.

"I have just the book for you, Lizzie. I know it's one your mystery book club will be dying to read." She deadpanned the line but then started laughing as she pulled a book from the New Arrivals shelf. "It's *Chapter and Hearse* by Lorna Barrett, and any book club that has 'cheese straws' in its name should read this. It's book number four in the series, but no reason you can't start there." She placed the book in Lizzie's hands and waited.

Lizzie scanned the back cover. "If you recommend it, Jensey, then I'll buy it. Now, can you suggest an author who might interest a sixteen-year-old who's also a reluctant reader?"

Jensey crossed an arm over her chest, rested her other elbow on it and leaned her chin on her hand. Her short, curly black hair—Lizzie often wondered if it had been dyed—framed her heart-shaped face. Whenever Lizzie read that description in a makeover column, she always thought about Jensey. Today she wore a turquoise cropped sweater and necklace with a knee-length pencil skirt and black boots. Always stylish. "Umm, a challenge. I love these questions. A girl?"

"Yup. And she's smart. Just not reading the right material that'll get her hooked."

Jensey walked over to the mystery section and ran her hands along the spines, stopping at Cleo Coyle. "This is your author. She's got an independent woman who runs a coffee shop with her ex. The dialogue is snappy, and the plot's just the right degree of complexity. And then there's the coffee aspect—most teens I know inhale specialty coffee these days."

"Thanks again. This'll do nicely." Lizzie chose the first book in the series, *On What Grounds*, scooped up the latest Avery Aames cheese shop mystery for herself as she walked past the New Arrivals display again and took her purchases to the front desk.

Jensey was cornered by a new customer entering the store, so Lizzie was served by her part-timer, a young girl she'd not met before, roughly around Andie's age but without the face jewelry. Lizzie thanked her and, purchases tucked into her tote bag, walked to the door and glanced out the window. Her hand froze on the doorknob.

A couple stood across the street, under the Makin Realty awning, locked in a passionate embrace. *It looks like . . . no, it can't be.* She waited, holding her breath. The couple pulled apart, and Lizzie gasped. Jacob Smith and some unknown but very attractive blonde, about five-foot-eight, dressed to kill in navy jeggings and a leopard cape.

Lizzie had to move away from the door as a couple entered the bookstore and when she looked back out, Jacob and the stranger were walking along the sidewalk, away from her. The woman had her arm wrapped behind Jacob, along his waist, and they were in deep conversation.

Lizzie remembered to wave to Jensey, then walked hurriedly to her car, looking back at Jacob and Madame X a couple of times until they disappeared around the corner. She unlocked the Mazda, slipped behind the wheel and sat, lost in thought. Who was the blonde? Certainly not a stranger to Jacob. What was his game? Should she tell Sally-Jo? No, probably best to ask Jacob if she got a chance. She'd hate to see her friend hurt. Again.

She glanced at her watch. Her next stop would be to see her mama. Since she'd be busy all day Sunday helping Molly with the party, she'd decided to switch her visiting day. But she had to go home first and deposit her frozen purchases. She'd stow all thoughts of Jacob out of her mind, as well.

Traffic was light for a Saturday and she made it home

quickly. Groceries put away, she ran upstairs to get changed. The cats were startled by her fast entrance, poised to take flight off her bed, but quickly settled back down to resume their naps. She explained her plans to them as she chose a fuchsia sweater set to go with black pants. Her mother loved bright colors, and she always tried to wear something cheerful for each visit.

It took less than fifteen minutes to reach Magnolia Manor, and Lizzie found her mama sitting in the sunroom by herself. All of the other residents had gone into the dining room for lunch. Lizzie had phoned ahead, and her mama's lunch was brought out quickly once she'd settled herself.

Much to Lizzie's delight, her mama seemed to be focusing today, listening to the chatter and nodding from time to time. The care staff at the Manor had decided that today, Evelyn Turner would wear a bright red cotton sweater set and taupe pants. Her thinning salt-and-pepper and auburn hair, pinned behind her ears by matching flower barrettes, looked freshly washed. Her face remained void of most of the wrinkle and lines a fifty-seven-year-old would sport, grim testimony of a mind that no longer worried. A tentative smile, as if she'd been practicing all morning, stayed on her face. She even asked for another helping of strawberry swirl ice cream for dessert.

After lunch, they went for a walk around the gardens. The flowing back lawn led to a pergola covered with lacy vines, affording shade to the padded patio furniture. Lizzie led her mama to the lounge swing, and they sat in companionable silence for quite a while.

When she noticed her mama's eyelids drooping, she suggested they go back to her room. She helped her onto the bed, slipped off her shoes, covered her with a light afghan and quietly closed the door as she left. The receptionist promised to let the staff know that Evelyn was sleeping in her room. Lizzie left, feeling much more uplifted than she usually did after her visits.

Later that evening, Lizzie packed up the books that cluttered the kitchen table, checking the wall clock at the same time. Ten thirty. Time to head to bed, even though it was a Saturday night. Her cats would be pleased, anyway. She stashed the side plate with the remnants of her dinner, a field greens and cherry tomato salad, into the sink. It could wait till the morning's dishes.

She'd closed the kitchen window earlier, when the sun had set and she'd felt a chilly autumn breeze blowing across her. That had called for a cup of hot herbal tea. She drank the remaining quarter cup of liquid, now cool but still tasty, and added that to the sink.

Hopefully, the weatherman was right and tomorrow the thermometer would take them into the midseventies again.

Out of curiosity, she checked her mailbox before heading upstairs. Nothing. The phone rang as she pulled her nightgown over her head.

"Hi, Lizzie, it's Mark. Hope I'm not calling too late."

"Oh, hi. No, it's not too late. I am sort of surprised, though."

"I just got home from a call, so my brain's still in work mode, I guess. I thought I'd check and see if your master sleuths had turned up anything more."

Lizzie wished she could see his face. He sounded serious. Was this leading to another lecture? "My sleuths. You make me sound like a PI agency. Well, nothing new has turned up, in answer to your question."

"You would tell me if that were the case, wouldn't you?"

"You'd be the first person to know if they found the killer," she said.

"That's not exactly what I asked."

"Have you found the killer?"

"I can see where this conversation is going. Nowhere. So I'll just say good night. Which is really what I called for in the first place."

"You did?" She pulled the neckline of her nightgown tighter.

He chuckled. "Pleasant dreams, Lizzie," he said, then hung up before she could respond.

She sat with the phone in her hand for several minutes before finally hanging up. What had he really wanted? She hoped it was exactly as he said. But he was a cop, after all, and high school was a long time ago.

Chapter Twenty

◇◇◇

How often must I tell you that nothing is trivial in crime.

MISS MADELYN MACK, DETECTIVE—HUGH C. WEIR

Lizzie mused about the possible outcome of the garden party as she drove to Molly's the next morning. She truly wished that none of the students were the thief. She didn't really know any of them very well, though, except for Stephanie, whom she was certain wasn't the culprit. Was it because someone needed money? They stole then pawned the stuff? But according to Molly, the missing items weren't overly valuable.

Maybe the person just wanted them . . . saw them, liked them and gave them a new home. That was entirely possible. She remembered a few years back when a small break-and-enter ring, comprised entirely of students from the middle school, was nabbed. Their parents couldn't afford the assortment of laptops, DVD players and other electronics that they stole, and they were certain the owners could easily have them replaced by insurance. Therefore, in their eyes, no one was hurt. She shook her head. What a crazy world sometimes.

Whoever this thief was hadn't taken into account the sentimental value of the items. No insurance could cover that.

Lizzie got out of her Mazda and locked it just as Sally-Jo pulled into the driveway. She waited while Sally-Jo parked so they could walk in together.

"Tell all, girl," Lizzie said.

"All. Let's see, it was hot wandering around that fairground yesterday afternoon, and it looked like every other fair I've been to over the years. And that's quite a few. Anyway, we eventually did talk to someone who'd actually socialized with Frank Telford and his wife, Enid, just after they had married. Gilda Cruise. She's a member of the Library Committee and staffed their bake table at the fair."

Sally-Jo stopped and dug into her shoulder bag, producing a small object wrapped in foil. "For you. It's Gilda's very own special recipe double chocolate, chocolate chip cookies. They're truly to die for. Anyway, Gilda said they'd lost touch over the years, but she did remember hearing at one point that Enid had left Frank. She thought there'd been a bit of a scandal but hadn't heard the details. Frank seemed to turn into something of a recluse after that. She was pretty much buried in kids at that time so didn't get too excited about any of it."

"Thanks for the added calories. I know I'll enjoy them, unfortunately. So, I wonder if the police know about Enid Telford."

"They must if they checked the vital statistics records."

"Funny that Mark didn't say anything."

"What, and get you out searching for her?"

Lizzie shrugged. "You're probably right. Well done. I take it spending the day with Jacob wasn't too much of a hardship?"

She thought fleetingly about seeing Jacob with the blonde the previous morning. Then he'd spent the afternoon with Sally-Jo. Busy boy. She longed to mention something but thought it better to try to get some more information before tattling. Sally-Jo seemed happy enough anyway, which was the main thing.

"Not at all." Sally-Jo smiled. "Now, what's the plan for this afternoon? Are we supposed to be keeping an eye on anyone special? What about Troy?"

"If he's here, then yes. I don't know if he's our prime suspect, but one of the items did go missing the night he stormed out of class."

They knocked and entered through the back door. Molly waved them in and went back to her discussion with a young man dressed in torn jeans and an equally ragged T-shirt. They could hear her giving him instructions as to where a tent needed to be set up on the far right end of the stone patio.

Bob Miller popped his head through the open doorway to the hall. "Oh, good. Some bodies. Would you young ladies mind helping me out for just a minute?"

"Sure, Bob," Sally-Jo answered for them both.

They joined him in the hallway where he'd climbed back up a tall ladder and was adjusting a camera in a small alcove. "Now, you, Lizzie, you go stand over there by that table with all those doodaddies on it"—he gestured at the Bedfordshire accent table at the foot of the stairs—"and Sally-Jo, you just take a look at that little monitor there on top of my bag. Tell me when you can see Lizzie and the table."

"A surveillance camera. We've gone high tech," Lizzie said with glee. "I didn't know Molly had called in the professionals for this."

Bob chuckled. "I've always wanted to use one of these thingies and never had any need on the job, so here we go now. OK, Sally-Jo, how's the view?"

Sally-Jo squatted beside the open duffel bag. "Just point it a little to the left . . . no, I mean your right, Bob. Okay, now down just a tad. That's got it. Why don't you come see for yourself if this is what you have in mind?"

"Good idea." Bob was already climbing back down the ladder. He kneeled down and peered at the small monitor and nodded. "Yep, that oughta do it. Now I'll just move that shiny brass statue over a bit, and the camera should just blend in."

Lizzie noticed he had a bit of difficulty pushing himself back up on his feet. She often found herself surprised at how so many folks she'd known all her life had aged almost overnight. Mama had seemed old for a long time, but Molly, and Bob, had been ageless for so long and now, here they were in their early seventies and showing some wear and tear. Not that they were old. Molly would have a fit if she heard Lizzie refer to her as such. Aging. Gracefully, in Molly's case.

"Did you and Molly find anything useful when you went to Stoney Mills?" Lizzie asked, remembering they hadn't spoken since their trip.

Bob cleared his throat. "Not really. I was talking it over with Jacob, and it was much the same information he and Sally-Jo found out." He sounded sheepish. "I'm sorry, Lizzie. I could give it another try."

"Hmm. Maybe. So are you recording this or what?" Lizzie asked.

"No, I'll just tuck myself away with the monitor in the library. Keep an eye on things from there. I'm not part of this party anyway."

"Just be sure to load up with eats before you tuck away," Sally-Jo suggested.

"Oh, I intend to, young lady. I surely intend to do that. Thanks for your help, both of you. Have you seen the setup outside?"

"No, that's our next stop, if Molly doesn't need us to do anything," Lizzie said. "Just let us know if you need any help."

Bob grunted as he carted the ladder toward the door.

Molly joined them in the hall, beaming. "Oh, I'm

enjoying this already. It's been awhile since I had a big garden party, and I do so enjoy them. How about this camera of Bob's?"

"I think it's a great idea, Molly," Sally-Jo said. "You can't argue with the camera's eye."

Molly nodded. "Thank you for coming early, but you know, there's not much to be done. I've hired people to take care of most of it. Why don't you just go outside and take a look. Let me know what you think or if I'm missing anything."

She went in the direction Bob had gone while Lizzie and Sally-Jo headed back through the kitchen and outside again.

The well-groomed lawn went on for about a hundred and fifty yards and was the ideal setting for the five white-clothed round tables, each with four chairs around them. At the right side of the patio, four long tables had been arranged in a row while to the left, the young man they'd seen inside, along with a helper, was placing the poles for the tent. A bar had been set up to the left of the doorway, with yet another young man placing boxes of soda bottles behind it.

He glanced over at them, grinned and held a bottle of tonic water in greeting. Lizzie recognized Dwayne Trowl from her class. She walked over to the bar.

"Why, Dwayne. Nice to see you. Is this a part-time job?"

"Yes'm. I tend bar off and on for Carleton Caterers. Have been for some time now. This and pizza delivery for Big Mike's Pizzas."

"Good for you."

"Yeah, I'm trying to get enough money to go to chef's school in Birmingham."

Lizzie tried to hide her surprise. "You like cooking?"

"Oh, yeah. It's a good job. There's a lot of opportunities if you're a big-time chef, not like a short-order cook at all. Like cooking someplace like here. Or at some big hotel. You know, the family roots go back to food and the land. Back to my grandpops."

Dream big, she thought. "Well, I hope you get there, Dwayne. And taking the GED is a large step."

"Oh, I'm counting on that, ma'am." He went back to unpacking bottles.

Lizzie spotted Sally-Jo walking in the flower garden at the back of the lawn. She joined her, and they followed the stone path that led back through the sculpted shrubs and around a large pond. Brightly colored koi of all sizes swam close to the surface, snapping at flies that landed periodically.

"This is absolute heaven," Sally-Jo said. "All it needs is a swing of some sort."

"Come with me," Lizzie said and led her even farther into the garden, through an arbor of gracefully entwined tree branches draped with hanging Spanish moss, to another smaller lawn area with a covered swing set placed to one side. Bunches of autumn-colored flowers bordered the space, giving way to a water feature with three levels of waterfalls, tumbling to a small pool.

"Wow! It gets even better," Sally-Jo exclaimed.

"I find it really soothing. Let's sit a minute and enjoy the view and the silence," Lizzie suggested.

They got the swing moving and sat, each deep in thought. Lizzie remembered how she loved to wander through the gardens and spend many an afternoon by herself, swinging in solitude, hiding out from reality, she supposed now. It had been a retreat when she needed to get away from the strain of trying to get her mama to talk to her, to become part of her life once more. Even as a teenager, Lizzie would often call Molly and ask if she could come over. She was never refused. And she'd often start out the visit in the backyard, by herself, mellowing out, then end it in the kitchen sharing a glass of milk and freshly baked molasses cookies with Molly.

It never seemed odd that even though Molly had a live-in cook and housekeeper, she often baked and tidied the rooms herself. That was Molly. In fact, Lizzie had learned the fine art of polishing the silver tea service from Molly. Even though Lizzie didn't own one. It was the sharing of the task that she'd enjoyed.

Sally-Jo broke the silence. "You've spent a lot of time here, haven't you?"

"Yes. It was like a hideout for me."

"I meant at Molly's in general."

"That, too. For the same reason."

"That's what I needed, a hideout from my five sisters."

"Hectic, was it?"

"Hectic and noisy. And I could never get any privacy nor have much of my parents' time and attention. We were always sharing everything."

Lizzie sighed. "I've often wished I'd had a sister or two, but I can't really imagine what it would be like, especially that many."

"Well, it was fun a lot of the times, but I often longed to just be alone. I really enjoyed going off to college, partly to get away. And then, inheriting Aunt Pearl's house was a dream. Of course, part of it belongs to my sister Janice, but I'm paying her monthly, like rent. So she's happy. And Auntie's summerhouse went to Donna and Carleen, while her money went to the others. It was an interesting way of divvying her estate, but then again, she was an interesting woman. I think we got the house because we visited her the most often."

"She sounds like a very thoughtful person."

"She was." Sally-Jo was silent for a few minutes. "I think I'd like to get a swing like this for my backyard. It would be lovely to have on a hot, sultry evening."

"Especially with a certain lawyer swinging by your side."

"Exactly." She made a face at Lizzie. "Now, don't you think we'd better get back and see if there's anything that needs doing?"

Lizzie linked her arm through Sally-Jo's. "Good idea."

Even though it was a bit early, a few guests had already arrived. *I wish they'd be this conscientious when it came to classes*, Lizzie thought as she greeted some of her students. Sally-Jo drifted over to the small platform where the guitar quintet was starting to set up.

By the time the buffet had been set out on the tables, most of the guests had arrived. Lizzie made a point of spending a few minutes with each of her students. She was pleased that the majority had come. However, she noted that Troy wasn't among them. Teesha appeared beside her at the fruit-punch bowl.

"This is real cool, Ms. Turner," she gushed. "I think it's so darn nice of Ms. Molly to invite us all. I've never been to such a classy party."

Lizzie smiled. "It's a treat for me, too, Teesha. I'm glad you could come. Here, let me get you some of this delicious fruit punch."

Teesha nodded and took a long drink after Lizzie handed her the cup. "See y'all later," she said between sips, and eventually wandered off.

Lizzie nodded, then got her own drink. She also picked up a plate and filled it with Asiago-olive rolls, a spinach mini-quiche and a couple of spicy cheddar straw triangles from the table laid out with tempting light food fare, and limited herself to one red velvet brownie from the dessert table.

Lizzie joined the girls from her class at their table. The chatter was mainly about Molly's wonderful garden and of course, the fact that she had invited them to her party. This would be the main topic of conversation for quite some time to come. Lizzie would bet on it.

She kept an eye on the back door, noting who went in, presumably to use the powder room. Lizzie knew that Bob had the situation in hand so she shouldn't be concerned, but she couldn't help but worry and wonder if the thief was part of this crowd. She sure hoped not, but what other explanation was there?

As sounds of a Boccherini guitar quintet filled the unseasonably warm autumn air, Lizzie relaxed, enjoying the conversation at the table. Molly looked to be having a wonderful time, too, surrounded by students every time Lizzie looked over. She wore a flowery red, green and white cotton summer dress, appropriate since the temperature was in the high seventies, and black sandals. She carried a broad-brimmed straw sun hat in one hand and a tray of chocolate truffles in the other.

By the time the caterers started clearing the tables two hours later, a lot of guests had already left. The few still around looked as though they were having a hard time tearing themselves away from the beauty of the place. Lizzie finally ushered the last lingering students out to the front driveway, then returned to the back and joined Molly, Sally-Jo and Bob, sitting on patio chairs, iced teas in hand.

"Any action, Bob?" she asked.

He shook his head. "Too bad. That camera's a beauty. Maybe I'll just leave it hooked up for you, Molly, for a couple of weeks, anyway. I'll bring over a recorder, too. You just have to remember to click it on and start the recording when the students arrive at night. Then, if anything disappears, we hopefully will have a video of it. You might want to leave that little table set up just as it is."

Molly nodded her assent. She stretched her long legs out in front of her and sighed. "Such a delightful afternoon. I'm glad nothing was stolen. That would have ruined it."

"It was a great success, Molly. The kids loved it. Most had never been to anything so elegant before," Sally-Jo said. "This was a really nice thing to do."

"That young guitar player in the quintet was wonderful," Lizzie added.

Molly smiled. "He is good, isn't he? I thought the students

might find it interesting that someone their age could be so talented and enjoy classical music, too. He's the son of my gardener, and I've been helping with his music lessons. He may audition for Julliard in the spring, so that's very promising."

Lizzie wasn't surprised to hear that Molly was assisting him. She'd be willing to bet that Molly would be the one paying his tuition next year, also.

Bob leaned forward. "Molly, you look dog tired. Why don't I just whisk you over to my place and I'll fry up some grouper I caught fresh this morning." He grinned. "Some small boiled potatoes with collard greens and it'll taste good enough to eat. You girls are welcome, too."

Lizzie looked at Sally-Jo, who raised her eyebrows. Lizzie said, "Thanks, Bob. That sounds so tempting, but I've got some prep work to do tonight. I think I'll just head home. Maybe pick up some takeout on the way."

Sally-Jo had a similar reply. "If there's nothing we can help you with, Molly, maybe we'll both get going and let you two get to dinner."

"I thank you both for your offers, but it will all be cleared and back to normal in no time. You run off now and enjoy your evenings, even if you're both working."

Lizzie gave Molly a quick kiss on the cheek, as did Sally-Jo; then the two gave Bob a quick wave and left.

"I think something was accomplished today, anyway," Sally-Jo said as she got into her car.

Lizzie nodded. "And a very nice couple they make.

Chapter Twenty-one

◇◇◇

The trouble with mornings is they come when you're not awake.

THREE FOR THE CHAIR—REX STOUT

Checking her mailbox as she left for school had become another of those morning routines for Lizzie. So she wasn't entirely surprised to find yet another large manila envelope stashed in it. What did surprise her was that Nathaniel Creely either hadn't seen this happen or hadn't let her know. She decided a quick check on him was in order, just to make sure he was okay.

He answered on the first knock, his Tilley hat in hand. "Oh, Lizzie. Good morning. How nice to see you. Is everything all right?"

"Yes, Nathaniel. I just thought I'd let you know, I found another envelope in my mailbox this morning." She knew he was proud of his independence and might get a bit miffed if he thought she kept as close an eye on him as she did.

"Oh my. How did I miss that?" He shook his head, then appeared to have one of those "aha" moments. "I did retire earlier than usual last night. I just wanted to be rested for today. I'm meeting some old friends, and we're taking a walk along the Pritchard Nature Trail. That must be what happened. I'm sorry."

"No need to be sorry, Nathaniel. I just thought I'd let you know. Enjoy your walk; it promises to be perfect walking weather today."

Nathaniel raised his hat in a jaunty wave. "I shall, I shall. You have an enjoyable day, too."

That was good, she thought as she backed the Mazda out of the drive. Getting out with his friends. He didn't need her help in finding activities at all.

Lizzie found her morning's assignment fairly straight-forward: observe and comment on a fifth-grade teacher, in her first year at teaching, who desperately needed some tips for handling the diversity in reading skills in her classroom. Lizzie admired the young teachers starting out in their cho-sen careers. Teaching was a difficult job, and doing it full-time was something Lizzie couldn't imagine for herself. Besides dealing with students as individuals, as well as a class in general, plus keeping up to date on the latest teach-ing techniques, teachers now needed to know the most recent technology, which was advancing in leaps and bounds. Anything Lizzie could do to lighten their loads was a good thing, and she worked hard at it.

She'd meet with this teacher over lunch, then send her the written notes later. That way, there'd be no delay in get-ting her suggestions implemented. The class time flew by, as did the lunch hour. Lizzie barely had time to make it to her afternoon class, which included Danny from the other day. She was anxious to ask if his parents had bought him the books yet.

When she met up with him after class, it turned out they hadn't. She dug into her bag and came up with another graphic novel, a version of one book on the required reading list, and gave it to him. "What I want in return," she said to him, "is a copy of the book report you'll be doing for your teacher. Now, enjoy."

His attempt at a blasé thank-you didn't quite mask his excitement. *I'll get him hooked yet*, Lizzie thought, and decided it was time to go home and do her own reading.

Lizzie poured herself a glass of pomegranate juice, then settled in her comfy chair by the window in the living room. She'd been dying to read the next installment of manuscript since finding it earlier but had resolutely left it at home to avoid temptation while at school. She pulled the pages of manuscript out of the envelope and quickly scanned what she'd already read before carrying on with the new pages.

Just as she feared, tragedy hit the family of three. The father, Harlan Fowks, unable to get any of his investment back and having lost his job because of the economic downturn, moved his family to a new town, hoping to find work. After months of trying and getting nowhere, he gave up and in despair committed suicide. Lizzie sat a few minutes, lost in thought, imagining what that must have been like for his young wife. Her thoughts briefly lit on her own mother, in her midthirties, with a young daughter and suddenly no husband. She'd reacted by retreating into her own world. A young woman of delicate sensibilities, as they would have said in years gone by. She shook her head and returned to reading.

Adele pulled her ragged coat closely around her body as she walked home. It was pretty cool for a fall night and her feet ached. She'd been on them all day, cleaning three houses that, lucky for her, were all on the same block. Now she just had the half-hour walk home.

She stopped in at her neighbor's and picked up the sleeping Carla, wrapping the blanket tight around her. The apartment was cold and dark when she finally let herself into it. She laid the baby in the crib next to the couch and turned on some lights. She kept her coat on, hoping not to have to turn on the heat.

She opened a can of pork 'n beans and heated it on the stove, and sat on the couch eating. It was nine o'clock when she finished, so she washed up the dishes, checked on Carla and then pulled the couch out, making it into her bed, and got ready to crawl into it.

The next day was her regular at the Johnson house in the upscale part of town. It took her a good hour to make it there. When she'd finished her work—it took most of the day to clean the two-story mansion—Mr. Johnson asked her into his study. He'd just come home from work and still had his overcoat on.

"Mrs. Fowks, I know you are in need of money, and I'm impressed with how efficient you are around here. I'd like to offer you a job at my office."

"Cleaning your office?" she asked.

"No. I need someone to do the filing and make coffee and anything my secretary needs help with. I have an insurance agency right downtown. I'll pay you two times what you make here." He waited while she thought about it.

She could hardly believe it. More money and easier work. And she wouldn't be so tired at night. She could enjoy the time with her daughter. She said yes right on the spot.

It would have been ideal, except for the extra duties he quickly added. Having Adele safely away from his wife's prying eyes, he coerced her into a sexual relationship, leaving Adele feeling sickened and insecure. Lizzie threw the manuscript down in disgust. *What a creep. Taking advantage of Adele's desperation. A true lowlife of the species.*

She stomped into the kitchen, startling Brie, who lay reclining on the kitchen table, enjoying the last few hours of sunshine. Lizzie stopped abruptly. "Sorry, baby. I didn't mean to scare you." She took a couple of deep breaths before grabbing the jar of almond butter out of the cupboard.

Jar and spoon in hand, she went out to the back patio and tried to put it all in perspective. It was just a story, after all. But whose? And why send it to her? And why was she reacting so strongly to it? Because of her own daddy's death? But the circumstances were entirely different, as was the way their mamas handled their grief.

Lizzie ate a couple of teaspoons of the thick almond butter and went back inside. She left spoon and jar on the counter and sought out the manuscript, grabbing a pencil on the way. Starting at the beginning of the story, she slowly read through the pages, circling all the possessives; then she went back to the start again and read only the circled words. A pattern began emerging. As the story evolved, the author seemed to be removing him- or herself from the telling of it and was no longer a participant. Lizzie wondered if that was because the story hit too close to home, becoming almost too painful to relive.

Or else, the writer was totally inexperienced and didn't realize he or she had made the switch.

Lizzie read it through again, this time searching for how much setting and extraneous observations were included. Hardly any. The writing was spare, almost as if journal entries had been embellished to read more like a novel.

Lizzie sat back. Was it a journal? Someone's true story? Often the basis for fiction. So that made sense, but why send it to her? Perhaps it was from one of the literacy students, but wouldn't that person want feedback? And if she/he could write this well, what were they doing in her literacy class? It just didn't add up. She needed Sally-Jo to read it again, now that there were more chapters.

Or maybe the book club should read it after all. There was a crime, maybe not murder, but fraud leading to suicide. And the manuscript itself was a mystery—what would happen next, and who was the author? Lizzie glanced at the clock and was shocked to see she had ten minutes to get to literacy class.

No time to change or eat dinner. She stuffed the entire manuscript into her bag, filled the cat dishes with dry food and left, peeling a banana, which she ate on the way to Molly's.

She arrived five minutes late and noticed the class was down by three, or they were even later than she. No Troy. Also missing were Dwayne and Teesha. That was surprising since they'd both been at the garden party and looked to have enjoyed themselves, even though Dwayne was working. Those two were often whispering at the back. Maybe they'd connected and had other plans for the evening. She hoped they'd all return for the next class.

"I have your written assignments about the unsolved murder ready to hand back. I want you to quickly read over my comments and then if anyone would like to share their paper with the rest of the class, we'd love to listen, and afterward, anyone who wishes can comment."

She was sorry Dwayne had skipped class. She'd be interested in his reaction to her notes. Although his writing skills left a lot to be desired, she'd been impressed with his imagination. Of all the papers, Dwayne's had been the most creative, suggesting that Telford had been about to extort money from Molly, and his brother had tried to talk him out of it, they'd fought over the gun, and it had accidentally gone off.

Sonny's hand shot up immediately, and he started reading his paper aloud before even checking Lizzie's comments. Although she didn't grade the assignments, Lizzie had pointed out that Sonny's lacked the structure they'd been talking about for several weeks now; however, it was equally imaginative, albeit implausible.

Jolene had a comment at the ready when he stopped reading. "We don't have a Mafia here in Ashton Corners. There's nothing for them to get their mitts into here. We don't even have any gangs."

"Says you," Sonny countered. "Whoever heard about the Mafia going around telling everybody they're in town? I like my story. It could'a happened like that."

Jolene shook her head, and Stephanie looked down quickly to hide her smile.

Jolene went next, and her story had shades of fantasy involved. Stephanie wouldn't meet Lizzie's eye, so Lizzie decided not to put her on the spot. She felt Stephanie's paper lacked anything more than the facts, anyway, and wondered if there was a reason for that.

Lizzie then pulled out a stack of Rapid Reads books from her tote. She'd been so impressed with this series of books for reluctant readers, she'd talked one of the program's private donors into funding her special purchase.

"These books should not take y'all too long to read, some of you may even do it in one sitting, and don't let the size of print fool you. These are books for adults, with topics that'll hook you right away. Now, we have a variety of titles here. I want you to each choose one from the display on the coffee table, then start reading, finishing them at home. If you don't get the one you want this week, don't worry because we'll be swapping around next week. After reading them, I'd like you to answer the questions on this sheet that I'm now passing out. I'd suggest reading over these questions first, so you'll know what to keep an eye out for when reading the books. The assignment is due next class."

The books were thin, which when added to their dramatic covers, meant a quick acceptance by the group. The students quickly made their choices and settled in to start reading. After the break, a lively discussion ensued about Rapid Reads before the class ended.

As Lizzie stuffed her books into her bag, Jolene stopped in front of her chair. She shifted from foot to foot, until Lizzie stopped what she was doing and looked at her.

"Hey, Jolene. What can I do for you?"

"Well, umm, I was wondering. Well, I sorta've got this story, you know."

Lizzie's heart started pounding. Was Jolene the mystery author and about to reveal all? "Yes?" she said encouragingly.

"Well, umm, I know it's not really good. Yet. But I'll work on it and make it better. It's a story that's really important to me. And I was hoping you'd read what I've got so far and maybe give me some pointers? Umm, would you do that?" Jolene stuck her hands in the pockets of her camouflage army jacket and chewed her bottom lip. Her vibrant, red-dyed hair, worn in a ponytail, along with the black eyeliner that encircled both eyes, gave her the appearance of a preteen. Someone totally unsure of herself.

Lizzie smiled. "Of course, I'd be happy to. What's it about?" Then she worried it might be the true story of Jolene's own family. What would Lizzie say after reading it?

"It's, umm, it's like a fantasy story. Sort of sci-fi, also. About this planet and this young couple who escape there after the Troglelytes attack earth. Set in the future."

She stared in earnest at Lizzie.

Lizzie tried not to show her disappointment, not just because this wasn't the author of the mystery manuscript but also because she really didn't enjoy reading fantasy or science fiction. She swallowed a sigh.

"Just bring it in next time, and I'll read it as soon as I can."

Jolene grinned, gave her a high-five and pranced out of the library.

Lizzie found both Molly and Sally-Jo in the kitchen. She gave the manuscript to Sally-Jo then said good night to them both and headed home, suddenly exhausted and wanting nothing more than a good night's sleep.

Chapter Twenty-two

◇◇◇

"One way or another," I mumbled as my head hit
the pillow, "I'm going to get my questions answered."

DECAFFEINATED CORPSE—CLEO COYLE

The insistent ringing of the phone tried its best to awaken
Lizzie, but she resisted as long as possible. Finally, her
brain kicked into gear and she rolled over, dislodging the
cats from their crevices around her legs. She fumbled with
the receiver, her heart pounding in her chest. A phone call
at that hour could only be bad news about Mama.

"Hello?" she blurted out.

"Elizabeth Turner?" She didn't recognize the voice,
couldn't tell if it were male or female even. But nobody
called her Elizabeth, unless it was someone she didn't know
very well. And it wouldn't be from anyone from Magnolia
Manor.

"Yes . . . what is it?"

"I think you'd agree that every life has a story, even
though some of those stories are more what the people want
you to believe, not what's true. Your daddy knew that. In
fact, his final story was about just such a person. That's why
he was in Stoney Mills just before his accident."

Lizzie heard the phone click and then nothing but a dial tone. She said hello a couple of times anyway, then turned on the light and grabbed the pen and pad from the bedside table. She took a couple of deep breaths to calm down and thought about what the caller had said. Then, she carefully wrote down every word she could remember, read it over, then turned off the light and slid back down under the covers. Her brain kept going over the words until they all became meaningless. She'd give it a go in the morning.

Lizzie woke up, heart pounding, gasping for breath. She sat up abruptly. *What's going on? Am I having a heart attack?* She lay back down and tried sorting through her jumbled thoughts. *Breathe slowly.* Her daddy. She sat back up. She'd gotten a phone call about her daddy.

She scrambled out of bed and grabbed the paper on which she'd written the caller's message. Had this person known her daddy? What had he been writing about? What was going on?

She kept rereading the message as she finished her breakfast of granola and fresh fruit. It just didn't make any sense. The voice hadn't sounded sinister, just anonymous and androgynous. Was there a connection to Frank Telford's death? Or to the manuscript she'd been receiving? *Another anonymous contributor.*

Maybe Molly could help make sense of it, but Lizzie had meetings all day. She scraped the dregs of her breakfast into the composting bin and rinsed her dishes. Back in her bedroom, she ditched the flouncy skirt she'd been planning to wear and settled on taupe straight-legged pants and a multicolored long-sleeved crepe blouse. She added a cinch belt, some hoop earrings, and comfortable brown flats since she'd be hoofing it between classrooms most of the day.

She made certain she had all the books, test papers and other materials she needed, stuffed her lunch in her tote and left for school. Neither cat tried to get out the door, a sure sign they'd finally settled into the back-to-school routine.

She had to force herself to concentrate on each student and teacher she spoke with, finding her mind wandering to the now-memorized message. She hoped her subconscious could come up with an answer while she did her work, but the memory of the late-night call refused to stay in its allotted place. Finally, the end-of-day bell rang and she raced off to Molly's.

She was annoyed with herself for not calling first when it became apparent Molly wasn't at home. She'd give her a call later. What she needed was a cold drink and a quiet place to think. She realized, with a sinking feeling, that might have to wait. Officer Amber Craig drove up as Lizzie walked back to her car.

"I'm here to see Ms. Mathews," she told Lizzie.

"Well, you're out of luck. She's not here."

"In that case, you'll do. Would you mind following me down to the police station?" Lizzie looked skeptical. "Or you could climb into the back of my smelly cruiser and we could talk here."

"I'll see you at the station," Lizzie said and left before Officer Craig got back in her car.

They entered the station at the same time, Lizzie through the front door and Craig through the back. Mark looked up from his desk as Lizzie was escorted past his open door and over to Officer Craig's desk. Lizzie avoided looking at Mark, which was hard to do since she sat in a chair facing his office.

"I want you to tell me all about the little snooping trip that Molly Mathews and Bob Miller took to Stoney Mills." Craig leaned on her desk, pen in hand, ready to make notes.

"I assume Chief Dreyfus told you about that, so he can also tell you what they found. Which, I think, is nothing. I'm certain he must have interviewed them. Or, I guess he asked you to do that, which is why you were at Molly's today." Lizzie felt a streak of irritability run through her body. She wouldn't make this easy.

"I don't need you to tell me why I was there, Ms. Turner," Officer Craig said through gritted teeth. "Just tell me what you know."

"I already told you, I think they didn't have any luck. They found nothing." Lizzie sat erect in the chair, trying to appear more confident than she felt.

"You think. I'll bet you know. I think you're the instigator here. That you've sent your merry book clubbers off in search of a killer. Which is not only interfering with a police investigation, it's also stupid. You all could get yourselves hurt. Or killed."

"Stupid?" Lizzie rubbed her temples. She could feel a doozy of a headache taking hold. "If that were true, we might be a bit foolhardy or overzealous, but stupid?" She stood up, trying to keep her voice down.

"Sit down, Ms. Turner," Officer Craig growled.

Lizzie felt a hand on her arm. "Maybe I could have a word with Ms. Turner, Officer Craig," Mark said. He pivoted her and held tightly to her arm until he'd guided her to a chair in his office.

"I'm sorry, Mark. That woman just gets me going." Lizzie looked at him, a suitably contrite expression on her face. "I am sorry."

Mark smiled. "You two are like oil and water. I think I'm going to have to take on all the questioning of you. Now, do you know anything else about what Molly Mathews and Bob Miller found in Stoney Mills?"

"Just as I told Officer Craig, they didn't find a thing. Except that Frank Telford was a recluse. Which you probably already knew." She waited for him to confirm that, but he said nothing. "So, I'm wondering, why was a recluse in Ashton Corners to start with?"

"That's the question, Lizzie. You don't happen to have an answer, do you?"

"Only what he told us at the house, which was exactly nothing. So, where do you go from here?" She wasn't about to tell him that Sally-Jo and Jacob had also taken a stab at it.

"We're still trying to dig into his life, but there's not much to go on since he dropped out of society about thirty years ago."

"Why then? What happened to make him do that?"

"I'm trying to find out, believe me, but we're having a hard time finding someone who knew him, and of course, as I'm sure you know, the local paper lost all their old files in a fire about fifteen years ago."

"What caused the fire?"

Mark looked at her a moment. "Are you thinking it's tied in, some sort of conspiracy?" He sounded amused. He leaned back in his chair and crossed his arms over his chest.

"No." She sat straighter. "Well, you never know, but I guess it's highly unlikely."

"So, I should be looking at what happened fifteen years ago to precipitate the fire that may have been set to destroy any information referring to Frank Telford, who was then killed fifteen years later?"

"Well, when you put it that way . . . ," she said. "Did he have any next of kin?"

"No, just his former wife—they were divorced—but nobody else."

"Did anyone claim his body?"

Mark shook his head.

"What happens to it?"

"Well, the county will give him a burial. They'll do it on the cheap, no service, inexpensive casket. There's a portion of the local cemetery reserved for such situations."

"That's so sad."

Mark shrugged.

Lizzie shook off her melancholy mood. "Do you still think someone in the book club might be involved?"

"We haven't found a connection yet. But we can't ignore the fact that he was killed outside Molly Mathews's house during a book club meeting. I'm focusing more on Telford, and Officer Craig is looking at the book club end of it. She thinks that's where the killer's to be found."

"Of course she does."

"Look, I know you believe none of your group is involved. And I suspect you and some of the others will continue to nose around, but I want to know what, if anything, you find out. Will you do that?" He stared at her. She had to say yes. "And won't do anything that could prove to be dangerous?"

She nodded this time.

"Good. Now how would you like to grab some dinner and maybe a movie tomorrow night?"

"Tomorrow night?" she croaked with dismay.

He nodded.

"I'd love to, but I teach literacy on Mondays and Wednesdays."

He sighed. "Well, what night don't you have something?"

"Um . . . Thursdays are open."

"Thursday, I have to attend the City Council meeting. How about Friday?"

"Sorry, choir. Saturday?"

"Unfortunately, I'm working this Saturday."

"The chief of police has to work on a Saturday night? What do you have officers for?"

"Well, the older ones have families, and the younger ones like to go out on the town on weekends. Besides, I don't have anyone to free up my time for." He cocked an eyebrow and stared at her. "If I did, I'd want to give them plenty of notice about a shift change."

She hardly skipped a beat. "What if you did have someone to do something with, say, a week from this Saturday?" She couldn't believe she said that.

"I'd assign the shift to someone else, well in advance." He smiled. "Which is what I'll do."

"Good." She stood up and turned to leave, then walked to his desk instead. "By the way, can you check into an old police report for me?"

"Probably, but it may take awhile if it's not been entered into the computer system. When did it happen?"

"In 1990. Mark, I want to know what the police found about my daddy's car accident."

He looked at her a moment before answering. "Can I ask why?"

Lizzie took her time replying. "Because I received a phone call in the middle of the night." She took the message out of her purse and shoved it across the desk. "I wrote it down as well as I could remember before going back to sleep."

Mark read it slowly, then looked at her. "Have you had anything like this happen before?"

She shook her head.

"Do you remember what happened to your daddy?"

"Only what Mama told me. That Daddy had been on his way home from work and was coming over Broward Hill when someone, trying to pass another car, hit him head-on. He died instantly." Lizzie suddenly felt like she was about to burst into tears. Where had that come from? She'd talked about his death many times over the years. She must be overtired.

"That doesn't sound too sinister."

"No," she admitted, feeling more in control again, "but why did I get this call?"

He came around the desk and put a hand on her arm. "I'll look into it. See what I can find out."

She smiled. "Thanks, Mark." She resisted turning around to wave as she closed the door behind her.

When she got home, she tried phoning Molly. No answer.

She had a moment of worry, hoping everything was okay, then reasoned that Molly was entitled to a private life, one that Lizzie knew nothing about. Who knew, maybe Bob Miller had talked her into some further snooping, maybe even going undercover.

Chapter Twenty-three

◇◇◇

"What's the matter?" I asked as we made our way
not toward the carriage house, but to the truck. "Has
something happened? Something more?"

PLASTER AND POISON—JENNIE BENTLEY

The next morning, Lizzie added another quarter mile to
her run, taking a left on Partridge Lane rather than going
straight along Jackson. This section of the town was home
to mainly older, retired couples or young ones just starting
out. The housing prices here had remained fairly stable during the recession. There wasn't much movement, among the
older homeowners anyway, at the best of times. And fortunately, this area had not been hit by foreclosures, as some
of the newer ones had in the past few years.

The houses along this street were mostly built in the
thirties, a fact underscored by the still-present white clapboard that had been so readily available in those days. Her
favorite was a two-story, with yellow trim and a yellow gate
that brought some pizzazz to the traditional white picket
fence. The gardens were awash of color in the summer,
mimicking an English cutting garden. Now, in the early
throes of fall, gold chrysanthemums and orange azaleas set

the tone, with several small cedar bushes a background of greens.

She waved at the owner, a wizened white-haired woman who often was out snipping away at the flowers when Lizzie ran by, even at that early hour. Interesting how many people she knew to wave at or say hey to as she ran. The easy camaraderie added to the run and made her happy she'd chosen to return to Ashton Corners.

Nathaniel Creely waved her over as she walked past on the way to her place. "I have some freshly baked cheese scones I thought you might like. And a cup of coffee to go with them, of course."

What Lizzie really wanted was a tall glass of water and a shower, but she wasn't about to pass up his invitation. "Sounds wonderful." She turned up his walkway and did a couple of stretches before joining him on the porch.

"That smells so good. You know, this is why I have to keep running each morning. I just can't say no to such wonderful treats."

Nathaniel chuckled. "And it's such a pleasure to have someone to bake for, my dear." He leaned over and served her, then himself. "Now, take a bite and enjoy, then tell me the latest news."

Lizzie did as instructed, taking an extra few moments to savor the melting of the cheese in her mouth. She took a sip of coffee and looked at Nathaniel's expectant expression. Something was different. His glasses were pulled down and rode on the tip of his nose. That was it. His mouth, as usual, was open slightly in a small "O" shape, as though he wanted to be ready for any exclamation.

"Well, you know I got another bit of the manuscript. It's a very gripping story. It reads almost like a journal to me. I've given it to my friend, Sally-Jo Baker, to have a read and see what she thinks. But there's still no clue as to who wrote it and why I'm getting it."

"I'm sure the author will make it all clear when the time is right," he commented. "But I can see it would be a bit perplexing. How is this business about the murder progressing? How is Molly handling it all?"

"There doesn't seem to be anything new, or at least, the police aren't saying if there is. Tim LaBelle was saying the other night at choir that the name Frank Telford sounded familiar, but like you, he can't place it either. You haven't remembered anything about him, have you?" She finished her cup of coffee and refilled both their cups.

"You know, as you said it, the name Telford Construction flitted through my mind. I don't know why. I don't even know if it existed, but there you go." Nathaniel looked pleased with himself.

Lizzie smiled. "That could be a clue, Nathaniel. I'd planned to go to the newspaper offices today anyway, so I'll see if I can find anything in their files about the company. These are delicious scones, by the way."

He beamed. "Yes, I'm quite pleased with them, if I do say so. I try a different filler each time, but it's always good to go back to basics. Have another."

Lizzie didn't have to be told twice. In fact, she thankfully took a plate of them back home with her.

A quick shower and change of clothes, a check that the cats hadn't totally devoured all their dry food, and she left for school, since breakfast had already been attended to.

Her second appointment of the day, with a sixth-grade girl, Jewels, who had a twelfth-grade attitude, was sorely trying Lizzie's patience. It took all her self-control to refrain from simply slamming her books shut and marching the girl, smoky eye shadow, ruffle top and all, down to the principal's office. Perhaps she should talk to Jewels's teacher, see if she had any pointers.

Lizzie had just pulled a short reading comprehension quiz out of her tote when the fire alarm blasted into the room. Jewels let out a shriek and dashed to the door. She was down the hall, having totally ignored Lizzie's calls, by the time Lizzie had grabbed her purse and followed.

Orderly lines of noisy children exited into the schoolyard and front boulevard. Sirens could be heard in the distance. Lizzie found the principal and asked if there really was a fire.

Herbert Slocam shrugged his shoulders. "Who knows?" he admitted as he made his way over to the first fire truck that screeched to a halt in front of the school.

Lizzie did a quick search of the grounds for Jewels and finally located her with a group of the older girls, giggling and busily texting away, at the far end of the paved area of the fenced-in schoolyard. A group of office staff stood off to another side. Lizzie went over to them and asked if they knew anything more. No one did. They stood in a bunch, watching the school for signs of smoke, until about twenty minutes later when the all-clear alarm sounded and teachers and staff attempted to round up the students and herd them back indoors.

By then, it was time for lunch. Lizzie went back into her allotted office, noticed Jewels had been by to grab her knapsack, packed up her own books and left. No classes or appointments were scheduled for the afternoon, so she headed over to the offices of the *Ashton Corners Colonist*, on Main Street, right next door to the police station.

The young receptionist gave Lizzie a cursory glance before picking up the phone and telling the editor, George Havers, he had a visitor. Lizzie watched the young man as he read through the "Lifestyles" section of last Thursday's newspaper, stopping every now and then to clip a story and stick it in one of many file folders spread across his desk. His face showed signs of recent acne problems. Dark curly hair matched the dark-framed glasses he wore.

She didn't even hear George walk up beside her. "You know, I don't totally trust computers," George said, touching her arm in apology as she jumped. "I like the good old-fashioned backup system, file clippings having been a newspaper staple for many years. It's good to see you, Lizzie. It's been awhile."

"Hey, George." Lizzie smiled up at him, realizing she hadn't seen him since she'd returned from college. He hadn't changed, though, except for the added gray in his thick, wavy hair. He hadn't shrunk any, still towering over her at his six-five; the black-rimmed glasses were the same, too.

When Lizzie was a girl, George had been a young cub reporter, fresh out of high school, who was always coming by Lizzie's house, or so it seemed, hanging on every word her daddy uttered. After Daddy died, she'd see George around town covering various events, but had never really connected with him for longer than a few friendly words in passing.

"And you, George. I hope I'm not disrupting your work, but I needed to talk to you about some old stories, and I'm glad to see your filing system. Maybe you'll have what I need."

"That sounds intriguing and you know, a newspaper man can never turn away from intrigue. Come into my office in the back here and we'll talk. Would you like some coffee?" he asked as they passed a half-full drip coffeemaker.

"No, thanks. I've hit my caffeine limit for the day already." She followed him around some empty desks, each with a computer screen and keyboard and not much else. George's desk, in contrast, was piled with paper and file folders. He caught her staring at it.

"I work best in clutter. And I truly can state that I do know where everything is on that desk." He chuckled. "Now, what's on your mind?"

"Well, I'm wondering if there might be any stories from, say, the 1960s or '70s involving Frank Telford."

"You mean, aside from the ones about his recent death?"

"Exactly. No one seems to know much about him in Stoney Mills."

"And just what is your interest, if I may ask?" He started

flipping through the sheaf of papers to the left of his blotter.

Lizzie hoped she wasn't awakening a journalist's curiosity by asking about Frank Telford. She didn't want Molly to have to deal with any more publicity, but she needed information and this seemed a good place to search for it.

"I was part of the book club meeting at Molly Mathews's house the night it happened. I'm concerned that Officer Amber Craig is treating us all like suspects, and I'm also concerned she might overlook something in her zeal."

"Ahh, yes, she reminds me of a Jack Daniels terrier: just sinks her teeth in and shakes things around."

"A pit bull, I was thinking."

George laughed. "Close enough. You could be right about her, but Chief Dreyfus seems on top of it. He was in asking the exact same question."

"Good. And what did you tell him?"

"Not much, I'm afraid. I found some ads for a Telford Construction and a new business development, with a Stoney Mills phone number that's long out of date. That was in 1966. We didn't do a story on it, so I guess it didn't merit any follow-up. Sorry."

Lizzie sighed. So Nathaniel was right. Score one for him. "Oh well, you never know. He was a very secretive man, I think. Thank you, anyway." She stood up to leave.

George put out his hand to shake. "Anytime, Lizzie. And don't be a stranger, you hear?"

Chapter Twenty-four

◇◇◇

Unfortunately, though I was itching to have at it, I
got a little sidetracked in my quest for the truth.

TOMB WITH A VIEW—CASEY DANIELS

This time she heard him. She leapt out of bed after a quick
glance at the clock. Two thirty A.M. The cats scattered as
she ran downstairs, not bothering to grab her bathrobe. She
yanked open the front door as a bicycle turned from her driveway, left on Sidcup, and tore away from the house. She followed as far as the street but lost sight. She started shivering
and realized she didn't have slippers on. Although the days
were blessed with a lingering summer sun, the nights showed
the season's true colors and warned that it really was autumn.

She glanced at Nathaniel's darkened windows. He'd be
in bed by now, she thought, running back to her front door.
She retrieved the manila envelope from her mailbox,
grabbed a sweatshirt from the hall closet and poured a small
glass of brandy.

Might as well read it since I'm wide awake now. As soon
as Lizzie sat in her favorite chair, Brie leapt to snuggle in her
lap, while Edam stretched out on the top of the backrest.

Lizzie started reading.

Adele Fowks stood in absolute silence, staring at her boss, the father of her child. She couldn't think of what to say. She didn't want to plead, but she had to, for her children's sake.

"You can't fire me, Henry. I need this job. I have Carla and now this baby to raise. Your baby."

Henry raised his right hand and slapped her, knocking her back against the desk. "Don't you say those words out loud again, you hear, girl? And I will not have you in this office, tempting me anymore. If my wife finds out about this, I'll beat the living daylights out of you. See how easy it is to find work then. Just get out of my sight. Pack up your things and get out. And don't come running back, trying to get money at any time."

Adele, holding on to her stomach and crying, ran over to her desk and looked through the drawers, taking all her personal belongings and putting them in her handbag. She looked back through the open door at Henry, but he had his back turned to her and was standing looking out the window.

She sobbed as she took one last look around the room. She struggled into her coat, tearing off one of the buttons, and took up her handbag and walked out into the night.

Lizzie didn't look up until she'd reached the end of chapter twelve. She was startled to see it was only three o'clock. She felt as if she'd been visiting in the story a longer time. As she moved to stretch, the cats leapt off and, giving her a look of disdain, sauntered into the kitchen, where she heard their chomping on dried food a few seconds later.

She wished she had left the reading until the afternoon. She knew she'd have a hard time sleeping after being in the Fowkses' world, where the mother, desperate after being fired when she told her boss about carrying his child, swallows an entire bottle of sleeping pills and dies. The child,

Carla, finds her mother and runs next door for help. With
no family around to take her in, Carla is put into foster care
and begins a journey filled with rejection and sadness.

Lizzie was glad there were only three chapters tonight.
She didn't like where the story was headed, especially since
she was pretty certain it was all true. *Why do I think that?*
A gut reaction, she realized. She also realized she hadn't
yet spoken to Sally-Jo to see if she felt the same way. She'd
ask her friend her opinion tomorrow . . . no, today, for sure.

It wasn't until the lunch break that Lizzie was able to track
down Sally-Jo. She waited, a tad impatiently, until Sally-Jo
had finished talking to one of the male teachers, somebody
new whom Lizzie didn't know. "So, tell me what you thought
about the story?"

Sally-Jo sat down and poked about in her brown bag
lunch. She pulled out a sandwich in a plastic bag, along with
a paper napkin. She pushed her glasses up over her forehead
to sit atop her head. "Story? Oh, you mean the manuscript.
So, why do you think it's a true story?"

"I'm trying to keep an open mind."

"No you're not. I think part of you has decided it's true.
I'm not so certain, but it does read like a journal with an
attempt to fictionalize it. Sort of Truman Capote-ish.
Although nowhere near as well written. That makes it even
creepier, doesn't it? Having it anonymously left in your mailbox and all. I wonder if you'll ever learn who's leaving it."

"Well, I got another three chapters overnight. I've no idea
how this ends, but I suspect it's moving toward a denoue-
ment pretty soon. Unless it turns out to be a saga of redress
and redemption."

"It's bugging you, isn't it?"

"Absolutely. I'm curious, and it's an upsetting story."
Lizzie took a bite of her tuna salad wrap. "It's just that so
many odd things have happened recently. First the murder

in front of Molly's. Then the manuscript starts arriving. And then the phone call I got the other night."

"What phone call? You haven't mentioned it before. Who called and what did he or she say?" Sally-Jo dropped her sandwich and leaned forward.

"Well . . . ," Lizzie hedged. Maybe she shouldn't have mentioned the phone call. It was probably just a coincidence. But what if all these events were connected—the murder, the manuscript and the phone call? She wanted Sally-Jo's take on it, so she told her.

"Man, that's creepy," Sally-Jo said when Lizzie had finished. "He—or she—is not threatening you, but obviously this person wants you to look into that story your daddy was working on. And you have no idea what the story was about?"

"No. I think I'll ask George Havers at the *Colonist* if he knows, though, or if he can check it out for me. He worked with Daddy at one time, so he may know where to look. I'm hoping. Anyway, you do agree it's strange all this is happening at the same time?" Lizzie looked at Sally-Jo hopefully. Part of her wanted Sally-Jo to agree while another part wanted to hear that, no, it was nothing odd, that sometimes odd things happened in threes.

Sally-Jo took a couple of minutes in answering. "I'm not sure what to think or say, Lizzie. I do believe in coincidences, but on the other hand, there's someone who's behind each of these events. Whether or not they're tied in, is another matter.

"Maybe it's time to tell Chief Dreyfus about the manuscript," Sally-Jo went on. "I'm assuming you haven't told him because you haven't mentioned it."

Lizzie nodded. "You're right, I haven't. I'll tell him next time I see him."

"And, Lizzie, if you're feeling at all nervous about being alone, you're welcome to move into my house for a while. I've got plenty of spare rooms."

"Thanks. I'm okay. I've got Edam and Brie, with Nathaniel Creely next door keeping an eye on things." Although he hadn't seen the delivery last night.

Lizzie hurried over to Molly's after school for her tutoring session with Andie. After about twenty minutes with nothing more than monosyllabic answers, Lizzie's concern about Andie's mental state increased to the point where she finally asked what was wrong.

"Nada."

"Sure. That's the impression I'm getting." Lizzie watched a few moments longer as Andie slouched in the chair, head down, book open, looking studious except for the fact the pages hadn't turned since she'd arrived. She certainly looked the same as normal, or what was normal for Andie. Her black hair sported yellow streaks today, her black T-shirt was covered with yellow and red eyeballs, her jeans looked as if one more laundering would do them in, and she wore a fingerless lace glove on her left hand. Her black Puma sneakers looked to be brand-new, though. Not a speck of mud or grass stain on them. Teens did have their priorities, after all.

Andie lacked spark. There was none of that assertive-bordering-on-aggressive energy that often had Lizzie wondering if she'd last the session or just suddenly leap out of her chair and burst out the door.

After a few more minutes of watching, Lizzie said, "I don't want to pry, Andie, but I can tell something's bothering you. I just want you to know that if you'd like to talk about it, now or some other time, I'm happy to listen."

Andie looked up at her, opened her mouth but then shut it again. She tapped her right foot a couple of times, then shut her book and stuffed it back in her backpack. "It's not working for me today, Lizzie. Can we just skip this session? I'll come in another time if you want."

Lizzie nodded. "Sure. We'll figure that out later. And remember what I said. Bye for now."

She watched as Andie trudged out of the room. Something pretty serious was getting her down. She wondered if it had anything to do with Stephanie, or maybe it was rooted at home. She was tempted to pay Mrs. Mason a visit and see how things were going. However, she also realized that if Andie found out, she'd probably never open up to her about any problems. She'd just wait it out and hope for the best.

Chapter Twenty-five

◇◇◇

And after that, all the plans go right out the nearest window.

WORMWOOD—SUSAN WITTIG ALBERT

Lizzie groaned and reached out for the ringing telephone beside her bed. She managed to get one eye open and groaned again when she realized the clock showed three A.M. *Mama*. She jolted totally awake. She snatched the receiver, croaking out, "Hello?"

"Did you figure out what story your pa was covering when he died?" The same voice. She was sure. Then the dial tone.

She switched on the lamp and wrote it down. Then tried to get back to sleep, but the question played on a loop in her brain. No, she hadn't, was the answer, but it looked like she'd better talk to George Havers again.

What was the story and who was the caller and why was it so important to him? Or her? What had her daddy been up to? She glanced at the clock and groaned again. She had to get up in less than three hours.

She tried all the tricks she knew. Thinking of the fifty things to buy if she won the lottery. The fifty places she wanted to visit. The fifty activities she had to try before she died. She even counted sheep. The next thing she knew, the alarm woke her.

A run, a shower, and a protein drink for breakfast, followed by two cups of coffee had her feeling almost ready to take on the day. She fed the cats and gave them each a quick brushing. Edam wound his way around her legs as she removed a handful of fur from the brush and deposited it in the garbage. He followed her upstairs and stretched out on the black skirt she'd laid out on the bed. She mentally slapped her forehead for leaving it there. She knew that black clothing was a cat magnet in this house. After relocating Edam to the afghan on the chair, she brushed the skirt with a damp sponge and then dressed quickly. She grabbed her school gear and opened the front door—and found Andie sitting on the top step.

"Andie, what are you doing here?"

"I thought you could drop me off at school and we could talk on the way."

"Sure. I'm on my way now." Lizzie locked the door and walked over to the Mazda, Andie following her.

They got in and Lizzie waited until they'd both belted up, then asked, "Is there a problem?"

Andie shook her head. "Not with me. It's Stephanie."

Lizzie backed out of the driveway cautiously, then said, "I'm listening."

Andie stared straight ahead and sat hugging her black skull-and-crossbones backpack. She was dressed in her usual black jeans with the torn knees, but her top was a pale blue T-shirt, with a skull on the back for good measure. "You know we've been hanging out a lot lately?"

Lizzie nodded although she hadn't been entirely sure.

"Well, she doesn't really talk a lot about herself, ya know? She tells me about working at the diner, and, you'll be happy to hear this, she says the job stinks so I should stay in school and get a good job after."

Lizzie glanced over. Had Andie been seriously thinking of dropping out? Her parents would be none too pleased. Neither would she. She said a silent thank-you to Stephanie.

"She's a smart girl."

Andie shrugged. "Maybe so, but she's also a scared one."

"What do you mean?"

"I guess I should have told you all about this yesterday, but I was still puzzling it out, ya know?" She glanced at Lizzie, who nodded even though she didn't really know. "Well, every now and then she gets a call on her cell, she looks at the number and then ignores it. But she sure gets upset when she reads the number. I asked her about it, and at first she said it was just a wrong number, but after the next few times, she said it was someone she didn't want to talk to. And she pulled out her knitting—ya know how she goes at it when she's all tense?"

Lizzie had noticed but not thought about it. She admired Andie for being so observant and sensitive to her actions. "Yes," she answered anyway.

"And then she usually has to rip it all up because it's way too tight or just plain wrong. Anyway, that's been happening a lot lately."

"Why did you say she's scared? There's a difference between upset and scared."

Andie drew in a deep breath. "Because she'd been lying down for a short nap when I was over there yesterday, and I woke her up at the time she asked for. I had been sitting around reading while waiting." Lizzie perked up at the mention of reading but didn't want to ask what.

"She went to the can, and I saw her pillow had slipped off to the floor, so I picked it up and fluffed the other one, too, and . . . there was a knife under it."

"A knife."

"Holy sharks, yes, a big honking knife like the butchering kind. Don't you get it? I think she sleeps with a knife under her pillow because she's scared."

Lizzie stepped on the brake and glanced belatedly into the rearview mirror to make sure no one was looming behind her. "A knife?" she repeated.

"Yeah. So what do you think I oughta do?" Andie whispered.

"You didn't ask her about it, I gather?"

"Well, duh . . . yeah, I asked. And she got all mad at me and said it was none of my business and to stop bugging her. I wasn't bugging her at all. I hadn't been on her case or anything. She just blew up and hit the bathroom and slammed the door behind her."

"Then what did you do?"

"I left. I mean, I thought about sticking around and seeing if she would talk to me, but, like, she'd told me to leave her alone. And I thought, ok, I'll give her time to cool off and then talk to her later. But when I phoned her place last night, she didn't answer. I think she's still pissed off with me. So, if she is, she might as well get really pissed off when she finds out I told you about it and asked you to go see her. Which is what I'm doing." Andie stopped and took a deep breath. "Will you go talk to her?"

"Of course I will. And I'm glad you told me, Andie. It sounds like she needs her friends, and if she's in trouble, maybe we can help." She pulled up in front of the high school on Magnolia Street.

"And you'll let me know?" Andie asked as she got out of the car.

"I'll try seeing her after school today, and I'll give you a call when I have news. Don't you worry about it, Andie. You did the right thing, and we'll try and sort it out."

Andie made a peace sign with her left hand before shutting the door.

Lizzie drove over to the parking lot at Ashton Corners Elementary School and sat in the car for a few moments going over her conversation with Andie. She knew how disturbing it must be for her. The fact that Stephanie had a knife handy must mean she was terrified of someone. But who? Probably someone from her hometown. Lizzie didn't think she'd made that kind of enemy in the short while she'd been in Ashton Corners. Who then? The father of her child? A relative? Or did she have an unknown stalker? That could and did happen, even in moderately quiet Ashton Corners.

She had to admit, she wasn't quite sure how to handle this. If Stephanie wouldn't confide in Andie, and they seemed to be on close terms, then it was doubtful she'd just up and tell Lizzie. One thing was certain: Stephanie had to tell them what was going on in her life before they could be of any help to her.

Maybe Molly could talk to her again. Molly had a calming effect on those around her and just seemed to know what to say. Yes, Molly was the best bet.

Meanwhile, she had progress reports to work up on some sixth-graders she'd been following for the past two years. They were all nice kids, eager to learn but lacking the right tools to do so. She'd taught them some study skills that hopefully had made learning a little less of a challenge. It seemed to be working so far. She was really looking forward to the interviews this morning. She knew the other two students she had scheduled for the afternoon would probably leave her with a major headache.

After school Lizzie drove over to Molly's, hoping to catch her in. She hadn't had a chance to call ahead as a series of minor crises had robbed her of her lunch hour. She parked next to the garage and luckily found Molly out in back, gardening.

"Hi, honey," Molly called out as Lizzie approached her. "I just have to get these daylilies split. They're all taking over this here corner and though they're real colorful, I don't want them crowding out my shasta daisies next year." She'd been kneeling on a padded cushion and put out a hand to Lizzie to help her stand.

"They're gorgeous, Molly. I just love that shade of yellow. Your green thumb really shows."

Molly chuckled. "Well, it's Marv's green thumb, really. And for a gardener, he's mighty kind to allow me to putter around, even though it is my garden. You know, they can be quite obsessive about their babies. Now, let's take a tea break and you tell me what's on your mind. You don't look too sparkly right now."

She led the way into the kitchen, stepping out of her soiled red Crocs and into some red Birkenstocks at the door.

Lizzie sat at the kitchen table and told her about Stephanie. Molly stopped pouring the iced tea into the glasses and looked at Lizzie a full minute before continuing. She said nothing until she placed the tea and a plate of butter pecan cookies on the table.

"My goodness. What's that girl going through, anyway? And if she's that upset, it can't be any good for the baby."

"I agree. I thought maybe you could talk to her, Molly. I doubt she'd tell me anything, but I'm sure you can coax her." Lizzie stared at the plate of cookies but resisted taking one.

"I'll be happy to do what I can, but she may not feel ready to confide in any of us just yet. She didn't want to talk about her hometown last time I asked. We haven't known her very long, after all. But this is much more serious and it can't go on. I'll phone the diner to see if she's working and if not, I'll go right over to her house. If she's not answering the phone these days, I'll just take her by surprise."

"Thanks, Molly. I knew you'd do it, and I'm sure she'll be relieved to open up to someone." Lizzie continued staring at the cookies until Molly pushed the plate a little closer to her. Lizzie sighed and grabbed one, breaking it in half and popping one of the two pieces into her mouth. She sighed again as the rich pecan flavor invaded her taste buds.

"Will you give me a call, before I go to choir, if that's possible?" Lizzie asked.

"Surely." Molly got up and brought a plastic ziplock bag back to the table, slid the remaining cookies into it and handed it to Lizzie. "These will give you energy for singing."

Lizzie thanked her, gave her a kiss on the cheek and left so that Molly could get ready to visit Stephanie.

At the corner of Yancy and Pike, Lizzie made a quick decision and turned left, then right again, taking Main into town. She'd bet George Havers was one of those editors who stayed way later than his paycheck covered. She parked in front of the newspaper office and went in, suspecting George hadn't left for the day. The front desk sat empty, but when she hit the small bell sitting on the counter, George poked his head around his office door.

"Lizzie, back again so soon? I'm pleased. Come on back here, and we can talk while I tidy some things up."

"Thanks, George." Lizzie walked to the office, where she sat on a stool and watched while George closed some file folders and stuck them in a filing cabinet in the corner. Then he moved some storyboards featuring different sections of the newspaper, most likely used for displays out in the community, over to the same corner.

"Watching you do that," she said after a few minutes, "just gave me an idea about maybe a partnership we could form—the paper and the literacy program. Maybe we can work out some way to get subscriptions or at least copies for our students. They should be reading the paper, maybe most already do. I guess I should check that first. Anyway, it's just an idea."

"I like it, Lizzie. I'm happy to get involved with literacy any way I can. You set up a plan with what you want, and I'll see how I can make it happen."

Lizzie smiled. "Great. I don't know why I didn't think of it before. I'm actually not reinventing the wheel here. It's been done in many places. I just haven't thought to own it before. But that's not why I stopped by."

Now that she was here, she wasn't quite sure what to ask. Except the obvious question. But what if it opened a can of worms she wasn't prepared to deal with? Just because an unknown voice set her to this, didn't mean she had to follow through. But, she admitted to herself, she was curious not only about why she'd gotten the calls but also about the story the caller had referred to. She took a deep breath.

"I'm trying to find out what story my daddy was working on when he died. Do you know what it was, by any chance?"

George leaned back in his chair, frowning. He clasped his hands behind his head and thought. "Not offhand. I don't even remember if I even knew at the time. He'd sometimes ask me to do research for him, but I wasn't working on anything with him then. Maybe your mama would know." He sat up abruptly. "I'm sorry, Lizzie. I wasn't thinking when I said that. Why don't you leave it with me and I'll see what I can come up with."

"Thanks, George. I'd appreciate it. I was also wondering about his car accident."

George sat up even straighter but looked uncomfortable. "That's a long time ago, Lizzie. Why is it important now?" He paused. "Is there a connection?"

"I got a phone call in the middle of the night. This is the second time the caller has done that. The first time he—I'm actually not sure if it's a male or female because the voice was muffled each time, but I'll say he—the first time he called he asked if I knew what story my daddy was working on when he died. Last night he asked if I'd found out yet. Of course, I haven't."

"Have you told Chief Dreyfus about the calls?"

"Not about the second call. He's aware of the first one, though."

George nodded. "I'll see what I can find out and give you a call if anything turns up."

"Thanks." Lizzie waited a moment before asking her next question. She took a deep breath. "Was there anything odd about the car accident? Any chance it wasn't an accident?"

"As I recall, it was a pretty straightforward investigation."

"Would you happen to have a copy of the newspaper story on file still?"

George folded his hands on his desk and looked at her without speaking. Finally, he said, "I know just where to find it. I kept a copy. I really admired your daddy, you know. He inspired me to become a reporter. I couldn't believe it when he died so young and at the peak of his career. And, of course, with such a young family."

He turned around and clicked the mouse for his computer, which sat on a desk behind him. He clicked a few more times, and a newspaper story appeared on the screen. He stood up and motioned her to the chair.

She sat down, not really sure if she wanted to read it after all. The newspaper page had been scanned. There were two stories, the initial news story of six paragraphs and an obituary that ran half the newspaper page.

"Why, it's your byline, George. You wrote the stories."

"Yes."

Lizzie read through them slowly, trying not to feel any emotion, reading strictly for the facts. She felt tears in her eyes as she turned back to him. "What a wonderful tribute, George. Thank you."

George smiled sadly. "I wanted to be the one to remember him and his career. Now, did you find what you were looking for?"

"I remember being told it was a head-on crash. But not a whole lot else. I guess there was no doubt it was an accident?"

George shook his head. "Look, I'll print you out a copy if you like."

She nodded, and he produced it for her in short order. "Thanks, George. I appreciate . . . everything. I'd better let you get on with things so you can get home for supper." She wondered what his wife and three kids thought about his long hours. They must be used to it by now. She didn't know Sandra Havers well, had only met her briefly at their wedding fifteen years ago, but had liked her immediately. She pictured them as having a very happy, loving family life. Of course, Lizzie pictured everyone as having that.

George walked her to the front door. "It must be worrying for you, but try not to let it bother you, Lizzie. I'll be in touch as soon as I have something to tell you. And if you get another call, please let me know. And the chief."

He gave her shoulder a friendly pat and she left.

She glanced at the police station as she walked to her car. Should she go in and talk to Mark? He might not be there. Or . . . he might. She decided against it as Officer Craig pulled into the lot beside the station. That was one conversation she could do without.

Chapter Twenty-six

✧✧✧

The message light was blinking when I opened the door, carrying a few groceries and the results of several errands.

DEATH LOVES A MESSY DESK—MARY JANE MAFFINI

Lizzie found it surprisingly hard to concentrate at choir practice. That added to her already melancholic mood. Choir had always had a redemptive power for her, able to set things right in her mind, if not in her world. But tonight she'd slid too far off the grid. She couldn't reel in her thoughts, all about her daddy, trying to bring him to life in her memory, and to make sense of his death. Before the mysterious phone calls had started, she would think about him only every now and then, particularly on the anniversaries of his birth and death. She'd long ago come to terms with it all. Or so she'd thought until the late-night caller had rattled her peace of mind.

Why was all this happening? First, Telford's death, now the reference to her daddy's death. And, oh yes, the manuscript. She shook her head, surprising Krista Barlow, standing beside her. Lizzie kept her eyes focused on the music and willed her mind to follow the notes. Or, at the very least, to get her through the two hours without appearing the fool.

* * *

Lizzie's Saturday morning "To Do" list seemed to be morphing into twice its usual length, the more items she ticked off. Shopping for groceries at the nearby Winn-Dixie ended in a trip to the Natural Lifestyle Shop around the corner, for some of the health food items she'd not already found. Stopping in at the Ashton Corners Public Library to pick up a book she'd reserved led to a visit to the Friends of the Library book sale in the activities room, which wasn't a bad thing in itself, except that she left with a "Fill-a-bag-for-five-dollars" bargain. Her next stop, a task she'd taken on at choir last night, meant a drive to the west end of town to pick up the program flyers they'd need for the benefit concert.

By the time she headed home again, she was tired, hungry and trying to keep her mind from sliding into that rut of worrying about the calls, the manuscript and the murder.

The phone was ringing insistently as Lizzie opened her front door. She grabbed the receiver, not bothering to check call display. Hopefully, it would be Molly with news about Stephanie.

"Hello?"

"You're a hard one to get hold of, Lizzie." Paige sounded a tad annoyed.

"Paige, I'm sorry. I've just had so much on my plate lately. I meant to call you last night, but I was wiped by the time I got home. And I've been out, driving all over town, trying to combine all my errands into one trip. How are you?" So, not Molly. Maybe she hadn't had a chance to visit Stephanie as yet.

"I'm miffed, but I'll admit it's more to do with a husband who's gone fishing with the guys for the weekend and a plumber who didn't show up when he said he would this morning."

"Yikes. What's your plumbing problem?"

"I'm getting only a trickle of water in the bathtub. Last

night we hauled buckets of water up for the kids' bath and arranged for the plumber. But I'll be damned if I'm going to do the same tonight."

Lizzie couldn't picture her petite friend carrying even one bucket of water. Anywhere. "Did you try calling him again?"

"Of course. It went to voice mail, so he has three messages from me waiting for him when he finally gets around to checking them." She sighed loudly, then took a moment to ask the kids to take their Popsicles outside. "I'm sorry . . . I just needed someone to rant to."

"And a good one it was. I have an idea. If he doesn't appear by dinner, why not come over here? We'll have something light and easy and you can bathe the kids here."

"Oh, sweetie, you're a lifesaver. I'll call you to confirm. See you later."

Lizzie smiled as she hung up. That would brighten up the end of the day. Meanwhile, she had a two-week buildup of cat fur and dust balls to deal with. She pulled her old Electrolux vacuum out of the small hall closet under the stairs, fit the attachments together and attacked the main floor. By the time she'd finished the top floor and also scrubbed the main bathroom, she needed a break. Fortunately, the back patio beckoned, and she grabbed some crackers and cheese, along with a cup of green tea, and pulled a chair into the sunshine to soak up some Vitamin D along with her lunch.

By the time Paige rang the front doorbell, the house stood spotless and welcoming and Lizzie had changed into clean jeans with a lime green dolman-sleeved cardigan and black T-shirt. She poured them each a glass of wine, along with some apple juice for the girls, and they all sat outdoors while the sun still reached the patio.

Over dinner, Lizzie told Paige all about the phone calls and her visit to the newspaper office, while Jenna and

Cate—and their two dolls—carried on their own conversation at their smaller, kid-sized table, placed beside the adults' table. Paige had stuffed the table and two tiny chairs in the back of her SUV, knowing it was the only way the two adults could enjoy any amount of conversation at their meal.

"Oh, Lizzie, sweetie," Paige said, reaching for a second piece of cornbread, "isn't that opening old wounds? What did you expect to find? That your daddy had been killed while investigating a story? Don't you think the police would have found some indication of that at the time?"

"Well, you never know. They might not have had a reason to suspect anything other than an accident. But I guess the fact that it was a head-on crash confirms it. I just want to double-check on everything these days. There are a lot of odd things happening—first the murder, then the manuscript, then the phone calls."

"Hmm. It could all be coincidence. I'm a great believer in that. For instance, what are the chances you'd run into Mark Dreyfus again and that you two would be all involved in a murder case?"

Lizzie was happy to change tracks, get her mind on more pleasant things. She paused, to add some drama, before answering. "And what are the chances we'd finally be going out on a date?"

"You're kidding. No, you're not. Tell all, girl."

"Next Saturday night. And that's all there is to tell at the moment."

"That is so exciting. And only ten or so years later." She switched her attention to the smaller table. "Cate, I know you're tired, chickpea, but I'd sure be pleased if you'd finish all your salad. You, too, Lizzie."

"Yes, Mama," Lizzie answered in a perky voice. "I know, it does seem strange. But you know, this Mark is not the same guy I had a crush on in high school."

"Of course not. You didn't even know him. Aside from this hunky body in a football uniform."

"And a great smile."

"Hey. And all that padding. Especially around the butt."

"And curly black hair. But that's all gone now. You know, he's shaved his head?"

"No, I didn't, but I'll bet that makes him even sexier. Oh, that boy just oozed sexual tension. He had you panting, and I have all the notes to prove it."

"Oh, no, not those notes again. I want you to go right home and destroy them. Or better yet, give them back to me." Lizzie tried to look stern.

"Hah. Not going to happen, sweetie. Just suck it up." Paige jumped up. "Jenna, that's quite a mess you've made, child. Let Mama get a dishcloth and wipe it up, then we'll tackle your T-shirt."

Lizzie watched her friend go about the cleanup, talking to her kids the entire time. She'd always felt Paige was great mama material. She'd had a good example to follow. Lizzie, on the other hand, used to feel she herself would probably be totally inept in that role. She felt she made a better teacher than she would a mother. Paige looked over at her and smiled.

"A penny," she said.

"I think it's i-c-e c-r-e-a-m time, don't you?"

"Ice cream! Yes!" yelled Cate.

Paige said, "We gave up spelling her favorites a long time ago."

After Paige bathed the girls and they'd left, Lizzie pulled out the manuscript once again. She read it through, then went upstairs and turned on her computer. No listings for Harlan Fowks, Adele Fowks or Carla. She searched on "Telford Construction" yet again. Nada. She read through every hit for a Telford of any gender, hoping to come up with a relative. Nothing seemed to fit. How could someone be so isolated and alone in this modern world? And why did he want to be?

Her growing frustration reached the point where it was either throw the monitor out the window or call it a night. She chose the latter.

Chapter Twenty-seven

◇◇◇

Having spent a restless night . . . I got up early and crept downstairs.

EXPOSÉ!—HANNAH DENNISON

Lizzie's usual Sunday visit with her mama left her feeling even more down. She'd found Evelyn Turner messing through the drawers of her bureau, fretful and searching for something. When Lizzie asked what she was looking for, Evelyn looked blankly at her, then resumed emptying one drawer at a time, then putting things back but in a jumbled manner.

Lizzie waited her out and eventually Evelyn sat down in her favorite chair and stared out the window. Lizzie got up and re-ordered all the drawers, knowing how important it was that everything be in its expected place.

When she'd finished, she sat across from her mama and read another couple of chapters in *Mansfield Park*, until the afternoon tea bell sounded. Maybe Mama needed to take part in the tea ritual with the others, without having to try to figure out who this visitor was. Lizzie knew the importance of routines in her daily schedule.

She left feeling as fidgety as her mama had been. She needed a distraction, something to take her mind off Mama, off the murder, off school.

She walked out to her Mazda parked in the side lot and sat behind the steering wheel for several minutes before finally inserting the key and starting it up. She eased out onto the street and found herself taking the old Slocam Road route that ran beside the Tallapoosa River, away from town. She drove for about an hour, passing through small lazy areas with only a general store and a gas station to mark the spot, through forested areas that gave way to pasturelands where the road branched inland from the river, then back along the quiet grassy banks as the road found its way to the water.

She stopped and got out of the car to stretch, realizing that her mind had been as free-flowing as the surroundings. She took a deep breath and a final look around her, then drove home, suddenly hungry and wanting nothing more than a quiet evening on her own.

After supper, Lizzie quickly washed up her dishes, leaving them in the dish rack to air-dry. The leftover spaghetti with pesto sauce went in the fridge. She wondered briefly what Evelyn had for supper and pictured her back in her room, staring out the window at the rapidly approaching evening.

That thought put her back on track. She ran upstairs and rummaged through the hall closet until she found the box where she'd stored her childhood. Not much had been kept. But in it she found the scrapbook Mama had kept highlighting her daddy's career. Every article he'd written or that was written about him had been lovingly added over the years.

She hadn't looked at it in ages, she realized. Just touching it brought tears to her eyes. *Buck up, Lizzie.* She ate a couple of teaspoons of almond butter while waiting for the water to boil for a cup of hot ginger tea, then sat down to read from the beginning. He'd started out writing for the *Ashton Corners Colonist*, part-time while still in high school, then went away to college in Birmingham where he wrote for their newspaper, and then got his first break with a short op-ed piece in the *New Yorker* magazine. His first job as a reporter was with the *Birmingham Herald*, but he switched to magazine writing when he'd married Evelyn Ross and settled down back in Ashton Corners.

He'd covered Elvis Presley's funeral and the murder of John Lennon and interviewed Sally Ride, the first American woman in space, as well as several visiting dignitaries. His final published story had been a tourist guide to the Old South. Of course, there was no hint anywhere in the box as to what he'd been researching at the time of his death.

Lizzie lingered over the photographs of the young Monroe Turner and wondered what he would have looked like in middle age. She tried to recall his voice or any mannerisms but came up blank. Frustrating. But it had been a long time ago.

The doorbell rang and jolted her back to the present. She glanced at the clock—eight thirty P.M.—and wondered who'd drop by at this hour. She pulled back the sheers covering the window and peeked out, spotting an Ashton Corners Police cruiser in her driveway. Annoyed, she prepared to stonewall Officer Craig and opened the door.

"Sorry to just stop by without calling first, Lizzie," Mark said, hat in hand.

It took her a few seconds to refocus. "I'm surprised, but come on in, Mark. Is this official?" She looked at the uniform.

He gave a small laugh. "No, I've just finished for the day and was heading home and saw your light on."

"I thought you lived in the other direction."

"I like to take a small drive around to unwind before going home. And I was hoping you'd be in."

"Have a seat." She indicated the living room. "I was just

having some hot tea. Would you like some? Or can I get you a beer? I have some Coors and Olde Towne Pilsner on hand."

"A Coors would go down real great right about now."

She was back in a flash with the beer and a glass in case he wasn't one to drink out of the bottle. "And what are you doing, working on a Sunday? No, you don't have to answer. I think you already told me—family time for the others, right?"

He nodded and gave her a small smile. She noticed how fatigued he looked after at least seven straight days of work. His shoulders had a slight hunch to them, rather than his usual ramrod straight stature. His eyelids drooped, just a tad. And his uniform looked like it had gone through a lot of movement during the day.

Mark glanced at the open scrapbook as he sat down. "Your daddy's stuff?"

Lizzie nodded. "I was just looking to see if there were any notes or anything tucked in the scrapbook that might give a clue as to what story he was working on when he died. I've had another phone call."

Mark sat up straighter. "What did the person say this time?"

"It was a shorter call but basically, he just said the same thing."

"And did you recognize the voice? You think it was a male?" He sounded all official again.

"No, it was sort of muffled, but it sounded like the same caller as before. I'm just calling the person a male. Makes it easier. I was sort of rattled, so I asked George Havers to see if he can find anything out about the story my daddy was working on."

Mark stood up, walked to the window and looked out. "You should have called me right away, Lizzie."

"Probably. But it wasn't really menacing or anything."

"Just scary?"

"Right." She shifted on the couch. "Now, you may think

I'm way off base here, but it just seems sort of strange to me that Frank Telford is murdered, a rare occurrence in town, and I start getting these phone calls."

Mark sat back down, next to Lizzie this time. "There's nothing to tie them together, is there?"

"No. But then there's also the manuscript."

Mark raised his eyebrows in question. Lizzie shrugged and got up to get the latest chapters from the end table where she'd left them after rereading them early that morning. "I didn't think these were tied in either, but it's part of a story about something that happened quite a long time ago. I'm guessing in the 1960s or so. Three chapters are delivered to my mailbox in the middle of the night each time. I've had twelve chapters in total now. It's a chilling story about a guy who was duped out of his life savings, couldn't face it and committed suicide, leaving a wife and small daughter. The wife gets a job, has an affair with her boss and is fired when she reveals she's pregnant. She commits suicide, and the daughter is put in foster care. That's as far as it goes . . . so far."

Mark sat in silence for a few moments. "That is a sad story, but why do you think it's connected to the other things you mentioned?"

"Well, it reads more like a journal that's been fictionalized—mainly because of the grammar, things like that."

Mark interrupted. "I leave all that to you. Never my forte in school."

Lizzie smiled. "Well, I could be right off base, but it got me to wondering."

Mark drank some of his beer and sat thinking, then had another drink. "It sounds a little far-fetched to me, but I'll look into it. I'm happy to get any leads I can at this point. Nothing else seems to be panning out. I'll talk to Havers in the morning. Maybe I can help by putting in some official requests for information somewhere along the line."

He finished his beer just as Brie jumped into his lap. He absently stroked the cat as he sat thinking. Lizzie liked that.

"You'll be walking away with a furry uniform, Chief," Lizzie warned him.

Mark looked down at the cat. "That's what clothes brushes are for." He smiled at her. "Are you nervous about being here on your own?"

She laughed. "You're the second person to ask me that. Sally-Jo Baker invited me to stay at her place. But I'm sure I'm okay here. What do you suggest?" She bit her tongue. How could she have been so bold as to ask that? If only she could hit rewind. It sounded as if she were flirting. Maybe she had been, subconsciously.

Mark chuckled. "I can sleep anywhere. A couch does the trick for me." He stared into her eyes.

She had the distinct feeling he was about to kiss her. And what surprised her even more was the realization that that was exactly what she wanted him to do. She leaned toward him at the same time as he moved, only to have the telephone shatter the moment.

She smiled awkwardly, swallowed hard and went to the phone.

"Oh, hi, Molly." She'd been hoping to hear back from Molly. Too bad the timing was so lousy. Also, she was reluctant to have this conversation with Mark in the same room. "How is everything?" She'd try and keep her questions as neutral as possible.

She realized Molly hesitated a moment before answering. *She must be wondering what's up.* "Well, it took a lot of doorbell ringing and coaxing, but Stephanie finally opened the door and let me in. Then it took some more time before she'd admit to me that she's been getting those calls, just like Andie said, but she wouldn't tell me who they were from. I can't help but thinking it's to do with the baby, maybe the baby's daddy and the poor child doesn't want anything to do with him."

"That sounds a likely scenario."

"And, furthermore, I'd say she won't be telling us anytime soon where she hails from because she's worried one of us might give her whereabouts away." Molly snorted. "As if I'd let some overbearing lout know where she's living."

"I'm sure you're right, Molly. I just wish there were something we could do about it."

"Well, I'm not about to give up on her. But it sounds to me like this is a bad time for you to talk?"

"You've got that right."

"A certain young police chief is there maybe?"

Lizzie smiled. "You are one smart woman."

"All right then. Enough talk for now. You go get back to your young man. G'night, honey."

"G'night." Lizzie didn't even bother trying to correct her. Not her "young man" at all.

Mark had finished his drink. "Is everything all right with Ms. Mathews?" He sounded genuinely concerned.

She shrugged. "Oh, yes. It's just that she's a mama hen to many of us and takes her role seriously." She eyed his empty glass. "Can I get you another Coors?"

"No, thanks. I'd better pass. Wouldn't look too good if the chief, in uniform, got pulled over or worse yet, had to go directly to a call. I'd better get going, but I'll take a rain check if you don't mind?"

She walked him to the front door. "Just so you know, I keep tabs on them once they're given out."

He smiled at her. "Oh, I do plan to make use of it." He pulled open the door, then paused. "Are you sure you're feeling okay about being here alone?"

She nodded. "I'm perfectly fine. I don't feel at all threatened, just curious."

"Well, give me a call tomorrow first thing if you get a call or if another of those manuscripts appears. You hear?"

"I'm all ears."

"Oh, there's more to you than ears, lady." He gave her a quick kiss on the lips and left.

Chapter Twenty-eight

◇◇◇

"That's the thing," he said after a moment. "It could have been anybody."

NIGHT OF THE LIVING DEED—E. J. COPPERMAN

Lizzie slept fitfully, half listening for either the phone to ring or the mailbox to shut. At dawn, she realized since neither had happened, she felt a bit disappointed. *How dumb is that?*

The drive to school took longer than usual as Bryer Street had been blocked off by the police for a huge flatbed truck and trailer easing a modular ranch house along the road. The rooftop slowly wove its way under the huge branches of the Spanish oak overhanging the street. Folks had come out of their houses and stood on verandahs to watch, and a smattering of children, who would be late for school, were rooted to their spots along the sidewalks.

She knew the prefab house was destined for the empty lot about halfway along. That had been the address of the Kliborn House for many years, possibly a century, but it had finally given way to neglect and disrepair after the last family member died. The new owners had decided the cheaper route was to raze the place and then, to be the owners of the first modular house in this area.

As interesting as the entire process was, Lizzie needed to get to her first appointment, so she made a U-turn, along with several other cars, and took the longer, unblocked route through the center of town to school.

Her morning consisted of sitting in on classes, and her afternoon was another long, drawn-out yawn of a school administration meeting. Her three-minute report was accepted without comment, another reason to wish she had skipped the whole process. She couldn't make the quick escape she'd planned on, though, and ended up sharing coffee and listening to a litany of complaints from some of the other consultants.

By the time she made it home, there was no time to change or eat dinner. She found the manuscript on the end table where she'd last left it, and stuffed it into her tote, filled the cat dishes with dry food and left, peeling a banana that she ate on the way to Molly's.

This evening's literacy session sported full attendance for a change, always gratifying to a teacher. Of the three women and three men enrolled, Lizzie felt half of them really wanted to be there while the others knew that regardless of their take on the class, they had to complete it if they wanted to pass their GED.

She was wondering if Troy would talk to her during break and tell her why he'd skipped class. She hoped he would but thought it unlikely. Part of her job was to be aware of their home situations, too, but officially, there was nothing she could do until he'd missed four classes. And since he wasn't one to chat with her on a regular basis, she knew she'd never know the reason for his absence.

Stephanie smiled shyly as she took her seat. Lizzie was

pleased to see her there. Obviously, Molly's talk did some good.

Last Wednesday's assignment had been aimed at building their reading comprehension strategies. She'd asked them to read their chosen Rapid Reads novels and then answer a series of questions about ideas and themes, distinguishing between facts and opinions, and identifying cause-and-effect relationships. Tonight, the students would "grade" each other's efforts, a task Lizzie hoped would draw them all into discussions as they challenged and defended answers.

Stephanie pulled Lizzie aside at the break. "I'm sorry, Lizzie, but I'm going to head on home right now. I'm right sorry for missing the rest of the class."

"Don't worry about it," Lizzie said, putting her hand on Stephanie's arm. "Are you feeling all right?"

Stephanie looked a bit uncomfortable. "Yes'm, it's just that I don't like walking home alone after dark. That's all. I'm sorry."

"I should have thought about that. Look, I can easily drive you home, if you'd like."

Stephanie shook her head. "No, not tonight, thanks. I've already gotten my mind on going home right now. Sorry.

"Maybe next time, okay?" Stephanie added softly.

"Sure," Lizzie answered. She had the feeling as welcoming as a ride would be to Stephanie, it would also mean close quarters, giving Lizzie another chance to question her.

On her way home, Lizzie thought again about the manuscript. Not knowing who had written it was driving her nuts. And what was she supposed to do with it, she wondered. Since she hadn't been asked to critique or edit it, she'd done only a little bit of both. She had tried to make sense of it, but with little success.

Sally-Jo, unfortunately, was of little help as she seemed to take it at face value, simply someone's attempt at writing a story. Maybe she was right, but Lizzie couldn't shake the feeling that the manuscript was a link to something more important.

Maybe she should ask the book club to read the manuscript, she thought yet again. Only this time she'd actually follow through with the idea. They would be totally unbiased. She would not include any of the mystery surrounding its appearance, just ask them for comments. Maybe throw in some leading questions but basically, just have them read it or listen to it, and see what they think.

Call an emergency meeting for tomorrow. She'd hold it at her house if Molly wasn't able to host them. She should have thought of this earlier and asked while she was at Molly's. Oh well . . . she'd call Molly first thing tomorrow.

The cats beat her down the stairs the next morning and waited impatiently beside their bowls. She fed them and changed the water dish before getting dressed for her run.

She couldn't believe how beautiful the morning was. Often, Indian summer stretched through the fall months, closing in on winter. If someone wanted four distinct seasons, Ashton Corners, Alabama, was not the spot to live. But for those who savored the warm days and crisp nights, as Lizzie did, it was the perfect place. She noticed how the bright green leaves of the elderberry had given way to a flurry of colorful earth tones and that the usual sweet peas and dahlias often found in many summer flower beds had been replaced by goldenrod and forsythia sage.

The smell in the air was entirely different also, drifting from sweet to tangy. More a promise of chestnuts roasting on an open pit. Her mind played with comparisons as she snaked through the sleepy side streets until she found herself in front of Stephanie's apartment. It had not been a conscious decision to run over here; in fact, the distance was likely longer by half than her usual route. She checked her watch. Even if she dared to knock on the door at this unseemly hour, she didn't have the time to follow through and try to get Stephanie to talk.

Chapter Twenty-nine

◇◇◇

Come along, madam. It's time to put our feminine wiles to the test.

A DEADLY DEALER—J. B. STANLEY

Everyone had sounded eager to get together again, when Lizzie finally reached them with the suggestion to reconvene the book club. Especially Molly.

"You know I so enjoy having people here," she said that evening, as they finished putting the glasses on trays and the sweets on plates. "It stops me from just sitting around and brooding about this whole business."

Sally-Jo gasped. "Molly, are you still worrying yourself? You know the police have other avenues of enquiry by now. You don't think you're still the primary suspect, do you?"

"Well, you never know how that Officer Craig's mind works. She's called me up a couple of times in the last few days with what she calls 'follow-up questions.' They're really just the same old thing but presented in a different way. Now, if she's not trying to trip me up, I'd say we're wasting a good salary just having her sit around and rethink things."

Lizzie chewed on her bottom lip. She hadn't realized

Officer Craig was still hounding Molly. They needed to find out the identity of the murderer, and the sooner the better. She absently grabbed a cheese straw from one of the plates and felt Molly's hands on her back.

"Now, you go in and visit with Bob and Jacob. Someone needs to keep those two in line. I'll just finish up here, and Sally-Jo can help me carry it all in."

Lizzie nodded and gave her hands a quick wash in the sink before joining the two men in the library. "Sorry to leave you on your own, but we were just getting the food ready," she said as she entered the room.

"That's the best excuse in town, Lizzie," Bob said with enthusiasm. "But I notice your hands are empty."

Lizzie laughed. "Molly thought I should play hostess while she finishes the last touches. I'm glad you were able to come tonight. Both of you." She looked at Jacob.

"I'm betting," Jacob said, "that rather than discuss fictional murder plots, we'll be focusing on one very real one." He quirked an eyebrow at her.

"Not hard to figure that out, I guess," she answered. "I'll just wait till everyone's arrived so I won't have to say it twice. In the meantime, read any good books lately?"

He laughed. "You mean, besides the assigned reading? Then, no . . . only law books and they haven't been overly interesting, I'm afraid. Just useful."

Lizzie looked at him a few moments before answering. She was picturing him standing across the street from the Book Bin, kissing the beautiful blonde stranger, a part of her wishing she were bold enough to ask him about it right now.

"One out of two isn't bad," she finally said just as the doorbell sounded. "Oh, I'll get that."

She rushed off to the front door. Andie and Stephanie arrived together and followed her into the room, just as Molly and Sally-Jo came from the kitchen with the trays of drinks and food. Greetings were followed by the serious business of choosing snacks. Lizzie watched Jacob watching

Sally-Jo. Surely he couldn't be two-timing her. But just who was that woman, in that case? When Lizzie had finished her cheese straw, she decided to get down to business.

"The reason I called you all here—I've been dying to say that—"

"So to speak," said Jacob, and everyone laughed.

"Um, yeah. Anyway, I've mentioned to a couple of you that I've been receiving chapters of a manuscript in my mailbox, usually every couple of nights. In the middle of the night, I might add. All very secretive." She looked around the room. She'd decided, at the last minute, that reading it aloud would be a faster process than everyone taking it home for a day or so.

"Who's the author?" asked Jacob.

"Is it a mystery?" Stephanie chimed in.

"Everything about it is a mystery," Lizzie said. "In fact, I have no idea who's writing it. At first I thought it might be a student from my literacy class or maybe even Andie." She looked over at her. Andie shook her head vehemently.

"But it's a very unusual story. And I would like to read it to you without saying anything more about it. Get your opinions on it. The chapters are very short, so it shouldn't take too long. Would that be all right with you all?"

Everyone nodded their agreement. Bob piled his plate high with pecan cookies and cheese straws, and Andie refilled her drink. Then Lizzie began reading.

She'd check with them at the end of each chapter to make sure she should read on and all agreed. When she finished the twelve chapters, it was going on ten o'clock.

"Now, first impressions?" she asked.

Jacob leaned forward and spoke first. "You know, I understand it's a novel, but it sounds almost like a journal. Of course, that could be partly from the way you're reading it."

Molly nodded. She'd sat beside Jacob on one of the settees and was watching him. "I'd agree with Jacob. It's very intriguing. I think we're leading up to some gruesome deed here. But it doesn't have the flow you'd find in a novel. What do you think, Sally-Jo?"

"Oh, I've read it and at first, it was just an interesting read. But, particularly now that I've heard it aloud, I'd add my vote to the journal."

Stephanie had been knitting away quietly. "But who dropped it in your mailbox and why?"

"Those are my questions, too, Stephanie." Lizzie noticed that Stephanie seemed much more at ease tonight. Maybe the phone calls had stopped, or perhaps she just was relieved she'd told someone about them.

Lizzie looked over at Bob. "What do you think, Bob?"

He roused himself from some deep thought. "I don't honestly know what to think, Lizzie." He shook his head. "I just don't know."

He looked bewildered, not a very Bob Miller look, and he hadn't finished his plate of goodies. Lizzie wondered what, if anything, that meant.

"Do you mind if I borrow it?" he asked. "I'd like to have a read. It's sometimes hard to get everything when it's read out to you, ya know?"

"Sure." Lizzie stuffed it all back in the large manila envelope and passed it to Bob. "Anyone have any suggestions?"

Andie sat at the edge of her seat. "We could stake out your place when the next one's due. See who brings it."

"It's a possibility, but that might be tonight and it's a school night for you." She looked at her watch. "In fact, I think you'd better get on home or your mama's not going to be very happy with me."

Andie snorted. "She's at some social club or something. Won't even know what time I get home."

"But I'll know, and I think you should get a good night's sleep on a school night."

Andie looked so crestfallen that Lizzie added, "But thank you, I do appreciate the offer. Maybe you could do some more online searches if you have some time tomorrow. See if you can find any reference to a story about a male suicide in, say, the mid-1950s to 1970s, and keep the search to southern Alabama."

"That'll get you a whole whack of hits, I'm sure," Jacob said.

"But I don't think they'd all make the newspapers, would they? This might have if they wanted donations for the family or if the land scheme was famous enough," Lizzie suggested.

"I'll do it," Andie said, "even if it's hundreds of hits. I have two free periods in a row tomorrow—just the way the timetable works out this week—so lots of time to do it. All right, I'll head home if you're ready, Stephanie."

Stephanie nodded and put her knitting away in the bag. As she pushed herself out of the chair, Jacob jumped up to give her a hand. She smiled her thanks and once standing said, "Maybe I can call around to the others in the literacy class and work into the conversation a question about the story, see if any of them are the writer?"

"That would be great," Lizzie said. "Thanks, both of you, for coming out tonight." She and Molly walked them to the door. "Is everything all right with you, Stephanie?"

"No phone calls today at all." She smiled. "We'll see." She thanked Molly and left with Andie close behind.

"Do you have any idea at all what's behind this manuscript?" Molly asked before they headed back to the others.

"None. Yet. How are you feeling about everything, Molly?"

"Actually, much better now that I'm not just sitting around waiting for Officer Hotshot to slap the cuffs on me." She hooked her arm through Lizzie's and started walking back to the library. "You know, I meant to tell everyone earlier on but just didn't get the chance. I got to thinking: Claydon and most of the fellows his age were in the local Elks club. So I wondered if Frank Telford had done the same. I called Saul Carstairs, one of Claydon's old cronies, and asked for a contact in Stoney Mills, which he gave me. Then I drove over there this morning and talked to this fellow, Arthur Lee. He remembers Frank Telford, says he was quite the flashy businessman but says he dropped out of the Elks in the late 1960s and he didn't talk to him after that. He became real antisocial, never acknowledging anyone when he'd stop in town for shopping."

"Did I hear right, Molly?" Bob asked as he came through the door. "You went over to Stoney Mills on your own, investigating? Are you getting foolish in your old age, woman?"

Molly's jaw dropped open. "Foolish? Are you calling me foolish, Bob Miller?"

"Well, you're not Agatha Christie or Miss Marple or any of those fictional folks you like to read so much. And there's a killer out there. Next time you decide you need to take a little trip to do some investigating, you call me, do you hear now? We'll do it together."

He shook his finger at her and stomped out the door.

"Why I never," Molly gasped.

"He's got a point," Lizzie said. "That was a clever connection, but you could have put yourself in danger."

"Oh, pshaw. We've got to try to figure this out. There's just too many strange things happening—the murder, the manuscript and your phone calls. I hope you're locking your doors at night, young lady."

"Oh, I am all right. And better than that, I had a police officer offer to sleep at my place—on the couch, I might add—last night."

"Not Officer Hotshot, I hope."

Lizzie laughed. "Not on your life."

Molly smiled. "Good lad."

Chapter Thirty

◇◇◇

The line between winner and loser was pretty thin, and the paths were pretty crooked.

PHANTOM PREY—JOHN SANDFORD

Lizzie added a new worry to her insomnia mélange that night. Bob Miller had certainly been quiet after Lizzie finished reading. What was going on in his mind? And why did he want the manuscript? To read it, of course. Very plausible. But was there something in it that struck a chord with him? Or was she so desperate to find a meaning that she was attaching too much value to others' actions?

And what about Jacob Smith? She'd totally forgotten the episode with the mystery woman until she'd seen him tonight. Of course, it wasn't really any of her business. But she'd also seen the way he looked at Sally-Jo. He had feelings for her. And she knew it was mutual. She just didn't want her friend to be hurt. Again. Especially since it was only last year, before she moved to Ashton Corners, that Sally-Jo had broken her lengthy engagement. From what she'd told Lizzie, that was the best thing she'd done in a long time, although it had taken his having an affair to force her decision. Two two-timers in a row would be two too many.

Lizzie managed a few hours' sleep, a short run and a long shower. While she ate her breakfast, George Havers phoned.

"I managed to find Enid Telford for you," he said without preamble.

Lizzie swallowed the last of her toast. "You did? I didn't even know you were searching. Where did you find her?"

He chuckled. "Well, it sounded like you were in the middle of an intriguing story, and the newshound in me couldn't let it pass. So I started digging. Seems she's on her third husband now, although she may not know it. She's living at the Shady Pines Nursing Home in Stoney Mills. I checked and that's a private assisted-living facility specializing in patients with Alzheimer's. And her name is Enid Hannaford these days."

"That's good work, George. I'm truly impressed and thank you for doing that."

"I'm betting you'll be wanting to talk to her, and I'm hoping that if this all comes together in an interesting story, you might let me in on it."

"Of course I will. And have you had any luck with tracking down the story my daddy was working on?"

"No. Nothing, I'm afraid. I may have a lead on an old colleague of his. I'll try to get in touch and ask him, but it's quite possible Monroe hadn't told anyone what he was doing. You have to be prepared for that. A lot of the guys didn't share leads in those days. Didn't want anyone stealing their stories. Guess that's just as true these days," he added.

"Well, keep in touch. And thank you." Alzheimer's. Lizzie shuddered. If Enid Hannaford was like her mama, she wouldn't be much help. She finished eating the last bit of toast. Maybe she could take a drive over to Stoney Mills this afternoon. Her schedule was free. She'd intended to work on a presentation she was planning for the next professional development day, but that could wait a bit longer. She wondered if Molly might like to go for the ride. A phone call got her an affirmative answer. She promised to swing by and pick her up at one P.M.

"**N**ow, are you sure you're wanting to be talking to this woman?" Molly asked for the third time as they pulled into the parking lot at the Shady Pines Nursing Home. "It might be upsetting, you know. I know how hard it is for you to visit your mama."

Lizzie swallowed hard. "Thank you, Molly. But I'll be fine. This needs to be done." Lizzie wondered if Molly might be the one who would be upset. She really had no idea if seeing Evelyn Turner was a hardship for Molly. "Would you like to wait out in their garden? It looks lovely and it's a perfect afternoon."

"Now, I didn't come all this way, although it was a pleasant drive, just to sit outside and look at a bunch of chrysanthemums, young lady."

It had been a nice drive. They took old Highway 2, which wound its way lazily through the countryside, past some horse farms whose prosperity showed in the large, Southern-style homes, the ones with the large wraparound front porches and pillars, nestled far from the road but within viewing distance. Lizzie felt like a tourist every time she drove along this road. It was so easy to place herself in long-ago times, strolling along the lawn with perhaps a carriage coming up the driveway to call. She was torn between losing herself in the fantasy and preparing questions, if she were able to ask them.

She remembered the many Sunday drives her family had taken in her childhood. Her daddy had loved driving, and her mama packed the best picnic lunches of any of her friends' mamas. And Mama had loved wide-brimmed straw hats with a scarf tied around, that matched the ankle-length dresses that flowed as she walked. Molly may have sensed those memories or been lost in her own. They rode along in a companionable silence until just outside the town limits, when Molly had asked her question.

When they checked at the front desk, Lizzie had a moment's regret that she may have been foolish in not phoning ahead. But the middle-aged woman at the desk didn't seem to find it odd they'd just stopped in.

"Why, Mr. Hannaford is here visiting her, too. Do y'all know him? She's in fine spirits today, and I know she loves company when she's like that." The receptionist rang down to the room and a few minutes later told them that Mr. Hannaford would meet them in the hall outside room 20. They found their way to him and introduced themselves.

Hannaford showed his years in his stooped back and deeply lined face. He wore a camel-colored sports jacket, white shirt, plaid tie and brown pants. Tasseled brown loafers completed the debonair look. Lizzie wondered if he, like she, took special care in what he wore when visiting his wife. Or if this was his usual attire. His smile was engaging as he pumped their hands and looked up at their faces. "My wife is very talkative today."

Lizzie let out the breath she'd been holding. Not like her mama then.

"However," he went on, "she doesn't always know where she is. It's like her mind just flits around in the universe of time and, if we're lucky, it will join us for a portion of its journey." He smiled sadly. "I've grown used to it, so I try to take great sustenance from those moments when she's back here with me."

Lizzie found herself sharing with him her own experiences visiting her mama. He nodded sadly. "That would be truly difficult on a person." He reached over and squeezed her hand. "Now, how do you know Enid?"

"Oh, we don't know her, but"—Lizzie looked quickly at Molly—"it's about her first husband, Frank Telford. We were just hoping to get a bit of information about him."

Hannaford looked puzzled. "Oh, I didn't know him at all, and she hasn't talked to me about him. I'm not sure if you'll get anything from her. What's it about?"

"Well, he died about three weeks ago," Lizzie said. Hannaford looked surprised.

"Yes," Molly jumped in. "He was murdered in front of my house."

"Oh my." Hannaford let out a small whistle. "How disturbing for you. Did they catch who did it?"

"No," Lizzie told him. "Not yet. I hope it won't disturb your wife if we talk to her. We won't mention his death if you think that's best."

He scratched his head. "I rightly don't know what to say. Let's just see where she's at and then play it by ear. If I think she's getting agitated, I'll just change the subject, all right?"

"Fair enough."

He led the way into a brightly decorated room with large windows overlooking a courtyard, complete with bubbling water feature. "Enid loves looking at the fountain," Hannaford told them, as he ushered them to the two tub chairs near the window.

"Enid, dearest," he said loudly. She turned from the fountain, and her face lit when she saw her two guests. "These ladies are Lizzie and Molly, and they're here to have a visit with you. Isn't that nice?"

"Oh my, yes. I love entertaining, don't I, Michael?"

Hannaford looked a bit pinched as he sat on the bed. Lizzie wondered where to start. Maybe niceties about the weather.

Enid made the decision for her. "Were you at that big dinner party we gave last spring? You look so familiar," she said to Molly.

"No, dear," Molly answered. "I missed that one, but I'll bet it was a dandy."

"Oh, yes," Enid said and clapped her hands like a little girl. She looked back at the fountain and fell silent.

Hannaford asked, "Enid, dearest, would you like some tea? Maybe your guests would like some, too?"

Enid turned to him slowly. "Why, I think that would be lovely, Jack. You two will join me, won't you?"

Lizzie and Molly accepted, and Hannaford shuffled down the hall to arrange it. Lizzie wondered if it was Jack or Michael doing the ordering. This seemed as good a time as any to start questioning her.

"Ms. Hannaford, we were hoping you might tell us a bit about your first husband, Frank Telford?"

Enid stared at her so long, Lizzie was certain they'd lost her. Finally she spoke in a soft voice. "I barely think about him at all. I don't like to remember, you see." Lizzie saw the pain in her eyes and decided not to push it.

"But you're happy here?"

"Oh, yes. They're good to me and as you see, I have a very thoughtful husband. Yes, Jack is very thoughtful. Frank . . . Frank was thoughtful, too, at first until . . . it was so unfortunate . . . I left him." It took a few minutes before she started talking again. "Do tell me what you're planning to wear to the New Year's Gala this year? I hear they're hiring a big band from Birmingham and all the tickets are already sold out. Dear me, I haven't a thing to wear. I'm hoping to get to the city any day now and choose a new gown."

Molly and Lizzie exchanged a look just as Hannaford reappeared. He looked at them, then at Enid. "Oh, oh . . . she's gone, is she?"

Lizzie nodded. A knock at the door preceded a nurse's aide pushing a trolley into the room. She efficiently set up the tea and plate of cookies on the small round table that sat between them all, then left.

Hannaford handed a glass of iced tea to his wife. "Tea, Enid?"

She smiled. "Why thank you, Michael. I do so love a glass of iced tea after an afternoon's ride. Now, what did you say your name was?" she asked Lizzie.

"Elizabeth Turner."

"Lovely name. My best girlfriend in grade school was named Elizabeth. Elizabeth Tyson. Why, the same initials as you, dear." She giggled, then looked at Molly. "And you are?"

"Molly Mathews." She passed the plate of cookies to Enid and Lizzie, then took one for herself.

Enid ate hers in silence. Hannaford refused a cookie but drank thirstily from his glass. "Where did you say you ladies are from?" he asked.

"We're from Ashton Corners," Molly answered.

"That's a nice drive. Did you come along the old 2?"

Lizzie nodded but she kept watching Enid. Her face gave away that her mind was working at something.

"I don't usually go too far these days," Mr. Hannaford said. "Our house is close to here, so I just take a taxi. Gave up driving a long time ago."

"Claydon was here one day," Enid said.

Molly almost dropped her glass. "What? Who did you say? Claydon? Claydon Mathews?"

Enid ignored her. "And that nice young man, Jefferson. Jefferson Perkins. Ohh, my. Oh, I'd better hurry and get ready or I'll be late for the dance. Mama doesn't like me to keep my young man waiting, you know." She tried to push herself up out of her chair and knocked over her glass. "Oh, I've got to hurry."

Hannaford got to her and took her hands in his, shushing her and leading her over to the bed. Lizzie picked up the glass and used the napkins as best she could to mop up the mess.

"Just leave that, I'll have someone take care of it," he said to them. "I think maybe you'd better leave now, though. I think she needs to rest."

"Yes, we'll go. I'm sorry if we've upset her, Mr. Hannaford," Lizzie said. "I'll mention at the desk that this needs to be cleaned up."

He smiled gratefully at them, and they left quickly. Back in the car, it took awhile before Molly finally spoke. "Now what in heaven's name was she talking about? And how on God's earth did she know Claydon?"

Chapter Thirty-one

◇◇◇

"What do you want?" Rutkin shouted. "You want
trouble? You want trouble? That can be arranged."

A COLD RED SUNRISE—STUART M. KAMINSKY

Lizzie let Molly off at her house, after seemingly setting
her mind at ease. She pointed out that Enid hadn't said
Claydon's last name and there must be many going by that
name in the county. And she'd been flitting between men's
names all the time. Molly finally agreed and was back in
good humor, thinking about the treats she'd be setting out
for the literacy classes that night.

When Lizzie got home, though, she went straight to her
computer and did a search for Jefferson Perkins. She'd tried
to ease Molly's anxiety, but she thought it was just one too
many coincidences. There were only a couple of references.
One listed him, along with two others, as a stockholder in
an unnamed land development company in the county. The
second was a short obituary in the *Weekly Post*, the local
newspaper in Stoney Mills. She copied down the date of
Perkins's death as well as the names of the other two men.
She searched on the latter, and both men showed up as

deceased, although long before Frank Telford. She shut
down the computer in disgust. She felt no further ahead.
And there'd been no mention of Claydon Mathews in any
of the articles.

What did it mean? Or was it strictly the ramblings of a
mind that wasn't lucid? She wasn't about to let Molly know
that she'd taken Enid seriously enough to try to track down
who Jefferson Perkins was.

She switched her computer back on. Maybe one of the
wives was still alive and could throw some light, if there was
any, on all this. She gave up after twenty minutes. She was
not highly skilled on the computer; she readily admitted
that. If the information was there, she didn't have the patience
to ferret it out. She called Andie and thankfully reached her.
After tasking her with tracking down Jefferson Perkins
and anyone named Claydon who might have connections
to him or Frank Telford and the wives of the deceased
investors, Lizzie had a quick dinner and left for the literacy
class.

Teesha had brought in some reading suggestions. Unfortunately, she hadn't moved much past the graphic novels,
but at least she had put some thought and effort into it. Jolene
actually had some questions about characterization, and so
Lizzie finished the evening a happy teacher.

"By the way," Lizzie said as they were about to leave, "I
want to remind y'all that there is no class on Monday night.
If you'll remember, that night was excluded from the schedule right from the beginning of the term since the community center classes are cancelled due to their annual general
meeting. But since all literacy classes need to advance at
the same rate, you get the night off, too. But don't forget to
come next Wednesday," she added for good measure.

There were a few laughs and chuckles, then good-byes.
Jolene hung back as the others left, and handed over an
envelope.

"It's my story," she said. "At least the first chapter. I hope you meant what you said about reading it. If you like it, I'll bring in the rest. I'm up to chapter ten now."

Lizzie smiled, hoping she looked more enthusiastic than she felt. "Of course I meant it. I'll try to get this read by next class, but I can't promise, okay? It all depends on how much work I have to do for my day students."

"That's cool. No rush. I'm just going to keep on going at it anyway. Night now," she said.

Lizzie had just gotten home when the phone rang. Molly's breathless voice announced another figurine had been stolen. And this time, the thief had been captured on tape. The police had been called and fortunately, it wasn't Officer Craig who turned up. The officer took the tape and was on his way to arrest Dwayne Trowl.

Lizzie looked at the phone in disbelief. Dwayne the thief? She'd thought for sure that since Troy was back, that's whose name Molly would say.

"Oh boy. Well, I guess we'll hear all about it after they question him," Lizzie said. "I am totally shocked, though. Why, he was a bartender at your picnic and nothing was stolen."

"I know, honey. I can't believe it either. But at least one mystery has been solved. Let's hope the other, more serious one follows suit."

Lizzie stopped by the police station the next morning on the way to school, hoping Mark would be in and tell her all about Dwayne. He was and he did.

"It seems he's a clever guy. He'd been hoping Troy would be suspected. That's why he never stole when Troy wasn't there."

"But why did he steal those things? They couldn't have gotten him much money."

"He gave them to his girlfriend, Teesha Torres. Seems she has an eye for glittery things and he wanted to keep her happy. Ahh, young, misguided love." He chuckled.

"Do not laugh about this, Mark Dreyfus." She'd almost stamped her foot, she was so upset. "He was just telling me at the garden party on Sunday that he wanted to be a chef, go to cooking school, and he had big plans. Now what's going to happen to him?"

Mark sobered quickly. "Sorry, Lizzie. Well, these are misdemeanor items, totaling less than five hundred dollars. And he doesn't have a previous record. Maybe the judge will have a long talk with him and look kindly on young love." His smirk was back.

"Did Teesha ask him to steal them, did he say?"

"No, he didn't, and I don't think he's about to, do you?"

She shook her head. "No. I sure hope she didn't, though. Oh boy . . . that stupid kid."

"That's exactly what he is. But I'm glad this was sorted out so Ms. Mathews doesn't have to worry about it anymore."

Lizzie looked at Mark and felt better. "Exactly. That is a good thing."

"Would you like some coffee? It's not as good as Starbucks but not as bad as they make out in all those cop shows."

"Thanks for the offer, but I've really got to get to class."

"We still on for Saturday night?" he asked, a smile playing at the edges of his mouth.

"Absolutely. What did you have in mind?"

"Well, you did sort of do the asking . . ."

Lizzie blushed.

"Sorry, I couldn't resist teasing you a little." He laughed. "Saturday's the final night of the FallFest, so I thought we might eat at the Black Tomato, then wander around the booths and maybe take in the big show at the main stage. Tell me you like Cajun music, now."

Lizzie laughed. "I love Cajun, and I love the idea of taking it all in. What time?"

"I'll pick you up at six?"

"Great. See you then."

Mark walked her to the front door of the station and gave her arm a light squeeze. "See you then."

Lizzie found it hard to concentrate on work that day. Fortunately, she had no appointments scheduled. She'd planned to finish putting together her workshop and needed to access the school library to do so. What with recent cutbacks, there was no longer a librarian on staff for her to check in with, so she commandeered what had been the librarian's desk in the small office and hooked up her computer. The shelves in the office appeared to have been co-opted for school storage. And a laminating machine was crammed in the corner with a small table nearby. A note with large black letters asked that the space be kept clear for use as a cutting surface.

After about an hour of busywork, she finally shut out thoughts of both Dwayne and Mark and concentrated on her PowerPoint presentation. She glanced at the clock as the lunch bell rang but planned to work straight through until she finished. Eventually she reached that point, read it all over a second time and emailed the entire package to the office to have them print out packages for the teachers.

She stopped by Molly's on her way home, wanting to fill her in on her conversation with Mark—well, the part that pertained to Dwayne, at least. She followed the sound of Molly's singing and found her out back, on her knees, digging around the daylilies again.

"I'm altogether surprised that you don't join our choir, Molly. You have such a beautiful alto voice," Lizzie told her as she settled into a nearby wicker chair.

Molly laughed. "You know, a little part of me wanted to

be a sultry singer in a smoky jazz club, but that was just the part that needed a small vacation from my real life every now and then. We all need those places to visit. What's yours, Lizzie?"

"I guess I never gave it much thought. I just immerse myself in a book if I want to do that. But if I had to choose a fantasy . . . umm . . . I think I'd like to be an artist, my easel set up on a white sandy beach in Aruba or some such place, and me there all by my lonesome, barefoot and painting."

"Why, Lizzie girl, I never did know you had a yen to paint. Why haven't you done something about it?"

"Probably the same reason you haven't gone to a club and asked to sing."

Molly nodded. "You'd have to find a new fantasy then. And, of course, there's always the threat of rejection. In my daydreams, I'm fabulous. In reality . . . well, it's better not to find out."

"Exactly. Now, I had a talk with Mark Dreyfus this morning and—don't you waggle your eyebrows at me, Molly Mathews. I was concerned about Dwayne Trowl, so we had a little chat. Now, if you don't press too hard on this, the judge may go a little easier on the boy."

Molly pushed herself up and brushed off the knees of her faded jeans, then shook her gardening gloves. The sleeves of her khaki canvas jacket had been pushed up to her elbows, and she took a moment to straighten them. "As I said, the objects weren't valuable. Some were sentimental, but when you come right down to it, they're just objects. Why did he take them, anyway?"

"To give to Teesha. He's sweet on her and she coveted them, I guess, and he wanted to make her happy."

"Humph. Like I said, it's not the items so much as the fact that he chose to steal from me. He violated my trust in having him in my house. That I cannot condone, so while I won't push, I won't ask for leniency either."

"Fair enough. He does have to learn the consequences of his actions. At least, he's out of jail on his own recognizance until the trial. I'm hoping he'll try to make it up to you."

Chapter Thirty-two

◇◇◇

My answer to stress is a tasty meal, an hour of watching the food network, and a good night's sleep. I got the first two but not the third.

THE LONG QUICHE GOODBYE—AVERY AAMES

"I want to talk about Janet Evanovich today. Not Shakespeare," Andie announced as she dropped her bag on the floor and slouched into the chair at the bridge table Molly had set up in the library.

"Evanovich is strictly for book club night. Shakespeare gets the daytime billing." Lizzie was secretly pleased that her unconventional attempt to interest Andie in reading seemed to be working. However, she still had to get the girl through a year of English lit.

Lizzie had done her own homework, though. She'd chosen a passage in *The Taming of the Shrew* quite similar to part of Evanovich's *One for the Money*. She asked Andie to read it aloud and watched with glee as Andie eventually made the connection between the two.

Andie fingered one of the many small silver loops in her right earlobe, which had remained hidden until that point, since her long black hair, recently rid of its customary colored streaks, hung loosely to her shoulders. A new look for her, but one that Lizzie liked. "Cool," Andie said finally. "This shrew babe is kinda her own boss and not taking being pushed around by any guy, just like Stephanie Plum, right?"

"I'd say so. What else do you find similar?"

"Well, you can tell they're nuts about each other, all that sexual tension even though they're saying otherwise. Like Plum and Joe Morelli." She bit into a molasses cookie she'd absently taken from the plate of freshly baked cookies Molly always supplied.

"So, I guess they sorta went through the same things we do these days," she went on once she'd swallowed. "But it's hard to figure out. If only he'd write so's you could understand it."

"You're right, but you know, the more you read Shakespeare, the easier it becomes to understand. Trust me."

Andie looked doubtful, but she went back to reading aloud. By the end of their session, she'd relaxed in her chair and was asking Lizzie questions about the time period.

"By the way," she added, "thanks for getting Ms. Mathews to go over to see Steph."

"Molly does have a knack for empathizing with others. And I know she's concerned about Stephanie, so she was happy to go over to her house. I hope everything will work out."

"Me, too." She pulled out her cell phone and checked it. "There's a message from Steph, sent about fifteen minutes ago. I had it on vibrate but had already stuck it in my bag." She punched her way into her messages. "Oh boy. She wants me to come right over. She says Officer Craig is there and giving her a hard time."

Lizzie gathered her own books. "I'll go over. Maybe I can help."

"Can I come with you? It was me she texted, after all."

Lizzie looked at her. "Of course. I'll just say bye to Molly and meet you at my car."

It took less than fifteen minutes to get to the apartment, but by that time, it was empty.

"Where's Steph? Do you think they took her in?" Andie sounded worried.

"I wouldn't put it past our Officer Craig. Let's go see."

Lizzie spotted Stephanie right away, as soon as they entered the police station. She sat with her arms hugging herself, looking thoroughly dejected, at Officer Craig's desk. She wore a bulky beige cardigan as a defense against the questions. Several strands of her hair had escaped her ponytail and now hung limply framing her face, emphasizing the look of terror it held.

Lizzie wanted to rush right over, but she knew that would only antagonize Officer Craig. Instead, she asked the young officer at the front desk if he would please go over and tell Stephanie that they were waiting for her. That would give her morale a boost, anyway. He appeared reluctant to do so but after some cajoling by Andie, gave her a quick grin and did it.

"You have a way with the young men in uniform, I see," Lizzie joked.

Andie smirked. "I've known Kenny Watson since grade school. He's only a couple of years older than me, and I've always teased him. I think he kind of likes it."

Lizzie nodded. She agreed. He delivered the message, and both an irritated Amber Craig and a relieved Stephanie looked their way. Lizzie gave a little wave, as did Andie. Officer Craig went right back to questioning Stephanie, so the two took a seat in the waiting area, positioned so they could see a bit of the desk. On the plus side, she wasn't being questioned in an interrogation room. However, she had been brought to the station, so things weren't great.

"Do you think we should call Jacob Smith?" Andie asked after about ten minutes.

Lizzie had been pondering the same thing. Would it help

or make Stephanie look guilty of something? Only Officer Craig knew the answer to that. She stood and asked Kenny if he would tell Officer Craig she wanted to have a quick word with her. Officer Craig glared at her when she got the message but walked over anyway.

"This doesn't concern you, Ms. Turner," she snarled.

"Oh, but it does. She's my student, and she doesn't have any family around. She's young and vulnerable, so I'd just like to ask you if maybe I should contact a lawyer to sit in on the questioning?" Lizzie tried to sound pleasant, like she was asking a totally innocent question.

"It sounds like a waste of money, unless she has something to hide. And it sure appears like she does."

"Oh, she doesn't, I'm sure, and he's a friend. He wouldn't charge." She hoped.

Officer Craig shrugged her shoulders, but Lizzie could see the effort it took to make it look like she was unconcerned. "Maybe next time. I have no further questions right now. But there will be a next time."

She abruptly walked back to her desk and told Stephanie she could go. Stephanie left swiftly, not saying anything until all three were out of the station.

"Oh my God. That was so awful. Thank you so much for coming, you two. I don't know what I would have done otherwise." She removed her scrunchie, regathered the loose strands of hair and retied her ponytail. Her eyes, normally done up in mascara and eye shadow, were instead rimmed in red. She began running her hands over her belly and a moment later, she started crying. Andie threw her arms around her, shushing her.

Lizzie said, "She's not the most pleasant person. Come on, we'll take you home and fix a nice cup of sweet tea and just relax."

Stephanie let herself be led to the car. She was silent the entire way to her apartment. Once inside, she sank onto the couch. Andie sat beside her while Lizzie checked the cupboard for tea makings. She wanted to let Stephanie relax and quiet down, but on the other hand, this might be the best time to get some answers from her. She was grateful to them for having rescued her from Officer Craig's clutches, after all. Lizzie felt a tinge of guilt, thinking that way, but she really did want to help the girl.

"Here, try this." Lizzie handed both girls a glass, then got her own and pulled over a chair so she was in front of them. "Now, Stephanie, I know it's been a trying afternoon for you, and Officer Craig is just going to keep at it until she gets the answers she's looking for. I think it would be far better if you just opened up to us. We're your friends. We don't want to hurt you or put you in danger, but we can't help you unless we know what's going on in your life—why you seem to be so scared, for instance."

Lizzie held her breath, hoping she hadn't made things worse.

Stephanie drank the entire glass of tea, then sat looking at the floor for a few minutes. Finally, she looked up at Lizzie. "I guess I'd better tell you. I do trust you and all. It's just, I'm just so confused about everything."

Lizzie nodded encouragingly. Andie reached out and grabbed Stephanie's hand.

It took her several minutes of chewing on her lips and looking around the room before she finally cleared her throat and spoke.

"I keep getting phone calls, and I'm sure they're from the daddy of my baby. But I don't want to see him. I don't want to see anyone from back home. I came to Ashton Corners to start a new life, to try to stand on my own two feet and bring up my child." She placed her hand on her belly and sniffled.

"Are you afraid of him?" Lizzie asked softly.

"Yes. No. I don't know. He's got a fierce temper, but he's

never hit me or anything. Just yells a lot. Like my daddy. Everyone back home thinks I should marry Trip—that's his name—but I know we'd end up just like my parents and be fighting all the time, and I'd be crying in my room a whole lot, and the kids would all be miserable.

"My grandpa and grandma, they're the ones I've lived with since I was six, they want me to marry him. They wouldn't hear of my getting an abortion, although I didn't really want one either. I just thought I did at first. But they're talking about disowning me if I don't marry Trip. But that's not the life I want for me or my baby. I may not be very smart, but I will work hard and make a life for us."

Lizzie's heart ached. She could hear the pain in Stephanie's voice and the determination. But she had chosen a really rough road. Being a single mama without much education meant long hours and a hard life.

"What would you like to do with your life, if you could be anything you wanted?" Lizzie asked.

Stephanie closed her eyes and thought. "I'd want to finish my schooling and maybe go on to college and become a nurse's aide."

It sounded so simple. Lizzie sighed. And wondered. Something to think about. "And I need to know if you know Frank Telford. That's what's at the bottom of all this police questioning, after all." *That plus the fact you won't tell them where you're from or anything about your past life.*

Stephanie stared wide-eyed at her and shook her head. "No, I don't know him. But when I first saw him he looked so much like a real close friend of my grandpa, that I thought he'd sent him here to track me down. I was so scared they'd found me out. I didn't take a closer look, so's I didn't realize it wasn't him." She shuddered. "I can't go back," she whispered, and started crying.

Andie patted her arm, shushing her while Lizzie went to get her some water. It was that simple. And complicated. At least she was relieved Stephanie had no connection to Telford. Now she had to make the police back off, and then maybe they could all figure out what to do in case Stephanie's past managed to track her down.

Chapter Thirty-three

◇◇◇

Society can make a union legal or illegal, but it can't do a darn thing about unruly hearts.

THE FROG AND THE SCORPION—A. E. MAXWELL

L izzie checked the bedside clock, hoping she'd finally fallen asleep and it was almost morning. Two A.M. That would be only ten minutes since she last checked it. The cats had long since given up on her tossing and turning, choosing to snuggle together for the rest of their sleep on the far edge of her queen bed.

She couldn't seem to switch off her brain. At times she'd be at Stephanie's apartment, listening to her pain. Then she'd be puzzling about the manuscript and the phone calls. Then, for good measure, she spent some time worrying about Andie, hoping the day would come when she would read just for the joy of reading.

And to top it off, snippets of the Rutter the choir had practiced last week seemed to be playing on a tape loop in her brain. And, of course, her mama entered the thought pattern, and she worried about whether she was doing everything she could to make her life good. And Molly came into it. Until the murder was cleared up, Molly would remain edgy, wondering when the police were coming to take her away.

She got up and padded in her bare feet down to the kitchen, pouring a glass of cold water from the filtered pitcher she kept in the fridge. She stayed, leaning against the kitchen sink, thinking for so long that Brie came down in hopes of a warm lap or some food, at the very least. She added some dry food to the cats' dishes and went back up to bed.

"Either I'm going to have to give myself a serious talking to, Molly, or maybe I should get you to do it," Lizzie said between bites of butterscotch pie, sitting at Molly's banquette after school.

"Why's that, honey?"

"Well, part of my brain is working with the kids, trying to unlock that desire or even just the ability to learn, while the other part is puzzling over this entire Telford thing. And now with Enid Hannaford in the mix, the entire puzzle is getting to that unwieldy state, rather than coming together. Have you had any further thoughts about our visit with Ms. Hannaford?"

"I've been thinking of nothing else all day, honey. That poor woman. I feel bad for her being in her state, but even more unfortunate is that wonderfully kind husband she has. And I can't for the life of me think of how she might have known Claydon. I never met her, and he certainly never mentioned her, nor Frank Telford, to me. And, he usually talked about what was going on in his life. He was a bit of a braggart, you know. Now, don't let on I said that." She winked.

Lizzie nodded. "No construction projects he may have been thinking about investing in?"

"Sorry."

"I'm hitting a whole lot of dead ends these days." She sighed. "No leads on Frank Telford. I've got an anonymous manuscript being delivered to me, and I can't find out anything about the author. And those telephone calls about what story my daddy was working on when he died. I've asked George Havers to look into that, but he's not had any luck either. It's all so frustrating."

Molly put her hand out to Lizzie. "You come with me, honey. We're going to have us a nice cool drink and we'll talk."

They took their glasses of lemonade and wandered through the gardens, beside the pond and out to the swing. They got a comfortable rhythm going before Molly spoke again.

"I've been debating whether or not to tell you this, but I'm now thinking you probably should know, not that I believe a word of it, mind you." She held up her hand to shush Lizzie, who had opened her mouth to talk.

"Now, I didn't talk to your daddy about his trips to Stoney Mills, but I did talk to your mama and she had her own theory." Molly took a deep breath. "She came over one night, about a week before he died, and brought you along. You came out here to play, and we sat inside, sharing a drink"— she tilted her glass at Lizzie—"and she said she'd come for my advice. She thought your daddy was having himself an affair with someone who lived in Stoney Mills and that's why all the trips there. Especially since he wasn't sharing any information about this story and that was highly unusual for him."

"An affair! That can't be true. He wouldn't. Would he?" Lizzie stopped swinging. She felt like the wind had been knocked out of her. How had her mama felt?

Molly shook her head in regret. "I told Evelyn that I highly doubted Monroe would have an affair, he was so devoted to the both of you. But she had it in her head and was wondering if she should confront him. I told her that suspicions were one thing, but she didn't have any proof and if she accused him without any real knowledge, she'd do that marriage unmentionable damage."

"So, what did she do?"

"Nothing. She fretted and she waited and then he had himself that accident. I think that's part of the reason she started this journey to wherever she is: she never knew the truth, and she couldn't forgive herself for the doubts that plagued their last weeks together." Molly wiped a tear away from her cheek.

Lizzie sat totally still for a few moments.

"I hope I did the right thing in telling you, honey. It may or may not have a bearing on the phone calls, but you're long overdue knowing what's been going through your mama's mind. I just kept putting off telling you because it's like a violation of her privacy and not something a daughter ought to be hearing."

Lizzie shook her head. "No, you did right, Molly. I just feel a bit off kilter right now. I'll have to sort it all through and decide what, if anything, to do." She glanced at her watch and took a deep breath. "Right now I've got to get home and get ready for choir tonight." She hugged Molly hard.

"Thank you for telling me, Molly." She left with tears in her eyes.

She managed to lose herself in the Rutter magic for a couple of hours. The choir director had emailed a list of the works they'd be focusing on each week, rotating them, honing sections of the night's offerings until, when strung together, it actually sounded like a well-polished piece. Tonight, the Rutter "Nativity Carol" had gotten extra billing. Lizzie immersed herself in her line, emerging at the break for some pleasantries and a sugar cookie, all the while willing herself not to think about her earlier conversation with Molly.

She snapped to attention when she heard her name called out. Stanton Giles, the director, looked bemused as he repeated what he'd just said. "I've decided to add another short piece to the second half of the concert. Another Rutter,

'The Christmas Lullaby,' as a quartet, and I'd like you, Lizzie, to sing the soprano line. Is that all right with you? It shouldn't require too much extra practice."

Normally, Lizzie would have declined. In fact, she never volunteered for any of the extra, smaller pieces. But put on the spot, as she was, she felt she had no choice but to agree. A small clump of butterflies took flight in her stomach, and she inhaled deeply to dispel them. Plenty of time for that, closer to the concert. She determined to stay in the present for the remainder of the practice and not be caught off guard again.

But later that night, she had a hard time falling asleep. She didn't think knowing about her mama's suspicions could help in how she interacted with her, but whether it had anything to do with the phone calls was another matter. Was someone, maliciously, trying to imply that's what Monroe Turner had been up to? If so, who was the caller? She didn't believe for a moment there was another woman, but if by any slight chance there had been, could she be the caller? Or even a relative, trying to cause trouble for whatever reason. And what possible reason could there be?

Her mind took off on fanciful flights as she probed possible motives. A half sibling wanting to make contact? Wanting to blackmail? Or just cause mischief? There was still the coincidence of the phone calls, the manuscript and the murder. Were the first two related in any way? Her father couldn't be anyone written about in the story. But was that the story he was investigating? Were the author and the caller the same person?

If so, why was it anything more than a tragically sad tale to her daddy? What would make it worthy of publication? Maybe she should show the manuscript to George Havers and see if he could find a connection. Maybe she should just put it to rest and go to sleep. Good plan, but like many a good plan, it didn't come together as hoped.

Chapter Thirty-four

◇◇◇

I hoped it wasn't an act. I was out on the same old
dead limb and I didn't bounce as well as I used to.

AMERICAN DETECTIVE—LOREN D. ESTLEMAN

The doorbell rang while Lizzie sucked back her second
coffee in a row. She looked down at her running shorts
and T-shirt, shook her head and thought, whoever it was
deserved to see her like this if they dared to come calling
at this hour on a Saturday morning. Of course, it could be
Nathaniel, about to take off on another adventure. She
cheered at the thought but got a big surprise when she
opened the door.

"Paige. What are you doing here at this hour, on a Saturday to boot?" Lizzie drew her friend in and gave her a
quick hug.

Paige laughed. "I'm in search of a good cup of coffee and
some adult conversation, that's what. Brad, on the spur of
the moment, took the girls out to McDonald's for breakfast,
so I thought, I'm out of here. Hope you don't mind."

"Not in the slightest. I've got some coffee dripping, as it
happens. Come on in, girl. This is like old times. Premar-
riage times." Paige wore dark denim boot-cut jeans with a

long-sleeved cream T-shirt and sleeveless brown quilted cotton vest. Her blonde hair had been caught back in a barrette, and black sunglasses rested on her head. She looked much the same as she had in senior year, except for the few added pounds. But they added to a look of contentment, Lizzie thought. Regardless of what Paige said.

Paige hovered while Lizzie poured her a mug. When they'd settled across from each other at the kitchen table, Paige asked, "What's up? I'm getting some strange vibes from you, Lizzie."

Lizzie finished the small amount of coffee in her mug left from earlier, then went to refill it before answering. "I didn't sleep well. Molly told me something yesterday, and I kept going over it all night." She gave a weak smile. "Good thing it's not a school day today."

"What is it, girlfriend? Can you share?" She reached over and touched Lizzie's arm.

Lizzie looked at Paige a moment before replying. They were childhood friends, but this was her mama's private business. But she had to talk it out with someone or burst. "She told me that Mama thought Daddy was cheating on her and that was why he kept on going over to Stoney Mills, the place he was coming home from when he had the car accident."

Paige looked shocked. She squeezed Lizzie's arm but took a minute to go over it in her mind before talking. "No way, sweetie. Your daddy wouldn't do something like that. I knew him, had all my life. He doted on you and your mama. I used to wish my daddy would hug my mama like your daddy was always doing. I thought y'all had such a happy family life."

"You used to think that? And here I always loved going over to your house and hanging around with your family."

"That was after your daddy died, I think. Oh, we used to play at my house before, but after the accident, you used to want to be around my parents a lot more, not be squirreled away in my room with some old board game."

Lizzie sank back in her chair. "Hmm, you may be right. And I appreciate what you're saying about my daddy, but we were just kids, Paige. We didn't necessarily know what was going on between our folks."

"Do you think that's why your mama's like she is now?"

"It's got to be part of it. Either she's feeling betrayed and then he dies, maybe adding more betrayal in her mind. Or else, she could be regretting her thoughts the last time they were together. We'll probably never know. Either way, it was enough to push her over the edge, I guess."

Paige sat silent, then went over to Lizzie and put her arms around her. "Oh, sweetie, I feel for you. But I'm sure in my heart of hearts that your daddy would not do something like that."

Lizzie nodded. "I feel it, too. But it's all so confusing."

Lizzie knew it would take her a long time to come to terms with it, even when she discovered, as she would, that there was no affair. But even that possibility had caused a slight shift in her world. Perceptions were brought out to be examined. Perceived truths, questioned. No wonder her mama had chosen to dodge it all. Maybe this would provide an answer to how to deal with Mama.

Paige sat back down. "You know, I think you've got too much going on in your mind right now. You need a vacation or at least something special happening."

Lizzie's smile spread slowly.

"Oh, go on, girl. Something's up," Paige said, perching on the edge of her chair. "Tell all."

"Nothing new. Just, tonight's my date with Mark."

"Oh my God, how could I have forgotten? I've got child-minder's brain, that's why. Yes, it is tonight, and where are you going?"

"To the FallFest. We'll have dinner first at the Black Tomato and then wander around, take in the late show."

"Sounds like fun. Just what you need. Now, what are you wearing?"

"Oh, I hadn't even given it any thought."

"Wear that new floaty white organza blouse, the one with the shots of blue and green through it, and a short, flirty skirt."

"Umm, maybe the blouse. I feel good in it, but I think black slacks will do."

"What! Think sexy when you're making your choice. He always did have an eye for the legs. Remember all those cheerleaders, now."

Lizzie laughed. "You are just the right dose of feel-good medicine, Paige Raleigh."

Paige smiled. "I'll take that as a compliment. It's what best friends are supposed to do, you know." She took another sip. "You got any sweets to go with this? I'm trying not to eat any in front of Brad so's he'll keep believing I'm sticking to my diet. He says I don't need to diet and in the same breath, says he knows I'll never follow through. He's right of course, but I don't want to cave this early on. But I have this craving."

Lizzie opened the freezer, brought out the cheese scones she'd gotten from Nathaniel and popped them in the microwave to warm them up. "I totally forgot about these. Nathaniel baked them. I'm glad you said something."

They munched in companionable silence, Paige emitting the occasional moan of pleasure and compliments like "So good." She licked her fingers before wiping them on the napkin.

"I shouldn't bring this up now that you're smiling, but I've been thinking as I've been eating," Paige said, watching Lizzie's reaction. "There's this murder, then you get that manuscript and then those phone calls. Now this. It's just too much coincidence, I'm thinking. Even for me, and you know I totally believe in that stuff. Fate, karma, kismet. That's what brought you and Mark back together." She raised her hand to stop Lizzie's comment. "Well, together. But all this other stuff. No wonder you can't sleep. Your brain is trying to make the connections because it knows . . . just too much coincidence."

Lizzie nodded. "I think you're right. But I can't seem to make those connections between them."

"Well, as a complete outsider, it looks to me like—you haven't gotten the ending of the manuscript yet, have you?"

Lizzie shook her head.

"Right. Well, I'll bet when you do, this dead guy turns up in it. Dead."

Lizzie stared at her friend. "Do you think the author is the killer? That's why I'm getting the book in parts? That's just too creepy. I've got Andie Mason checking on the Internet to see if the story parallels any news item. So far she's come up empty-handed."

"Hmm. It's just a theory. Maybe the wrong one."

Lizzie poured them both another coffee, her mind working on making connections.

Paige took a sip, then asked, "Have you thought to do an Internet search on your daddy? Maybe you'll find something there that might point to his last story. Maybe he was doing a series or something."

"Oh my gosh." Lizzie almost sloshed her coffee on the counter. "I hadn't thought of that. What a dummy. I've looked up his name before. I don't know why I didn't think of it for this. I'm going to check it right now."

Paige followed her upstairs to the computer set up in the spare bedroom. Lizzie booted up and drummed her fingers while waiting for the slow machine to come to life. Paige flopped on the daybed.

"I thought you were going to paint this room yellow," she said, casting a critical eye around. Paige had intended on being an interior decorator before Brad convinced her that having their family early was a good idea. She'd stowed the ambition but not the ideas. "That would suit your furnishings so much better."

"I know, it was on my summer list. Now it's on my fall

list. But there's always spring. Here we go." She typed in
her daddy's name and hit search. The hits ran on for several
pages. She checked the most immediate ones and those
dated just before his death, but didn't find what she was
looking for. Nothing that was referenced as part of an ongoing series, anyway.

"I'll have to take my time going through these. Maybe
later this afternoon." She gave Paige a hug. "You've made
me feel a whole lot better. Thanks for stopping by today."

"Glad to oblige, but I should be on my way. You've also
made my day, and I'm now ready to face the towering piles
of laundry."

After Paige left, Lizzie decided to get in touch with Bob,
to see if he had any new ideas about the manuscript, or at
least, to get it back. She tried calling him, but there was no
answer. She'd drive over, in case he was out back, fishing
off his wharf. When she arrived, his aging Pathfinder SUV
wasn't sitting in the driveway, and Bob didn't answer to a
knock or her calling his name. She lingered out back for a
while, enjoying the sound of the water rippling over the
rocks near shore and the sight of the sun playing off the
shimmering surface of the Tallapoosa as it meandered into
joining the Alabama River, on its journey to the Gulf of
Mexico.

She could understand why Bob loved living here. His
small house sat up on the embankment, in case of flooding,
but also to give him a spectacular view of water and the
treed shoreline across the river. As part of a federal reserve,
the area encompassed in this riverside vista would remain
the same, uninhabited and wild. Although Lizzie would love
a river view, this seemed a bit too secluded for her tastes.
She liked being able to see other houses, to talk to neighbors
out in the front yard and in particular, to hear the sounds of
children playing.

She heard a car drive up. Hopefully, Bob. She waited as
the footsteps along the path leading to the back grew louder.

It turned out not to be Bob, but instead, Jacob Smith, with a surprised look on his face that mirrored her own.

"Hi, Lizzie. I wondered whose car that was out front. Is Bob inside?" he asked.

"Nope. I stopped by hoping to find him here, and now I'm just enjoying his view. I'd forgotten you're neighbors, but not visible ones."

Jacob laughed. "Neighbors, in that I'm the next house along the road, but that's a quarter of a mile. I've got some-one real close on my other side, but Bob here's out in nowhere land. And he likes it like that."

"Yeah—keeps the fish happy, I hear. Do you have a few minutes to talk about all that's been going on?"

"Sure." He sat down in the weathered Adirondack chair next to hers. Flakes of paint had chipped off both, revealing a previous coat of green blending rather nicely with the newer rust color. "Have there been any new developments? Anyone else being grilled by our overly zealous Officer Craig?"

"Not that I'm aware. She was pretty rough on Stephanie, being an out-of-towner. I was actually wondering if Stepha-nie might be able to give you a call if that happens again."

"Sure. I'd be happy to go to the station with her."

"Have you been questioned again?"

Jacob snorted. "Nope. Fortunately. Officer Craig would make a good attorney, that's for sure. She gets something in her mind and won't let it go."

He grimaced at what must have been a memory of that encounter, and it turned his usual uncomplicated look, some-thing his clients must find trustworthy and reassuring, into something more menacing. Lizzie hadn't thought of him in those terms before. Was there another side to Jacob, one that might lead to involvement in a crime? And what about the mystery woman she saw him with in town? She wanted some details there.

Lizzie shifted uncomfortably. She didn't like thinking

along those lines. But she needed to know if he was hiding anything. "Where did you move from? I can't recall hearing that."

Jacob looked at her a moment before answering. He tacked a smile on. "I went to U. of South Alabama and stayed in Mobile for a short while."

Hmm, partial answer. "I went to Auburn and spent a few years working elsewhere but then came back home. You weren't tempted to go back home?"

"Nope."

"Why Ashton Corners anyway? I'd never have thought of this town as being a lawyer magnet."

He crossed his arms across his chest and looked out at the river when answering. "I'd been here as a child. On holidays. It was a good time and I remembered it, so I thought I'd like to try living here. Something smaller, slower paced."

"And you're glad you did?" she said with a grin, hoping to ease some of the tension that she noticed in his body.

He nodded. "It has its positive features. However, I didn't realize just how inquisitive folks could be. Just what are you trying to find out, Lizzie?"

She didn't know what to say to that. *I'm sorry, but I'm wondering if you're a two-timer . . . or even a murderer.* Maybe she'd better back off. Try again another time or another way. But she had to know about the woman.

"I'm really wondering about the woman I saw with you in town on Saturday two weeks ago." She watched the shocked look creep over his face.

"I know it's none of my business," she went on, "but you did look cozy. And Sally-Jo's a close friend, you know. It was probably your sister or something like that, and I'm going to feel real foolish, aren't I?"

Jacob sat staring at the river for such a long time, Lizzie wasn't sure he'd bother to answer. She'd really crossed the line this time.

"She's my wife, Lizzie," he finally said, still not looking at her.

"Your wife, as in 'still married'?"

"Yes. But we've been separated for a year now, which is part of the reason I moved here. We own a house in Mobile, and she's still living in it. I tried an apartment in town, but it was just too close. I thought getting away might help put everything in perspective, help us both make some decisions."

"Like whether to get back together or not?" Lizzie asked.

He looked at her. "Exactly. I thought I'd made the decision, especially after meeting Sally-Jo, so I told my wife I wanted a divorce. She came here to talk about it—well, it seems, to talk me out of it. That was her kissing me, actually."

Lizzie couldn't think of what to say. She wanted to know if that kiss had changed his mind. Instead, she asked, "Does Sally-Jo know?"

"Not yet. I had planned on telling her this weekend, but she's been so busy, I haven't seen her yet. Hopefully, tomorrow night. I know, I should have been up front right from the start, but I just so totally wanted it all out of my life. Can you understand? Do you think she'll understand?"

Lizzie thought about Sally-Jo's previous relationship, which had ended when she found out her fiancé was having an affair. She had no idea how this would affect her.

"I really can't say, Jacob. But I do know that you have to tell her, real soon."

"You're right and I will, I promise. Just, please, don't tell her before I get the chance?"

Lizzie agreed.

Jacob's smile was wobbly. "Well, I'd best be heading into town. That's why I stopped by, to see if Bob wanted anything at Clifford's Home Hardware."

Lizzie glanced at her watch. "Yikes. I've got too much to get done in too little a time period. I guess I spent more

time daydreaming and watching the water than I realized."
She had a final look at the river, with the sun now visible
lower in the sky, and then followed Jacob around to where
their cars were parked.

She stared at Jacob as he backed out, wondering how
betrayed Sally-Jo would feel when she found out.

Chapter Thirty-five

✦✦✦

It was worth the wait.

DIPPED, STRIPPED, AND DEAD—ELISE HYATT

Mark pushed the doorbell precisely at six o'clock. Lizzie liked that in a date, as she always tried to arrive on time wherever she was going. She'd chosen the floaty white blouse that Paige had suggested but teamed it with a pair of new dark indigo jeans and a cotton-knit blood orange jacket. She felt kinda foxy and was ready to have a good time.

Mark gave her an appreciative once-over, which set her toes to tingling again, and walked her to his Jeep. She turned to him as he started it up, about to ask him if he'd had any news about Frank Telford. She silently admonished herself. This was a date, after all, and murder had no place on it.

Mark apparently didn't have the same qualms. "Before you ask, I don't have any further news about Frank Telford. I did, however, meet someone who remembers talking to your daddy a few weeks before he died."

"Oh my gosh, who? And did they know what story he was working on?"

"It's Ms. Lillian Galbraith. She's retired now, but she was the reference librarian here in town when we were growing up. I used to bother her something fierce, but she never told my folks about it, and I sort of figured out she knew what my home life was like. She seemed to know a lot about the folks in town. So, I tracked her down at the Sherman Seniors' Home. She remembers him coming in several times and trying to get information on something. Unfortunately, she can't remember what. But she did suggest he go over to the Stoney Mills Public Library. Maybe that's where he was coming home from?"

"From what I hear, he made several trips over there, but that's a great lead. I'll go over there and see what I can find out. Thanks, Mark."

"My pleasure," he said as he pulled into the municipal parking lot just off Main Street and a couple of blocks from where FallFest had set up.

"I got the reservation at the Black Tomato, across the street, and then we can wander around after."

"Sounds great. And I'm starving. I just realized I didn't eat any lunch," Lizzie said, sliding out of the Jeep and waiting while he clicked the doors locked.

Mark groaned. "You mean, you're not going to be a cheap date?"

Lizzie laughed. "Sorry. Not tonight."

He took hold of her hand, and they crossed to the restaurant, where they were seated right away at a table overlooking the outside courtyard fountain and ordered drinks. Lizzie looked around the room. She'd always wanted to eat at the Black Tomato but hadn't done so in the year since it had opened. The décor was a modern mixture of black walls at two ends of the room, light gray on the others, platinum fixtures and bold splashes of orangey red for the chair upholstery, light coverings and of course, small bouquets of poppies on each table. She hoped the food was as memorable as the decorating style.

"I like this. It's very modern but still cozy," she commented.

"Just as promised in their ads. I've been wanting to come here for a long time. Couldn't find the right date."

Lizzie laughed.

"No, it's true. My brother, Mikey, has been trying to get me to sign up with an online dating service," Mark said as they waited for their drinks.

"What?" Lizzie couldn't hide the surprise in her voice. "You, Mr. Football Hero, Most Eligible Bachelor, and all that jazz?" She watched the subtle pink coloring infuse Mark's cheeks. It made him look young and shy, emphasizing the sexy dark brown eyes.

Mark shook his head and chuckled. "That was a long time ago, Lizzie."

"But there are still a couple of unmarried former cheerleaders in town. Well, one's divorced, so I hear. And what about the young and pretty Officer Intrepid?" She bit her tongue. She shouldn't have mentioned that one.

"Well, I don't date colleagues, especially those who work for me. Rule Number One. It can just mess up lives and careers so fast. And as for the cheerleaders and all, I may not have been away all that long, but it seems like a lifetime. Life's not full of parties anymore." He had been playing with the salt shaker but now looked at her. "I came back a changed man, Lizzie. I want a whole lot more substance in any relationship these days."

Their drinks arrived and each took a sip, then turned their attention to the menu. Lizzie couldn't help but feel pleased by what Mark had revealed. Not that she assumed they were headed toward a relationship. She was just happy to get to know the new Mark.

She ordered grilled salmon with mango salsa and mixed greens, then took a piece of hot, fresh cornbread that Mark offered.

"What was it like, Mark? Being in the army?"

A dark cloud passed over his face, and he took another sip. "I'll tell you someday, Lizzie. But not tonight, okay?"

She nodded. Okay, one topic to avoid. For now.

"I will tell you about the new little fellow in my life, though."

He was teasing her, waiting a bit before going on, giving her time to imagine all sorts of possibilities. None of which she wanted to dwell on. She looked expectantly at him.

"His name is Patchett and he's a sixteen-week-old bloodhound. I told myself he'd be useful on the job, but I really got him for the company. I used to have a hound when I was younger and man, they're some dog."

Lizzie could picture him with a dog at his side. Although he hadn't minded her cats, she knew he wasn't the type to own any. Not that you truly owned a cat.

"I can't wait to meet him. I'll bet he's so cute right now at this age and probably getting into everything."

"Into everything and wanting out at all hours of the night. I'm trying an experiment tonight and have him in his crate. I'm hoping he'll sleep till I get home. But I'm telling you to warn you, my conscience might get the better of me and I'll feel I need to go home and take him for a walk at some point."

"I could handle that," Lizzie said and toasted him with her glass.

He smiled and reached out for her other hand on the table.

Mark's roasted chicken with black-eyed peas and sweet potato casserole arrived, followed by Lizzie's order. They ate in companionable silence, decided to split a slice of pecan pie for dessert, had coffees and then walked the two blocks to the FallFest tents.

The entire south end of Pritchard Park, which covered two acres in the center of town, had been given over to the celebration. Named after one of the town's founders, Jethro

Clark Pritchard, the park featured a towering bronze statue in his image, guarding one of its main entries. The sun had just finished setting when they arrived, and Lizzie put her jacket on. A cool evening breeze had arrived with the setting sun, yet another reminder that even though the days thought it was still summer, the nights knew otherwise.

They walked hand in hand past the many craft tents, stopping to admire some wood carvings and later, a jewelry table. They could hear the bands starting up in the background as the crowds slowly started making their way to the main stage. The show that night featured a couple of local bluegrass bands and the Alabama Rivermen, one of the hottest blues groups in the country. It had been a small coup for the organizers to book them for the Ashton Corners event.

Running into so many people who knew them slowed their progress. Most looked surprised to see them together. "There'll be a new topic on the grapevine tomorrow morning, that's for sure," Lizzie said.

Mark grinned. "Yah. Hope you don't mind."

She smiled. "Not in the slightest."

They got in the ticket line, and Lizzie noticed Mark checking his watch on and off. "I'm guessing you're feeling a bit torn. Like maybe Patchett needs you?"

Mark looked sheepish. "That obvious, huh?"

"Listen, it would be fun to go to the concert, but I think a puppy is more important. Why don't we go take him for that walk?"

Mark squeezed her hand. "You're my kind of girl, Lizzie."

She smiled all the way to the car and his house.

Chapter Thirty-six

◇◇◇

It took me a moment to react. I was rooted to the spot with horror and couldn't seem to make my body obey me when my brain was commanding me to run.

A ROYAL PAIN—RHYS BOWEN

Lizzie spent the morning with her mother and stayed for lunch even though they were back to no responses. In between trying to think of things that might interest her mama, Lizzie thought about her date with Mark.

Mark's house turned out to be on Jardine Street, near the southern edge of town. He'd bought it when he'd returned to town and had been slowly renovating the sixty-year-old two-bedroom bungalow in his spare time. So far he'd managed to upgrade the kitchen with new appliances, slate tile floors, chopping block counters and a newly added dog donut bed tucked into a small alcove by the back door.

Lizzie had been impressed by what she saw as they toured the small bathroom, the focal point of current changes, the living room with the new paint job and awaiting a new floor, and the smaller bedroom, now his study, and finally the master bedroom. She gave it a cursory glance and walked a bit faster back to the living room with Mark chuckling right behind her.

Patchett had been eager to escape his confines and alternated between sniffing his way down the block and prancing, or the best a bloodhound could do along those lines. After the walk, they sat in the living room, each with a glass of brandy in hand, and talked until Lizzie tried to stifle a yawn and they realized the late hour. This time the goodnight kiss had been longer and more passionate.

Lizzie smiled at the thought, as she saw Evelyn back to her room. She settled her in a chair, turned on her radio and bent to give her a hug and kiss. "I may be back before next weekend, Mama. I may have some news for you. You just never know."

She drove over to pick up Sally-Jo, and then they were heading for Stoney Mills to search for a former librarian who may have helped her daddy with his research just before he died. Lizzie had gotten the idea while getting ready to visit her mama. Sunday usually attracted relatives into the seniors' homes, people were more talkative and could feed on each other's memories. Sally-Jo was keen to join in the search.

The plan was simple. Lizzie did an Internet search and downloaded a list of senior citizen residences in Stoney Mills. They'd do the rounds, wander around the great rooms and make small talk, hoping to find someone who either knew Frank Telford or Jefferson Perkins or could point them to a retired Stoney Mills librarian. And Lizzie realized that they were tracking two lines of enquiry: Telford and her daddy. Maybe they would intersect. Maybe not. Should be an easy task, though.

Not so. Their first stop, at the Rivercrest, took much more of their time than she had anticipated as the chatty residents all had something to say. Not, however, any of the information they wanted. Of course, sweet tea and cookies were being served, all afternoon as it turned out.

Sally-Jo, map in hand, gave directions as they drove to Quiet Pines, the second of five stops. "They're some mighty fine talkers just lying in wait at these places, you know. I think it might be fun to volunteer someday and just visit with them."

"That's sweet of you, Sally-Jo. I've seen notices for just such things in the paper from time to time. I'll admit, this is an eye-opener. It's a whole lot different from visiting my mama."

"Oh, sugar, I'll just bet it is. That must be heart wrenching for you. I was sorta wondering if you might find this too hard, visiting all these places." Sally-Jo reached over and patted her hand.

Lizzie shook her head. "Not at all. Just a tad frustrating, not being able to get the answers we're after."

"Yet."

"Right."

"I also think it wouldn't hurt to ask around about Carla Fowks, too. Try to find out if there actually was such a person."

"That's a great idea, Sally-Jo. I should have thought of that. We have a lot of unanswered questions about that manuscript."

"Well, Jacob's coming over tonight, so if we totally bomb out here, maybe he can figure out some way to track down people a lot faster."

Lizzie said, "Umm," and snuck a quick look at Sally-Jo, wondering how she would react to Jacob's announcement later this evening. She had tried putting herself in her friend's place but really had no idea how to react. She sighed and craned her neck for a look at the large white mansion to the right. It spoke to her of days of the Old South, true gentility, and women in hoop petticoats. "Wow, that's a beauty, isn't it?"

"It sure is," Sally-Jo agreed, "and it's also our next stop."

Lizzie pulled into the long curving driveway and parked next to a tall oak drenched in Spanish moss. A portico spanned the length of the front of the mansion and wrapped around the sides. Several sitting areas were configured for cozy conversations and a view of the sloping front lawn. "It sure does rival Molly's place."

"Mm-hmm. It's nice these old mansions are being used for good works."

To the left of the large front entrance hall, a comfortable waiting area held love seats and chairs, while to the right, a small white French Provincial desk displayed a sign-in book and a small placard inviting guests to go straight on through to the great room at the back.

"I always wanted to try calligraphy," Sally-Jo said, pointing to the placard.

"I don't have the patience. Give me PowerPoint any day."

They went through the large entryway, its double glass doors standing wide open, and followed the sounds of laughter to the back. About twenty people were seated or standing around in the great room, while a tiny, fragile-looking woman played jazz at a piano in one corner. A double-layered tea trolley sat to one side with pitchers of iced tea and extra glasses on it. The cookie plates sat on the numerous coffee tables between and in front of the dozens of chairs and settees.

Sunlight streamed in through the huge picture windows, and combined with the pale pink and greens in the room, gave the place a cheerful, airy feel.

"Very nice," said Sally-Jo.

"Probably very expensive, too," Lizzie suggested. "Well, let's go mingle, girl."

Lizzie picked up one of the plates and passed the cookies around to a small group seated at a settee and four chairs. It looked to Lizzie like three generations of one family. She asked if they minded if she joined them, and squeezed onto the settee when invited.

She started by introducing herself. "I'm looking for one of the former town librarians, and I'm just not sure which residence she's living in." *If she's even in one*, she silently added. "Worse still, I don't even know her name. She gave a small, self-deprecating laugh.

The oldest woman in the group, Nanny Carter she claimed she was, spoke right up. "You've come to the right person, girlie. I've lived in Stoney Mills all of my life, and I knowed who everyone is, even if we weren't ever introduced." She chuckled. "I used to own the one and only beauty salon for many years, and let me tell you, there wasn't much that escaped my noticing."

The others in the group laughed and agreed that was true.

"And I'm a great observer, too. For instance, I can see that you're surprised a beautician can afford to live in such a high-class place. Well, I saved whatever extra money wasn't going to my children, and I invested it wisely. I'm one smart cookie, you know. I'm now advising my chil'en and a lot of these old folks around here, on where to put their money. I'd be happy to do the same for you, too, sometime." She smiled and winked.

Lizzie, greatly encouraged, asked if she knew the woman.

"No, I didn't knowed no woman." She grinned. "Because it was a man. Malcolm Earnstly was his name. Still is, if I remember correctly. That is, he's still around. My best friend, Dolly Knowland, had a big crush on him when we were in middle school. He'd just come to town at that point in the early 1960s, a young'un himself, his first real job. Anyway, we used to hang out at the library a lot. But to no use. He broke her heart, Dolly's that is, by marrying Frances Murray. They had a small house just down the street from the library. Frances died some time back, right before Malcolm retired—he worked at that library his whole life—and he continued to live on his own until one day, he up and moved in with Frances's sister, Flossie Murray. He's still there, so I'm told. Now then, was that what you wanted to hear?" She looked pleased with herself.

"It most certainly was."

"She has a memory like a steel trap," said one of the

younger women, a daughter perhaps. Everyone nodded in agreement.

"And, just to prove it," Dolly continued, "they're a'livin' at 101 Main Street, right as you're entering town from the main highway. Now, another cookie would set just right."

Lizzie passed her the plate and continued to chat with them for a while, until she noticed that Sally-Jo had headed toward the door. Lizzie thanked them again, excused herself and caught up to Sally-Jo.

"Eureka," Lizzie said. "I have the name and address of the librarian."

Sally-Jo looked at her and smiled. "And I have a lead on Adele Fowks's daughter, Carla."

"Wow." Lizzie looked stunned. "You know what that means—if there really is a Carla Fowks, the manuscript is obviously a true story. I had a feeling all along it was, but now I'm feeling like I can't believe it."

Sally-Jo nodded. "I preferred it when it was a work of fiction. That story is just too sad to be true. But at least we know to keep looking."

"You're right. All these dead ends we've been hitting and now two leads in one day. But let's go find that librarian first. I need to know about my daddy."

They found the house easily, a modest white clapboard bungalow with a small front yard, and were delighted to find Malcolm Earnstly at home. They introduced themselves, and he invited them inside.

"You wouldn't necessarily find me at home on a Sunday afternoon," Earnstly told them, "but I had to get to trimming my shrubs in the front yard. You turn your back and those cedars just take over the place. It's not much, but it is my front yard."

"I can see you've put a lot of effort and care into it," Sally-Jo said.

They surveyed the small entry. The surprise was the color. Deep rose as far as the eye could see. The front room opened to the right, and a short hall on the left led to bedrooms and, at the end, the kitchen.

Lizzie began, after they had settled in the front room. "I'd like to ask you some questions going back to the time you were librarian, 1990 to be specific. Do you mind?"

He chuckled and his wire-framed glasses bobbed on a nose that was too large for his round face. Tufts of gray hair framed the sides and his ears, while the top of his head was a shiny bald beacon. "Not in the slightest. I'm quite flattered, although I may be a big disappointment, young lady. My mind's not as sharp as it used to be. Gone are the days when I could find a book without looking up the reference cards and even go direct to the page with a quote that someone asked about."

Lizzie smiled. "I understand, but it might be a big help."

"Ask away."

"Well, I'm wondering if by any chance you remember a man, he was a writer from Ashton Corners, and he may have been in the library doing some research."

"1990 you say? Anything special about this here man? Something that might twig my memory?" He scratched the top of his head.

"His name was Monroe Turner, he was thirty-eight years old, a tall, dark-haired man with dark-framed glasses. He often wore a gray fedora perched back from his face. He may have been working on a story for a magazine."

Earnstly sat in thought. It looked like he was chewing the inside of his mouth. It didn't take long before he connected.

"I do remember him. Of course I do. He was quite well known in these parts. He'd had some stories in *Life* magazine, as I recall. I read them all. I was quite flattered that he'd come to our library, in fact."

Lizzie let out the breath she'd been holding. "Wonderful. Now, do you happen to recall what he was researching?"

Earnstly thought some more. "No, I can't say it comes to me. I'm sorry. But if you leave me your name and number, I'll call if I do remember."

Lizzie smiled. "Thank you, I'd appreciate that." She wrote her contact information on a notepad she carried in her purse and gave it to him.

"Lizzie Turner. Hmm. Of course, you'd said that. Are you kin?"

"He was my daddy."

"Oh," Earnstly said, his already pale eyebrows disappearing in a frown. "I remember he died in a car accident, didn't he, not far from here?"

"That's right. It was on May 25, 1990. You wouldn't recall if he'd been in the library that day, would you?"

"No, I know he wasn't because I'd surely remember if I'd seen him the same day he died. I'm right sorry for your loss, Miss Turner."

"That's kind of you to say, Mr. Earnstly. And, it's Lizzie, please. We should go now, though. Thank you so much for letting us intrude on your day."

"Why it was a pleasure. Meeting Monroe Turner's daughter. A real pleasure."

They sat in the car a few minutes in silence. Lizzie said with a sigh, as she turned the key in the ignition, "At least I know Daddy was here on legitimate business. He was chasing a story."

"Say what?" Sally-Jo asked.

"Oh, I guess I didn't mention something Molly told me." She wondered if it was something she wanted to share with Sally-Jo. She decided it was. "You see, my mama thought maybe my daddy was having an affair, he kept going to Stoney Mills so frequently and not telling her why." She found the more often she talked about it, the less likely it seemed. "But he was on a story, although it is odd he wouldn't tell her about it."

"Maybe he was trying to protect her. It might have been

something dangerous. That is, after all, what your phone calls were about, weren't they? The story he was working on?"

Lizzie nodded. "I know the place but not the story. Guess I'll do some library research here one day after school. Now, what did you find about Adele Fowks's daughter? Should we try tracking her down while we're here?"

"Well, no one recognized her name, so I told the story—a father commits suicide and a few years later, so does the mother."

"And someone remembered that?" Lizzie shuddered.

"Uh-huh. But it's not a Stoney Mills story. It took place in Prescottville." Sally-Jo couldn't contain her excitement.

"That's about forty-five miles south, isn't it?"

"Something like that. Only my source wasn't sure if Carla grew up in Prescottville—his memory was kind of vague."

Lizzie thought a moment and then said, "It's getting too late to drive to Prescottville. I'll make time later this week." She put the car in gear and headed toward the exit before asking, "Do we know if Fowks is still her last name? Did she get married?"

Sally-Jo shook her head. "Haven't a clue."

"Well, maybe we can track it down in the county records, see if there was a marriage license. If not, maybe she's listed in the phone book."

Sally-Jo sighed.

"It's a good lead," Lizzie reassured her. "And at least we know now that the story is real. We're closer to the truth than before."

"Yeah, but there's still so much to find out."

Chapter Thirty-seven

◇◇◇

We all handle bad news differently.

BUZZ OFF—HANNAH REED

"How about we stop at the Rock Garden Cafe over there and have something to eat before heading home?" Lizzie asked as they drove slowly along the main street.

"I'm starving. Good idea. Jacob's coming over later tonight, but I've got plenty of time."

The restaurant was nearly empty. They both ordered an iced tea and an apple pecan chicken salad, and took their food to a table by the front window.

"So," Lizzie said, "to reiterate what we've found out today. One, my daddy was researching a story at the library here on at least one occasion. Two, Harlan Fowks lived in Prescottville and his daughter may still be there. We just have to figure out how to find her. And what? Ask her what happened to her daddy? Try to figure out how, if at all, that ties in with Telford's murder and our manuscript? And three, we've found out nothing further today about Frank Telford. I suppose two out of three isn't bad."

Sally-Jo laughed. "If I remember correctly, there's a song

with that title somewhere out there. But you know, when you lumped them all together like that, I expected you to go on about a connection. The more we learn, the more likely it seems. I mean, coincidence only goes so far."

Lizzie picked out a hot cornmeal roll from the basket that had just been set on the table. She added some butter and bit into it. "Yum. This is so good, I could be happy with three of them and nothing else."

"Calories, my girl. Think fewer carbs."

"Right," Lizzie agreed and took another bite. She laughed when Sally-Jo ate hers and rolled her eyes in delight.

"Okay, let's see how we can connect the dots then. We've both read the manuscript about Harlan Fowks. How does Frank Telford fit in? And how does my daddy fit in with both of them? If at all."

She thought back to the first few chapters of the manuscript. "What was the scheme that Fowks got involved with? How did he lose his money? Land development, wasn't it?"

Sally-Jo nodded. "I think so."

"Now, remember I mentioned the only thing about Frank Telford I'd found in the *Corners Colonist* was an ad for Telford Construction? Now, it may not be Frank's company, but I'll bet a construction company could be involved in land development. Don't you agree?"

Sally-Jo nodded again and leaned forward, excited. "That could be it. The connection. And maybe your daddy was doing a story on it. Maybe there was corruption or something like that and he was trying to blow it wide open."

Lizzie took a couple of bites of her salad, savoring the flavor. Everything tasted better when she didn't have to prepare it.

"You're right. We won't make assumptions nor jump to conclusions. First, we find out if Frank Telford and Telford Construction are one and the same. Then, maybe we can find a connection between the company and Harlan Fowks. As for my daddy, maybe if I assume that's the story he was

working on, I can find some way to confirm or deny it.
Although, according to what we know, the Fowkses' story
took place in the sixties, while my daddy was working on
his story in 1990. Were they the same story? If so, what got
him interested in it after such a long time? And regardless
of all that, I'd also like to know why he wouldn't, or couldn't,
share that fact with Mama."

They looked at each other a moment. Lizzie lowered her
eyes first. "Yeah, maybe he was doing the story and maybe
having an affair at the same time. I can't totally rule out
anything just yet."

They finished their meals and were back on the road
within an hour.

"I kind of enjoy driving at twilight," Lizzie said, trying
to find something soothing on the radio. She stopped changing the dial when she found the Mobile NPR station.

Sally-Jo was staring out the side window. "That's a right
pretty sunset over the river. See how it glows on the water?
No, I take that back. Don't see . . . I'll describe it to you."

Lizzie laughed. "Deal. This road's awful twisty. Your
role has now officially been changed from navigator to scenery describer."

"Well, there are no houses along this portion of the Tallapoosa River, listeners, and the sun is at the perfect angle,
glinting off the water and into this here reporter's eyes. The
usually fairly clear blue river waters have been enchanted by
a fairy's wand and sparkle with silvers and shades of pinks."

"Very nicely done," Lizzie said appreciatively, glancing
in her rearview mirror. "Continue, please."

"Well, if I look down the short but steep embankment, I
can see that glow continue on the wet rocks below. The tide
is obviously on its way out, leaving behind it a damp sheen
on the assorted vegetation and rock formations. Why do you
keep glancing in the rearview, Lizzie?"

"Just watching that car behind us. It seemed to come out
of nowhere and is gaining rapidly." She gasped. "It just cut

straight across that curve. I hope it doesn't catch us on a blind curve. I've nowhere to go to let it get by me."

Sally-Jo turned in her seat. "It looks like he's coming straight at us. Maybe you should speed up."

"I can't outrun something like that. This is just a little four-cylinder job. I'll just slow a bit going into that next curve and pull over as far as I dare."

She attempted to do just that as Sally-Jo gave her an inch-by-inch description of the car pulling up closer. "Good God, he's right in our trunk."

Lizzie glanced at her side mirror just in time to see this big black blur pull out beside her. Then, crash! The impact nearly knocked her car off the road. She hung on to the steering wheel, trying to keep her smaller Mazda from going over the edge. The rogue car veered into her once more, then raced off ahead as Lizzie fought in vain. The right front tire hit the verge, and the wheel yanked hard right as the Mazda nosed into a thicket of undergrowth. Lizzie and Sally-Jo were both thrown forward as the bumper smashed into something hard, setting off the airbags.

"Are you all right?" Lizzie asked, trying to extricate herself. Her hands shook so badly she had to take several deep breaths to try to calm down. She looked at Sally-Jo, who nodded despite the dazed expression on her face.

"Oh my God," Lizzie moaned. "You're sure you're all right? He did that deliberately. Oh, my poor car. Yikes, we'd better get out of the car in case it's not too stable. Let me go out first and check your side. You're sure you're okay?"

Sally-Jo finally answered. "Yup. The airbag did its thing. Now, if I can just get out of its clutches."

Lizzie groaned, more in frustration than pain as she cautiously pushed her door open, undid her seatbelt and wiggled out. The car sat at a forty-five-degree angle to the road, nose downward, nestled against a thick stump. She walked around behind it and checked the passenger side. Sally-Jo's window was still open. "It looks secure, but I can't tell what you'd be stepping out onto, so you'd better climb out my door, just to be safe."

She walked back around and helped Sally-Jo out, then grabbed her purse from the backseat. "I'll call the police."

She looked around first, wishing a car would come by. But not a big black one. She shuddered and suddenly felt like she'd never stop shaking. After a few deep breaths, she pulled her cell phone out.

"You keep an eye out for that big black car. If it's anything less sinister looking, flag it down. I'm calling Mark. It may not be his jurisdiction, but he can get us help."

She punched in his number and tried hard not to burst into tears when she heard him answer. In a shaky voice, she told him what had happened.

"Are you okay?" His voice sounded two octaves higher than normal. "Were you hurt? Either of you?"

"Not really. A bit bruised and shaken, but there's no blood or broken bones." She tried to make a joke of it but ended with a sob.

"Where are you?" Mark asked.

She gave him directions the best she could.

"I'll phone the local chief and get an ambulance on the way. I'm out the door as we speak. Just stay calm, sit down if you can find a safe spot and wait for help."

Lizzie and Sally-Jo hugged each other for a few moments, then found a couple of boulders not too far away and sat, as instructed.

The ambulance got there first, and the EMTs were giving them cursory checks when the Stoney Mills police cruiser pulled up. One officer went directly to the patients, while the other checked out the car. He then radioed for a tow truck and put out red cones to warn traffic of the single lane they'd encounter. He kept an eye peeled in case he'd need to direct cars along.

By the time Mark arrived, both women had been declared in good shape, although the EMTs strongly suggested they go with them to the hospital for observation. Both declined, but Mark assured the EMTs that he would take them to the Ashton Corners hospital on the way home. They had them sign waivers and then drove off.

Mark gave Lizzie a long hug and then went to talk to the officers. He identified himself and asked to take a look at the car that had just been hoisted onto the wrecker.

He took a minute to suggest to Lizzie and Sally-Jo they wait in his car, and then he examined the tire marks on the roadway and took a final look at the car's resting place.

Meanwhile, the officers were busy taking measurements and drawing diagrams in their notebooks. Mark asked that they send him a copy of the report, and then he drove the women back to Ashton Corners.

Lizzie sat in the front with Mark. He reached over and held her hand. "Tell me what happened," he said.

"Well, we were heading home from Stoney Mills"—he glanced at her sharply, which she ignored—"and I noticed this big black older-looking car coming up really fast behind us. When we came to that curve, I slowed a bit and pulled to the side as far as I could go, so he could get by us, but as he came alongside, he swerved right into my car. And then, he did it a second time. I lost control of the steering wheel with that one, and we ended up where you saw." She started shivering. He squeezed her hand. "I guess it's a good thing I'd slowed down, isn't it?"

Mark looked at her quickly but didn't answer. "What did you see, Sally-Jo?" he asked.

"When Lizzie mentioned this guy coming up fast, I turned around and sure enough, there he was. And all of a sudden, he pulled up beside us and slammed into us. And then a second time, just like Lizzie said. I couldn't see him leave. The airbag was blocking my view." Her voice shook. "He was nuts, Chief. Just plain nuts."

Mark drove in silence a few minutes then asked, "And what were you doing in Stoney Mills?"

Lizzie wondered how much she should tell him. Everything, she decided. Except maybe the bit about her daddy possibly having had an affair. She outlined the afternoon's events as Mark listened without comment. When she'd finished, he sighed.

"You talked to a lot of folks this afternoon," was his only comment.

"Yes, we did. Do you think one of them drove that car? It couldn't have been. They were all old folks. They couldn't drive like that."

Mark shook his head. "Now, if this is connected, and I'm not saying I think it is, they would all have younger relatives, wouldn't they?"

Lizzie had to agree with him. "So, you think it was tied in?"

"It sounds like it was. I mean, one swerve could just be carelessness. Maybe a drunk driver or something. But that second one was definitely deliberate. Maybe he was drunk and didn't want you reporting him after that first swipe. Maybe he tracked you out of town. They're both possibilities I'll be following up."

"You will? But it's not your jurisdiction, is it?"

"I'll just offer my assistance. I'm sure Burt Howard won't mind. I've done him a favor or two in the past."

"Burt Howard? Not the football player from Ashton Corners High School?"

Mark grinned. "Yeah, my old teammate. Comes in handy to have those old school connections once in a while. Now, I'm taking you both to the hospital so they can see if you have concussions or anything, and then I'll see you both home, if they let you go, that is."

Sally-Jo said from the back, "All right. As long as I get home in time to watch PBS *Mystery* at ten."

Lizzie smiled, relieved. Sally-Jo sounded just fine.

Chapter Thirty-eight

◇◇◇

The voices of the little gray cells are beginning to speak to Poirot.

APPOINTMENT WITH DEATH—AGATHA CHRISTIE

"You don't think the driver was trying to kill us, do you?" Lizzie asked as Mark pulled into her driveway. The question had been nagging at her all the way home.

They'd been examined in the emergency room at the Ashton Corners Memorial Hospital and released, although the intern had suggested that neither of them be alone overnight. Jacob had been waiting patiently in his car, parked in front of Sally-Jo's house, when they dropped her off.

"I sort of doubt it, Lizzie. Although he probably wouldn't have been upset if you'd landed in the river. But if he'd really wanted you dead, he would have turned around and finished the job." Mark shook his head. "I'm thinking it was more of a warning. The problem is, trying to find an older model black car with some front-end damage—I'd bet there are a lot of vehicles that match that description around this county. Now, I'm coming in and we're going to have a little talk and you're going to tell me in detail what you've been up to today.

"And then I'm going to sleep on your couch tonight. This time I mean it." He put up his right hand to stop her protest.

"I was just going to ask if you'd like a beer or tea."

Mark grinned as he turned off the ignition. "Beer. Talk. Sleep. Okay?"

Lizzie nodded and hoped he didn't see her smile.

The cats demanded to be fed before anything else could be done. Once she'd filled their bowls and refreshed the water dish, Lizzie got two beers out of the fridge and joined Mark at the kitchen table.

She ran through a travelogue of every stop she and Sally-Jo had made, of everyone they'd spoken with. Mark listened and made a few notes.

"I'd say you touched a raw nerve with someone today. It seems very unlikely to me that this is to do with something your daddy was writing, although we won't rule it out totally. So that leaves Frank Telford, which is the most logical, since he was murdered recently. Although, you may be onto something, tying Harlan Fowks and that manuscript with Telford. The question is, what is the tie-in?"

He took a long swig of beer and sat thinking. Lizzie was lost in her own thoughts. The realization that both she and Sally-Jo could have been seriously injured was sinking in. "Do you think my poor little car will be okay?"

Mark looked at her. "It's hard to say. It depends mainly on whether the frame's been bent. You'll probably need a new bumper at the very least. And new airbags. Maybe Harley Hoyt can fix it up. He put new life into my old Camaro."

"You still have that red Camaro from high school?"

"Yeah. I had it stored while I was away and then tooled around with it but wasn't getting very far. Harley gave me a hand, and now it's running just great. Have to do something about the paint job next, but that's costly."

"Wow, that was some flashy car, Mark Dreyfus. And double whammy when you were wearing your football outfit. A real chick magnet." She started laughing, feeling suddenly much better than she had in a few hours.

Mark joined in. "That was my aim, in those days. We'd all pile into my car and Ritchie Day's Mustang—remember Ritchie's Mustang?—and then spend the rest of the evening cruising down Main Street before heading up to Brower's Point."

"And we won't go into what went on there."

Mark shook his head. "We surely won't." He sat watching her for a couple of minutes. When he spoke, his voice was devoid of humor. "I'm going to start looking into all of these connections tomorrow, first thing. And I want you to promise me, you'll leave it all to me. No more excursions to Stoney Mills, asking questions. Just consider yourself lucky that it's me hearing this and not Officer Craig." A smile tugged at the corner of his mouth.

Lizzie looked at him and shuddered. "Yikes, you're right. I couldn't face going through that. And I'm quite happy to leave it to you, now that you're looking in the right direction." She yawned and tried to cover her mouth with her hands.

He looked like he was going to respond but changed his mind, shaking his head instead. "I'd say it's bedtime." He went into the living room and looked at the couch. "This'll do just fine."

"I do have a daybed in the spare room you can use."

"This is okay. I can make do with a blanket and a pillow."

Lizzie nodded and trudged upstairs to get them for him. When she came back down, he was checking all the windows and doors. She removed the extra pillows from the couch and set it up for him, watching as he removed his gun and laid it on the coffee table, within reach. She turned back to him, at the door.

"What about Patchett?"

"I made a quick call to my neighbor, who'll walk and feed him. Jeff's been keen to do it and has a key."

Lizzie nodded. "Thanks again, Mark."

He smiled. "A light breakfast will do me just fine."

The cats weren't quite sure what to make of the newest addition to the morning routine. Lizzie had fed Brie and Edam, then cooked up a breakfast of scrambled eggs, bacon, hash browns and toasted corn bread for the two nonfelines in the house.

They were just about finished when the phone rang. Lizzie answered and glanced up at the ceiling when she heard Bob Miller's voice. Of course he knew what had happened. Everyone in Ashton Corners was probably finding out about it at this very moment, she thought. She gave him the short version and assured him she and Sally-Jo were both fine.

"This is going too far, Lizzie. We need to have a meeting of the Ashton Corners Mystery Readers and Cheese Straws Society this very evening. Put our heads together and try to put an end to all this."

"Yes, Bob." Lizzie agreed when she finally got a word in edgewise. "Would you be able to call everyone about that?"

"That's what I'm going to do, and meanwhile, young lady, you stay around folks today. Don't go off secluded anywhere. And I'm going to give that chief of police a call and tell him to keep some cruisers in your vicinity."

"Why, he just happens to be here, Bob. You can tell him right now, if you want," Lizzie said all innocently.

"No, ma'am. I'm going to head on down to his office and have a talk to him."

"You might want to give him a couple of hours, Bob. He has another stop after here." She looked at Mark, eyebrows raised.

He looked down at his clothes and nodded.

"Thanks for calling, Bob. See you later."

Mark waited until she sat down again before talking. "I take it the illustrious former chief will be paying me a visit."

"He will. And I don't want to spoil it for you. He can tell you himself what you should be doing."

Mark grinned ruefully. "Seems that's the only kind of conversation I have with him."

"Seems Bob has not-so-fond memories of you. Would that be before, during or after your Camaro days?" she asked teasingly.

Mark turned beet red. "Yes."

Lizzie grinned. "More toast?"

Mark shook his head. "Thanks, but no. This was delicious, in fact a much better breakfast than I usually have, but I'd better head home and change so that I present a dutiful appearance for all my visitors. Now, stay close to people today. Don't go off on your own anywhere."

"That's what Bob said."

Mark grunted. "Did I hear there's a book club meeting tonight? At Molly's?"

Lizzie nodded to both questions.

"I'll have a car posted outside, and it will follow you home."

"Is this more personal service?"

"Afraid not, Lizzie. I'm guest speaker at the chamber of commerce meeting tonight." He shook his head. "Who would have thought it? Anyway, someone—I'm not sure who's on tonight—will be keeping a close watch on your place all night."

"Thanks, Mark. I appreciate it." She walked him to the door. "All of it."

He looked at her a moment, inspecting her face, then gave her a light kiss on the lips. Her lips tingled as she watched him get in his car. It was then she noticed the manila envelope sticking out of the mailbox. Mark wasn't a light sleeper, that was for sure.

She was dying to read the pages, but one glance at the

clock had her racing upstairs to get ready for school. She had a quick shower and threw on some black cotton pants and a taupe chintz blouse with small black polka dots on it, and grabbed a three-quarter-sleeved black sweater from the drawer. She cringed as a sharp pain shot up through her neck. She rotated her head slowly and did a few gentle shoulder shrugs before dressing. She'd have to avoid sudden moves for a day or so, it seemed.

She called Sally-Jo, hoping she hadn't yet left for school, and was pleased that she could get a lift in with her.

As soon as she hung up, the phone rang, and the caller ID showed it was George Havers. "Good to hear from you, George. What's up?" Lizzie asked.

"Lizzie, I'm sorry to bother you so early, but I wanted to find out how you are. I heard all about the accident. You're not hurt, are you?"

"Thanks, George, but I'm just fine. My car is another matter, though."

"Chief Dreyfus's office wouldn't give out too many details, and I'm not trying to pry for more, believe me. I just wanted to make sure you weren't hurt. I also wanted to let you know that I've not had any luck finding out what story your daddy was chasing. I'm real sorry about that."

"That's all right, George. I do know the story is the reason he was over in Stoney Mills so often and that it might have had something to do with Telford Construction and one of their development schemes."

"Telford again . . . hmm. That gives me a bit more to work with. Let me give it another try, and I'll get back to you as soon as I can. Bye now."

He'd hung up before she had a chance to answer. The phone rang again, but she let it go to message this time as Sally-Jo pulled up out front.

Word had spread. Several of the teachers stopped her in the hall, asking if she was all right. Even the principal, a quiet, dour-faced man in his fifties who had surprisingly

progressive ideas, stopped by the staff room at lunch to ask
how she was. By the time her day had ended, she was happy
to escape the concern of her friends. She noticed the police
cruiser parked on the street, with a view of the front door,
the back and the parking lot. She waved when she recognized Officer Craig. She bet that really burned her, having
to babysit Lizzie. That made Lizzie's day.

"Could you drop me at Hoyt's garage, please, Sally-Jo?
He has a loaner for me," Lizzie said.

"Sure thing." She yawned. "Sorry, I had a bit of a late
night. Jacob stopped over. And then Bob Miller phoned to
tell me, us, about the special book club meeting tonight. It's
sure a good thing that the literacy classes are cancelled
tonight. Talk about timing. Anyway, I'm gathering you won't
need a lift to the meeting tonight."

"No. Thanks for this, though. I appreciate it. Is your
shoulder still bothering you?"

Sally-Jo shrugged a couple of times. "Not really. I think
it's just sore to the touch. It hasn't stopped movement or
anything."

"And how is life in general?"

Sally-Jo looked over at her. "You know, don't you? Tell
me, how do you know?"

"It came up in conversation with Jacob . . . I sort of
backed him into a corner. How are you taking it?"

Sally-Jo sighed. "Well, I'm angry that he didn't tell me
he was married, but I guess I understand. I think it was moving a bit too fast, anyway. We'll still go out now and then,
but we need to take our time in getting to know each other.
And he can just get his life in order before anything deeper
forms between us."

"That sounds wise." She glanced over and saw that
Sally-Jo didn't look too broken up. "You know, changing
the subject, I'm real hesitant about saying too much tonight.
I don't want the others to get too involved, just in case this
escalates in any way."

Sally-Jo looked a bit shocked. "Oh my gosh, what do you think could happen?"

Lizzie shrugged. "Nothing, I hope. But if whoever ran us off the road hears that some of us are still snooping, who knows what they might do."

"I guess you're right. We'll tell them what happened but say the police are taking over from now on. That is right, isn't it?" She glanced at Lizzie, a worried expression on her face.

"Yes, it is," Lizzie assured her. She wondered, though, if the latest installment of the manuscript might have some answers that would tell her what to do next.

Chapter Thirty-nine

◇◇◇

It all seemed like too much of a coincidence to be coincidental.

PLASTER AND POISON—JENNIE BENTLEY

Lizzie should have realized by the weight of the envelope that it held only one chapter this time. She skipped to the last page. Nothing indicated it was "the end." Maybe this really was a work in progress and one chapter was all that could be managed at this point.

She started reading, moving over slightly in the chair to let Brie snuggle in beside her while Edam leapt onto her lap. She waited until they'd both settled and then read.

Her Mama's funeral hadn't been over by much when a lady in a black coat and hat with a feather in it came up to Carla and told her to get her coat and belongings. This was the lady from the Children's Welfare office that Carla had been told about. She looked around at her neighbors. There was no one she wanted to hug or say good-bye to, so she picked up her small suitcase and followed the big lady out the door and down the steps and into the big, black shiny car.

They drove straight to an older two-story house on the other side of town. Carla followed the lady into the house and was told that Pete and Harriet Hopfore were her new folks. And then the lady left. Carla could hear children upstairs. It sounded like quite a few.

Harriet yelled up for the oldest, a boy named Tony, to come on down and get Carla settled in her room. He told her to follow him on upstairs, showed her a room with four single beds, two big chests of drawers and not much else. He told her to drop her suitcase and come and meet the rest of the kids.

There were six in total, counting her and all foster kids. He then told her she didn't really have to bother unpacking her suitcase. Nobody stayed too long at the Hopfore house.

Her childhood was neatly tied up in a few lines about foster parents and moving around a lot until suddenly, at the bottom of the second page, Carla returned to her hometown, a young woman of seventeen, a young son in tow.

She eventually gave up trying to exorcise the ghosts of the past, escaping instead into a bottle. By the time her son, Duwo she nicknamed him, was himself a teenager, Carla had been through a succession of men, jobs and welfare workers. When Duwo was removed from her care, she checked into a rehab facility, and years later, back out in the world and sober, she started writing her life story as therapy, realizing that she needed to exorcise all the demons from the time of her parents' suicides. She'd spent so many years blaming the men who'd swindled him, she'd totally let it ruin her life. And her son's.

Insight often comes too late, she ended with in the final paragraph. The residual damage is sometimes the worst part of it all. And one must try desperate means to make amends.

* * *

"Hold up, folks. I call this meeting of the Ashton Corners Mystery Readers and Cheese Straws Society to order," Bob said above the chattering of six highly excited people in Molly's library.

Molly sat next to Lizzie. In fact, she'd stuck close to her, a plate of shortbread cookies in hand, ever since Lizzie had arrived an hour earlier. She'd pumped Lizzie for every detail about the accident and frowned at what she considered a less-than-satisfactory conclusion.

"It's one thing for a complete stranger to be murdered," she'd said. "That was pretty horrific. But when someone you care a great deal about is in jeopardy, that's the stuff of nightmares. I want you to promise me, young lady, that you will not put yourself in such a situation again."

"Stop investigating?"

"Well, that would be the smart thing to do. Leave the danger to the police. But I have a feeling you won't give up that easily. So my main concern would be the traipsing off and asking questions. I hate to sound sexist, but promise me you'll take a man with you next time."

Molly had looked so distressed that Lizzie had bit back her immediate retort and said instead, "That's probably a good idea, Molly. I'll see who's arm I can twist."

"I suppose if you asked Mark, he'd forbid you from doing it."

"That's a good guess. I'll think on it, Molly." She'd squeezed her friend's hand and gone back to setting the eats out on trays.

Now, they were waiting for everyone to quiet down. Finally, Bob said, "All right, you two. Let's have it. What were you up to yesterday before all hell broke loose?"

Lizzie explained the basics, while Sally-Jo added some of the color. When they'd finished, everyone sat silently for several minutes. Stephanie took a long drink from her glass of water.

Andie was the first to break the silence. "Well, that sucks. You're getting so close, I know it, and then that has to happen."

Lizzie nodded.

Andie drummed her fingers on the arm of the chair, then said, leaping up, "Molly, can I use your computer? I just want to see if anything new has turned up on all those names I've been searching on."

"You sure can, honey," Molly said and led Andie to the small anteroom off the library that she used as an office.

Bob said, "I'll check out Prescottville and also Stoney Mills again. I don't want you two anywhere near that town again." He looked over at Jacob. "Maybe you could distract our Sally-Jo here and get her mind off investigating. I know I'll have to work fast if we want Lizzie to back off." He looked at Lizzie sternly. "This is getting rough, little girl, and you don't want to be around it."

Lizzie took great care in choosing her words. "I'm curious as to what you know about all this, Bob."

"What do you mean?" he sputtered. His bushy graying eyebrows drew together as his mouth dipped in a frown. His glasses perched precariously near the tip of his nose.

"Well, it's been bothering me for a couple of days now. When we last discussed the manuscript, you seemed to drop out of the conversation, and you were the first to ask to take the story home to read some more." It had been bothering her, but she wasn't sure if she was making more out of it than necessary.

"I think this investigating thing is getting you going, girl," he finally said, with a small laugh. "You got to watch out, you'll be seeing conspiracies and bad guys all over the place. And speaking of which, here's your manuscript."

Molly had come back into the room during the conversation. "No, she's right, Bob. You were mighty quiet there. What is there you're not telling us?"

Bob looked at her and opened his mouth, then shut it quickly. "That's a fine thing, Molly Mathews," he huffed, "accusing me of all sorts. You two ladies don't know what you're talking about. Now, getting back to what I was saying, you leave the nosing around to me from now on. Meeting adjourned."

He grabbed his baseball cap from the floor beside his chair and headed for the door, snatching a couple of cheese straws from the table as he walked by.

Molly sat staring at the door he'd closed behind himself. "Well, I'll be."

Stephanie's knitting needles clicked faster. "I think y'all have gone and hurt his feelings."

"Harrumph," Molly said. "His feelings have such thick calluses grown around them, there's no fear of that. Now, how about we discuss books, since you're all here?"

Andie called out at that moment. "Lizzie, come on in here and have a look at what I found."

They all followed Lizzie and hovered while Andie read from the screen. "It's a Facebook page in Harlan Fowks's name. It wasn't here a few days ago when I checked. It shows his picture—here, take a look."

They all crowded around. "He looks to be in his late twenties or early thirties," Jacob said. "That's quite an old photo, though. Very grainy."

"That would be the right age for the Harlan in the manuscript," Lizzie said.

"There's nothing here except for this one posting on his wall," Andie continued. "If you want a study in injustice, here's Harlan Fowks. Died at age thirty-two by his own hand, unable to bear the shame and the hardship his family suffered because of his trying to better his lot in life. His real murderers are the unscrupulous land developers who sucked him into their schemes. Isn't it about time the real devils paid?' "

Andie finished reading and no one said a thing. Finally, she said with a small laugh, "They always say end a Facebook comment with a question. Try to draw readers in. Nobody's posting here, though."

Lizzie shivered. "That's so sad but also very scary. I'll tell Mark about it." She was suddenly very anxious to get home and reread those last pages of the manuscript.

Chapter Forty

◇◇◇

He had our full attention now, and he knew it. I felt a jolt of dismay.

DEAD OVER HEELS—CHARLAINE HARRIS

Lizzie glanced at the clock. One A.M. She yawned noisily as she set the manuscript aside. She'd wanted to check it out again and see if she'd missed anything. Nothing leapt out at her.

That's it, Lizzie thought. *It is the end, but it's also a beginning, perhaps.* Would she ever meet this person? And what was Carla's next move?

Lizzie slowly got ready for bed and crawled in but lay awake wondering what it might be. She was seriously thinking about stopping in at the health food store and snagging some organic sleeping pills. This had to stop. She needed her sleep, after all.

The phone rang, jolting her totally awake. Two A.M. She sat up and reached for it, wondering what her mystery caller would say this time. She thought she was prepared.

She wasn't prepared to hear Molly's voice, however. "Lizzie . . . I'm so sorry to wake you, honey, but I've just had the most upsetting thing happen. I just needed to talk to you while I'm waiting for the police."

"The police? What's wrong?" Lizzie screeched.

"Well, I'm hoping it's not much, but my house alarm just went off. The alarm company called to tell me the back patio door had been breached and that the police are on the way. I'm supposed to stay on the line with them, but I wanted to talk to you instead."

"I'm on my way over, Molly. Where are you? Upstairs, I hope?"

"Yes. I'm in my en suite, and I've locked the door. Oh, I hear the sirens now. I believe the police have arrived."

"Molly, stay put until the police have searched the house and come and find you. Don't go out in the hall. The guy may still be there."

"I know, Lizzie. I'll stay put. I can hear the police shouting downstairs. You shouldn't bother coming over."

"There's no way I'm not coming over. Where are the police now?"

"I hear them on this floor, probably in the hall outside my bedroom. Oh, they're in the bedroom. I'd better hang up now. I'll see you soon then."

Lizzie didn't even have time to say good-bye. She leaped out of bed, scattering the cats, and quickly pulled on some yoga pants she used for running, and a sweatshirt. She grabbed her purse and keys and flew out the door.

The red and blue strobe lights of the police cruisers welcomed Lizzie, though the police officers were less than happy to see her. She was explaining to one of the unknown officers that Molly had called her, when she heard Mark's voice call out that it was okay for her to enter the house.

"How is Molly? Is she all right?" she asked Mark as soon as she got to him.

"She's just fine, Lizzie. She's had a fright, but she's not hurt."

"What happened? She said someone broke in? Did you catch the guy?"

He put his hands on her shoulders. "Slow down and take a deep breath. Now, there was a break-in. Someone smashed the window in the back door and managed to stick his arm through and unlock the dead bolt from the inside, but he was gone by the time we got here. Guess the alarm scared him off. He left a calling card of some blood on the broken glass, though."

"Good. You can find out from that who he is, can't you?"

Mark nodded. "But only if he's in our data system, and it takes awhile, too. This isn't like a TV show, where it's all figured out in an hour."

Lizzie slumped. "I know. It's just such a frightening thing to have happen. Can I see Molly?"

"She's in the library with Officer Craig."

"That's sure to soothe her," Lizzie muttered as she went along the hall to the library. She flung the door open and was surprised to see Officer Craig kneeling beside a seated Molly. It actually sounded to Lizzie as if Officer Craig murmured soft and encouraging words.

"Molly, are you sure you're okay?" Lizzie asked, making her way across the room.

Molly rose and opened her arms to Lizzie. "I'm fine, honey. I shouldn't have bothered you. But thank you for rushing over." They hugged each other for a couple of minutes until Officer Craig broke the silence.

"I'll just get back to the investigation, Ms. Mathews." She nodded at Lizzie and left the room.

Lizzie looked at Molly, unable to hide her surprise.

"I know, I know," Molly said. "She's been very supportive and kind. Really a totally different side of our intrepid officer. Now, you have school tomorrow, and I'm already feeling silly for calling you. You should go home and get some sleep."

"I can sleep tomorrow night," Lizzie said, wrapping her arm around Molly's waist. "Let's see if we can get you a cup of hot tea, and I'll wait with you."

The young officer at the door to the kitchen advised them not to enter, so they returned to the library, where Molly opened the doors of a solid oak credenza tucked in a small alcove next to the door to the restroom. She pulled out a bottle of brandy and two glasses.

"Claydon had a stash in every room . . . for emergencies. I'd say this qualifies. I hope this brandy is still okay. I don't know when I last used it." She poured them each a small amount and took a tentative taste. "Seems fine."

They sat across from each other and sipped.

"I wonder if this is tied to the Telford case," Lizzie said.

Molly held her glass up to the light and watched the colors swirl. "Or it could be a random attempt at a break-in. They don't happen very often around here, but it's possible."

"But if it is part of the Telford thing, why break in here? Was Telford actually looking for something the night he came here and didn't find it? And this is his partner, giving it another try?"

"Oh, honey, you do like your mysteries, don't you?" Molly asked with a small laugh. "That would make a lovely Agatha Christie plot, though. The secret that only two know about, secretly hidden in the house of the unsuspecting widow, originally secreted away there by . . . whom?"

"Maybe one of them was a tradesperson working here at some point and needed a hiding place for this item?"

"Or maybe the widow had acquired something of value or incriminating and had hidden it. Which I haven't, by the way."

Lizzie sat forward, happy to play this game. "But what if that widow then tried to blackmail these two guys?"

"Why wouldn't they bump her off then, rather than each other?"

"Good point." Lizzie took another sip. "I'm glad you'll be safe, in that case," she said with a chuckle.

Molly smiled. "Safe from everything but our imaginations."

The door opened and Mark joined them. "I think we've gotten about all we can from here, Ms. Mathews. The guys will board up your door; you should get it replaced later in the morning. I'll have someone here very early to check the outside further by light of day and take some footprint impressions, if there are any. You might want to go to a hotel for the rest of the night, though."

"Or my place," Lizzie offered.

Molly shook her head. "No to both suggestions. With thanks. But I feel quite safe here. I still have my alarm system, and it worked beautifully. I wouldn't get any sleep anywhere else, not that I'll sleep the rest of the night anyway. Thank you, Chief."

Mark nodded and looked at Lizzie. "Can I give you a lift home?"

"No thanks. I do have my loaner car, and I've had only a tiny bit of brandy, I swear. I'll just hang around a bit until Molly's ready to call it a night." She walked Mark to the front door.

"I'm just relieved Molly's all right. Do you think he'll try to come back?"

"Not tonight, that's for sure. But it depends on what he was after."

"Do you think it's linked to the Telford case?"

"I've no way of knowing that, Lizzie. And don't you go trying to make any connections, you hear? I'm leaving a car here to follow you home when you're ready to go. There's still the matter of the car accident, you know."

Lizzie squeezed his arm. "I do know. Thanks, Mark."

Although she didn't like to dwell on it, she was thankful to see the headlights of the police cruiser in her rearview mirror as she drove slowly home in the dark.

Chapter Forty-one

◇◇◇

The realization settled in my stomach like ice, and I held my breath and inched back toward the front door. I should have moved faster.

TOMB WITH A VIEW—CASEY DANIELS

The next morning, Lizzie couldn't seem to get her brain functioning. Lack of sleep would do that, she thought. She'd spent too much time deciding what to wear and was now struggling to find jewelry to match the pale pink tank top and three-quarter-sleeved blouse she'd teamed with navy cotton pants and a pair of low-heeled navy slides. Silver hoop earrings would do the trick, she concluded. Less was often more with Lizzie when it came to jewelry these days. She closed the box, then opened it again and chose a hot pink shell bracelet to keep up her energy level.

The phone rang, and George was once again on the line. "I've got some surprising news for you, Lizzie. I found that development that Telford was putting together. There wasn't much but it was in the courthouse records because someone had tried suing the partners a couple of years before Fowkses' suicides. It was thrown out of court, not enough evidence. But the partners in TC Developments, as it was called, were Frank Telford; a Jefferson Perkins, who I couldn't find a lot of information about except that he's deceased; and Claydon Mathews."

Lizzie was speechless. She couldn't believe that Claydon had been involved in something underhanded that had led to two deaths. That had to be the connection between Telford and the manuscript. She managed to thank George for his help and then sank onto the bed. Was that what her daddy had been investigating? It would sure explain why he hadn't told Mama anything about it. How could he share such painful news about the husband of her close friend? Oh, Mama . . . no affair! She was certain.

But did it explain what Frank Telford was doing at Molly's house? Had she lied? Had she known Telford all along and was trying to save Claydon's reputation?

But who had killed Telford? The author of the story? Was that how she—or he—planned to make amends? But why share this all with Lizzie, if that were the case?

There were just too many questions. It was all too confusing. Lizzie couldn't believe Molly would lie to her, though. Not Molly.

She had to talk to her. She glanced at the clock. The reading demonstration she had planned for one of the fifth-grade teachers was over an hour off. She'd make time.

She grabbed her purse and tote and ran out to the courtesy car.

Part of her brain played with the manuscript. She was certain the answer lay there. Otherwise, why send it? She was certain it all tied together—Telford's scheme, Claydon Mathews being part of it, the story about Harlan Fowks and the tragedy his family suffered because of his association with Telford and Mathews. Where was Carla these days? And her son, Duwo? How old would he be, and was he with her? The answer stared her in the face, she knew it . . . but what was it?

She turned onto Molly's street. She hadn't counted on Bob being there, too. Oh well, she thought, pulling up behind his SUV, he'd been acting strangely because maybe he already knew about the connection. She'd make sure he didn't run out this time until he'd told all.

She stood beside her car for a moment, trying to spot the police cruiser that should have been parked somewhere close by. She'd noticed one farther down the street at what appeared to be a car accident, but where was Molly's protection?

She started walking toward the front door and glanced at the front seat of the SUV as she walked past. Bob wasn't in the house with Molly. He sat slumped over the steering wheel. She called his name, in case he was napping. No response.

Heart attack. Lizzie's own heart pounded as she pulled open the door and tried rousing him. Should she pull him out and start CPR? As she climbed on the pullout step and tried to reach behind him, she noticed a huge welt on the back of his head, with blood seeping from it. He'd been hit. She eased him back, made sure he was breathing okay. She reached in her tote to take out her cell but realized she'd left it at home. She'd have to use Molly's phone to get help. Or should she just run down the street and get the cop?

But what about Molly? Whoever had hit Bob might be in with her.

Lizzie had to get in there fast. The front door opened to her touch. She slid it partly open and went in. She could make out Molly's voice in the kitchen. Who was she talking to?

Lizzie decided to call 911 first. What she hadn't counted on was the intruder being on the phone. He heard the click as she picked up the receiver in the library.

"You'd better hang up. Right now. And get on back here to the kitchen or your friend is dead," a familiar voice ordered.

Lizzie's hand shook as she replaced the receiver. She knew that voice, and she knew he was serious. She looked desperately around for some inspiration as she walked toward the kitchen.

"Hurry up!" he yelled from behind the door.

She took a deep breath to steady her nerves and pushed open the kitchen door. "Dwayne Trowl," she said, trying to keep the jitters out of her voice. "This isn't the way."

Dwayne had Molly backed up against the kitchen counter. He stood about four feet from her, a large, menacing black gun in his right hand.

"Now you just shut up, Ms. Lizzie Turner, literacy teacher and nosy bitch. You get over there by Ms. Molly Mathews." He waved the gun at her, and she quickly obeyed.

Lizzie's heart pounded in her chest as she grabbed Molly's ice-cold hand. She glanced at her friend and saw that even though her face was deathly white, her mouth was pinched shut in that determined way of hers. Lizzie squeezed Molly's hand hard so that Molly looked over at her. Lizzie shook her head ever so slightly. She didn't want her friend doing something foolish.

Dwayne was checking out the back windows, his gun still pointed at them. "Is anyone with you?" he demanded. "What are you doing here?"

Lizzie thought she'd better keep him talking until . . . what? She wasn't sure, but she knew she had to do it. Maybe she could shock him, throw him off his guard. Hopefully, the truth could do that.

"I came here to tell my friend Molly the story about Frank Telford and TC Developments," she began. She had his full attention. "And about how a man named Harlan Fowks lost all his money with this company and eventually committed suicide. And how his wife eventually did the same, leaving a six-year-old daughter, Carla, all alone. And how that girl grew up and had a son . . . a son named Dwayne Trowl."

Molly gasped and Dwayne stomped toward Lizzie, stopping a few inches away, waving the gun. He glared at her a few minutes, without saying anything. She tried to read something in his face that would give her a clue as to what he was thinking. No hints there.

"Yeah? So how'd you find all that out? Who told you about my grandpops? You think you're also some kind of super spy?" He laughed and backed away.

"Your mama told me, Dwayne."

He stopped abruptly. The look in his eyes turned to bewilderment. "Whaaa? You're a liar! She wouldn't. No way. My mama wouldn't do no such thing."

"She's written a story all about it, Dwayne, and she's been sending me a few chapters every couple of days. That's why I'm here now. Yesterday's final chapter told me all about you."

"She didn't," he yelled, pointing the gun at her. "My mama wouldn't tell no one about all this."

Lizzie took a deep breath. "But I know the story, don't I?"

"You think you're so smart. Well, you know, I'm smart, too. I know you don't believe that, what with my taking the literacy class and all. You think I'm real dumb and you can trick me and get away. Well, there's a reason I took those classes, so's I could get into this house and see just what my family was missing out on. And I outsmarted the cops, too. I've got smarts where it counts." He tapped the side of his head with his gun.

Lizzie tensed, anticipating a gunshot that didn't happen.

"I figured what the cop outside needed was a distraction, and a neighbor was very obliging, leaving her keys in the car. So I just drove it down the street a bit and straight into a parked car. That got the cop's attention. I hid in the bushes and snuck back here. But that old goat came driving up at the same time."

"What old goat?" Molly demanded.

"I didn't mean to kill him, but he shouldn't have gotten in the way."

"Who?" Molly almost screamed.

"It's Bob, Molly. But he's not dead." She squeezed Molly's hand again. "And we don't want anyone to die today, Dwayne," she said, moving a step closer to him.

Dwayne backed up. "Just stop right there or I'll use this. I guarantee y'all that."

Lizzie stayed in place. *Just keep him talking.* "So, what's the point now, Dwayne? We know about what happened. I think you'd better just drop the gun, and we'll help you all we can."

Dwayne's face closed into a wicked sneer. He kept the gun pointed at her. He said in a low voice, "There you go, thinking you're so smart again. But do you know about the other guy?" He swung sideways to face Molly. "The other bastard who cheated my grandpops out of all his money and his life. That man was your husband, Claydon Mathews."

Molly gasped. "It's not true. Claydon would never knowingly harm anyone."

Dwayne straightened to his full height. "Well, it is true. They both swindled my grandpops, and he committed suicide and so did my grandmama. And it's all their fault. Frank Telford paid with his life, and you"—he waved the gun at Molly—"were supposed to pay with cash since your husband's already dead. But Telford wouldn't have none of it. He tried to stop me from telling you all about it. That just got him dead. Now, I'll just take that money. You've got plenty. I want it, right now."

"And do what?" Lizzie asked. "What will you do with us?"

He looked confused for a moment, just the amount of time it took Lizzie to grab the thick Agatha Christie compendium from the bookcase beside her and hurl it at Dwayne's hand. He let out a yelp and dropped the gun, which slid across the floor toward the door. He dove for the gun. Lizzie grabbed Molly's arm and pulled her into the hall. She heard the back door burst open and Bob's bellow.

They peered back into the kitchen and found Bob,

spread-eagled across Dwayne's back, both arms struggling toward the gun. Lizzie ran over, kicked Dwayne's arm away and grabbed the gun. The bang startled them all. Lizzie's arm had been flung upward by the kickback. She grabbed the gun with her other hand, too.

Dwayne lay absolutely still.

"I didn't kill him, did I?" Lizzie whispered.

Bob chuckled, then grimaced in pain. "Nope. I think you killed that there chair." Bob struggled up so that he was kneeling with one knee pushed into Dwayne's back. He grabbed Dwayne's left arm and pulled it behind him. "Do you think you could gently put that gun down way over there on the counter—real careful now—and then grab this guy's right arm and pull it toward me?"

Lizzie did as asked. Molly arrived with a tea towel in hand. "Here, let me tie up his hands," she said, kneeling beside Bob. "Lizzie, you keep sitting on him. I'm going to take care of Bob's head, here." She helped him stand and got him over to the banquette.

"You'd better call the police, too," Lizzie suggested.

"It's been taken care of, young lady," Bob said before laying his bleeding head down on his arms, crossed on the table.

Chapter Forty-two

◇◇◇

One thing at a time, she told herself. One thing at
a time.

CHAPTER & HEARSE—LORNA BARRETT

Mark finished the beer he was drinking as he finished
his story. Lizzie set his empty glass in the kitchen sink
and turned to face him. "You mean, Dwayne's mama sent
me the manuscript because she wanted him stopped?"

"That's how she tells it. She's been in and out of detox
and rehab several times over the years but for the past five
months, she's been living in a rooming house on Wilton.
She started writing the story as therapy and then decided to
send it to you when she got worried about what Dwayne was
up to. She knew he'd been scheming, and after he lost his
job, she said he just snapped."

"Did she know that Dwayne planned to kill Telford?"

"Not before it happened. No. Seems Dwayne wanted
money from Telford, who said he didn't have any. Dwayne
said he'd get it from Molly the night of your meeting. Telford
beat him to Molly's, then called him to say he'd be waiting
for him and not to go up to the house. When Dwayne got
there, they argued, Dwayne pulled out the gun he'd stolen

from Molly a few weeks before, and got so mad he shot Telford."

Lizzie bit her lower lip. "Why did he leave the gun . . . to implicate Molly? Did he want revenge so badly?"

"He hasn't said. What he did own up to was stealing the gun during one of the literacy evenings, along with something for Ms. Torres."

"This is getting complicated. How did Dwayne's mama know about all this? And how did she get the manuscript to me? And why me?"

"Dwayne confessed to his mama what he'd done, but she knew he still wanted money from Molly and she was afraid he might end up killing her, too, if Molly refused. She thought if she sent you the manuscript in sections, it would get your interest up and you might connect all the dots and stop Dwayne."

Mark crossed his arms and leaned back against the counter. "She couldn't bring herself to just turn him in. Since Dwayne was in your literacy group and he talked about you a lot, you seemed the likely recipient. She paid the kid next door to make the deliveries and told him not to get caught."

"Did she also make those phone calls to me?" Lizzie asked, hoping everything would be neatly tied up with no loose ends.

"She did. Now, she thinks she contacted your daddy at some point and told him what had happened, but her mind's so fogged up when it comes to certain times of her life, that's not a certainty. But it makes sense," Mark said, walking over to stand beside Lizzie. "Something or someone got him looking into the story. She hoped her calls to you would push you even harder to find out about Dwayne."

"And what about the Facebook page for Harlan Fowks? Was that Dwayne or his mama?"

"Dwayne thought that one up more to help ease his anger than anything else. He wanted some recognition for his granddaddy."

Lizzie sighed. "It's all so sad. Molly knew nothing about Claydon's involvement, and she's pretty heartbroken about it. She told me, though, that she's going to do right by Carla Fowks, or I guess it's Trowl, and sign over some long-term mutual funds that have a monthly payout. She's feeling really bad about all that happened to the Fowks family."

She leaned back against the counter, thinking. "About the only good thing that came out of it all was finding out my daddy really was working on a story, not having an affair. He didn't tell Mama about it because of her close friendship with Molly."

Mark stood and walked over to Lizzie.

"You know, when I told Mama this morning, she didn't say anything, but she was crying, Mark. She knew. She understood that Daddy really loved her after all." Lizzie felt the tears misting her eyes.

Next thing she knew, Mark's arms were wrapped around her. She hung on tightly. He tilted her head back and kissed her. Her arms tightened even more.

"You see what happens from holding things back and keeping secrets?" Mark whispered. "I got a lot of things I want you to know, Lizzie. But not all at once, okay?"

"Sure. But you know, there is one question I'd kinda like to know the answer to right away." She felt warm and wanted, and even a bit playful. "It's been nagging at me, and I haven't yet figured out how to bring it up."

She felt Mark tense up. "So, ask," he said.

Lizzie leaned her head back and looked at him a bit sheepishly. "Well . . . it's about your hair. Or lack of it. I mean, it's quite a contrast from when I knew you in school. I was just wondering if that's a remnant of army life?"

Mark started laughing so hard, she was shaking in his arms. He stopped, sighed and spoke. "When I got out, I wanted to shed everything that had anything to do with the army. Never again see a buzz cut. So I started growing my hair and was just going to see how long I could get it. But it occurred to me, a police chief with a ponytail wouldn't go over too good. And then, the high school Shave-a-Thon for Cancer Research happened along. And that was that. And then, the look sort of grew on me, so to speak." He grinned.

Lizzie nodded. "I kinda like it, too. Thanks for telling me. You get to ask me a prying question next time, but now we'd better get on over to the book club or who knows what rumors they'll start up."

Bob met them at Molly's front door. He sported a thick white bandage on the back of his head. "I just wanted to explain to you, Lizzie. I started getting a vague notion about what had happened way back then. I'd been away doing my stint in the army, so I wasn't here when it happened. But I'd heard some rumors. When I began suspecting Claydon had been a part of it, I knew it had to be kept from Molly. I guess I acted sort of the dunce."

Lizzie put a hand on his arm. "I understand totally, Bob. That's exactly what my daddy did. But you know, you've been acting a dunce in more ways than one." She looked over at Mark.

Bob nodded. "Yeah, I guess so." He extended his hand to Mark, who shook it.

"I saw you hovering at the door, Bob Miller," Molly said, coming up behind them. "I was afraid you might try to sneak out again. Good evening Lizzie, Chief." She nodded at them both.

"How are you, Molly?" Lizzie asked.

Molly sighed. "Well, I'm none too happy to learn these things about Claydon, but I surely do understand why he kept it all from me. I knew he wasn't perfect, but it shakes your faith in people when someone you trust can have such a dark secret." She shook her head. "Now, come on in and join the others. We're going to celebrate the fact that the case has been solved and it's all over.

"But before that, I've got a gift for you, Bob." She turned

to him. "It's a kind of thank-you and something I'm sure you'll find enlightening." She beamed as she handed him a small parcel, wrapped simply in brown paper.

He looked at her a moment and then at the gift a moment longer before ripping the paper off. The book had a brown leather-bound cover. When he turned it faceup, the gold-embossed title teased a chuckle out of him. *Poirot Investigates* by Agatha Christie.

Reading Lists

Lizzie Turner

1. Mary Jane Maffini—*Closet Confidential*
2. Avery Aames—*The Long Quiche Goodbye*
3. Lorna Barrett—*Chapter & Hearse*
4. Margaret Maron—*Sand Sharks*
5. Linda Barnes—*A Trouble of Fools*

Sally-Jo Baker

1. Annette Blair –*A Veiled Deception*
2. Krista Davis—*The Diva Paints the Town*
3. Julie Hyzy—*Grace Under Pressure*
4. Jennie Bentley—*Spackled and Spooked*
5. Hannah Reed—*Buzz Off*

Molly Mathews

1. Agatha Christie—*Murder on the Orient Express*
2. Ngaio Marsh—*Photo Finish*
3. Caroline Graham—*Murder at Madingly Grange*
4. Rhys Bowen—*Her Royal Spyness*
5. P. D. James—*The Murder Room*

Bob Miller

1. John Sandford—*Phantom Prey*
2. James Lee Burke—*Black Cherry Blues*

3. Lawrence Block—*Even the Wicked*
4. Tony Hillerman—*Skinwalkers*
5. Loren D. Estleman—*Sinister Heights*

Jacob Smith

1. Robert B. Parker—*Small Vices*
2. Randy Wayne White—*Sanibel Flats*
3. Michael Connelly—*The Black Echo*
4. Lee Child—*Die Trying*
5. Margaret Coel—*The Silent Spirit*

Andrea Mason

1. Janet Evanovich—*One for the Money*
2. Cleo Coyle—*On What Grounds*
3. Casey Daniels—*Don of the Dead*
4. Charlaine Harris—*Dead Until Dark*
5. Kim Harrison—*Once Dead, Twice Shy*

Stephanie Lowe

1. Janet Evanovich—*Finger Lickin' Fifteen*
2. Maggie Sefton—*Knit One, Kill Two*
3. Elizabeth Lynn Casey—*Death Threads*
4. Riley Adams—*Delicious and Suspicious*
5. Lila Dare—*Tressed to Kill*

Turn the page for a preview of Erika Chase's next
Ashton Corners Book Club Mystery . . .

READ AND BURIED

Coming soon from Berkley Prime Crime!

"Lizzie Turner, you'd like a signed copy of Derek Alton's award-winning book, wouldn't you?"

Lizzie looked over at the cash register, where Jensey Pollard, owner of the Book Bin, stood waving a trade paperback with a moss green cover at her. The store was empty except for a dark-haired man at the back of the store. Jensey took Lizzie's delay in answering to be a "yes" and called out to the man.

Lizzie watched him as he walked toward her. She didn't recognize him, but she was pretty sure she'd heard of the book, *Judgment*. She smiled, hoping to cover any look of bewilderment.

"I'm Derek Alton," he said, giving her the once-over as he held out his hand. He wasn't much taller than Lizzie, possibly around five-eight. His eyes drew her attention—they were such an odd shade of green, Lizzie was certain he wore contacts. His nose looked slightly off-center, but that gave him a slight bad-boy look, especially when paired with the short dark brown hair, graying at the temples. His smile looked practiced to her, but she supposed that after years of book signings, he would be a bit jaded.

Jensey came around from behind her desk. "You know, Lizzie, *Judgment* is a mystery of sorts. And since it won the Onyx, I think it would be grand if Derek spoke to your book club. What do you say, Derek?" She had come up beside him and put her hand on his arm.

He looked at her hand and then at Lizzie. "I'd be delighted, although I'm in town for only another week."

Lizzie tried not to look cornered. She didn't know how the rest of the Ashton Corners Mystery Readers and Cheese Straws Society would feel about a guest. "I'm sure everyone would be delighted," she said, fingers crossed. "We're actually having a meeting next Thursday, if that works for you."

Alton leaned back against the desk and appeared to be in deep thought. Lizzie had the distinct impression she was being studied and maybe that's what he'd base his decision upon. It made her slightly uneasy.

"I'd be happy to do it," Alton finally said. "I'm staying at the Jefferson Hotel. If you'll give me your phone number, I'll call you for instructions." He pulled a pen and small notebook out of his jacket pocket and wrote down what she told him.

He signed the copy of *Judgment* that Jensey handed to him then excused himself and left.

Lizzie stared at Jensey, not quite sure what had just happened. She felt like she'd been railroaded into not only buying a book she'd not planned to purchase, but also revising the book club schedule.

"I didn't realize you were having a signing here today, Jensey," Lizzie finally said.

Jensey giggled. "It wasn't really a signing. He just popped in, and fortunately, I had a few copies of his books on hand so he signed them. Your walking in at that moment was opportune, don't you think?"

Jensey looked pleased with herself. Lizzie sighed then smiled, paid for the book and the two mysteries Jensey had put aside for her—the latest from Ellery Adams and Janet Bolin—and left.

The phone was ringing as Lizzie opened her front door. She picked it up just before it went to the message.

"Derek Alton here. Lizzie Turner, I hope?"

She nodded, taken off guard, but quickly realized an answer was needed. "Yes."

"I hope you won't think I'm too forward, but I'd like to take you out to dinner tonight. I'd like to know all about your book club before I speak to them. It will give me a better idea of how to tailor my talk. Are you free tonight?"

Lizzie knew she had no plans but she hesitated. It wasn't really a date. But a part of her felt guilty thinking of Mark Dreyfus, the heartthrob police chief she'd been dating for a few months. But Mark was working tonight. Okay, from what she'd seen of Derek Alton, he was somewhat attractive, in an older, mature way, but this was really a business dinner. It made sense he'd want to know about the book club. She accepted.

He picked her up at seven P.M., and after a brief drive through town with Lizzie pointing out the main sights, drove back to his hotel, where he'd reserved a table in the restaurant. Lizzie was glad she'd worn her fairly recent purchase, a black pantsuit along with a platinum satin shell. The Shasta Room at the Jefferson Hotel was one of the classier spots in town. Ashton Corners, Alabama, had a good variety of dining spots, along with plenty of activities for all ages. But Lizzie didn't make it out to places like The Shasta Room very often.

Alton made a big show of examining the wine list after they were seated at a table for two. Although it was early evening and still light outside, the lights were dimmed in their corner, three tea lights were lit and a single red rose lay across her plate.

Uh-oh. Lizzie inhaled its fragrance and then set it alongside her cutlery. She adjusted the linen napkin the maître d' had placed on her lap and looked around the room.

The walls, ceiling, crown moldings and chair coverings were done in varying pale shades. Linens were all white with a discreet "S" embroidered at each corner. Table and chair legs were dark oak. The shots of color came from the centerpieces of red poinsettia, towering paperwhites and sprigs of holly that anchored each table. String music wafted softly through the air.

Alton ordered a bottle of wine, without consulting her, she noted, then immediately began talking about himself. All she was required to do was nod and interject the occasional exclamation, showing she was suitably impressed.

"I'm still getting requests to read from *Judgment* at every event, and my publisher is thinking of doing yet another print run, so I thought it would be a good time to write a sequel. What do you think?" he asked.

Lizzie reined in her wandering mind and replayed his question before answering. "That sounds like a clever move." It was all she could think of to say.

Alton poured himself another glass of the California Baco Noir and beamed. "Just what I thought. Now, let's order before we get too wrapped up in talking."

Lizzie balked at his suggestion he order for both of them, instead choosing lemon chicken with braised root vegetables while Alton ordered steak, done rare, and lobster tail.

"So, what do you do when you're not running the book club, Lizzie?" Alton asked after another long sip of his wine.

"I'm a reading specialist with the local school board," she replied. "And I do some tutoring and teach a literacy course at night school." She watched for a reaction.

Alton smiled pleasantly. "Interesting. I also taught, you know. Creative writing, of course. In fact, I still dabble at giving the odd workshop, but my novel writing is such a large part of my life, I hardly find time for other pursuits, even the more pleasurable ones." His smile slid into more of a leer, and Lizzie cringed.

"Have you started your new book?" she quickly asked.

He stared at a point behind her right ear. "Early stages, my dear."

She wondered what that meant, but he had already launched into describing the award ceremony when he'd received the Onyx for Best Fiction from the prestigious Hawthorne Society, even though it was close to eighteen years ago. Lizzie couldn't help but feel a bit sorry for him, that he was still consumed with that win after all these years. She wondered if he was a lonely man.

Their food arrived, saving her from further comments as he ate with gusto, stopping only long enough to refill his glass. Lizzie was still working on her first glass of wine by the end of the meal. She declined dessert, choosing a peppermint tea to keep her occupied while he ate a piece of pumpkin pecan cake. She tried to introduce the topic of the book club a couple of times, but Alton had slid into a silence punctuated by smiles and winks at her.

"Oh, look at the time. I should be getting home," she finally said, glancing over at the flashy watch on his left wrist. She couldn't read the dial but thought he'd never notice. "It was a wonderful meal. Thank you so much," she said as she gathered her clutch purse and jacket.

Alton stood abruptly and swayed for a moment, then grabbed her elbow and walked with her to the entrance. He stopped to sign the check at the desk then maneuvered her behind a tall ficus plant next to the coatroom.

"I'll see you home," he said, his hot breath brushing her left ear.

She moved away from him. "No, that's quite alright. I can take a cab. I really think you should just head up to your room."

He leered and grabbed her arm once again. "Good idea. Join me, won't you?" He leaned toward her to kiss her.

She turned away and removed his hand from her arm. "Thank you again for the dinner. Good night."

She rushed out the door and down the steps, asking the bellhop to get her a cab. He blew his whistle and one pulled into the driveway from the main street. Lizzie gave the cabbie her address then sank back and breathed a sigh of relief.

What a nightmare evening. What a letch. And they hadn't even talked about the book club. What an idiot she had been. Well, she'd just have to get the book club members on board for his visit and then act as if nothing had happened between them. Because, of course, it hadn't.

FROM THE AUTHOR OF *A KILLER PLOT*

ELLERY ADAMS

Wordplay becomes foul play . . .

A Deadly Cliché

A BOOKS BY THE BAY MYSTERY

While walking her poodle, Olivia Limoges discovers a dead body buried in the sand. Could it be connected to the bizarre burglaries plaguing Oyster Bay, North Carolina? The Bayside Book Writers prick up their ears and pick up their pens to get the story . . .

The thieves have a distinct MO. At every crime scene, they set up odd tableaus: a stick of butter with a knife through it, dolls with silver spoons in their mouths, a deck of cards with a missing queen. Olivia realizes each setup represents a cliché.

Who better to decode the cliché clues than the Bayside Book Writers group, especially since their newest member is Police Chief Rawlings? As the investigation proceeds, Olivia is surprised to find herself falling for the widowed policeman. But an even greater surprise is in store. Her father—lost at sea thirty years ago—may still be alive . . .

penguin.com